I0623927

ECHOES THROUGH THE VATICAN

Echoes Through the Vatican

A Paranormal Mystery

K. Francis Ryan

Penman House Publishing

Copyright © 2014 Roxann K. Brooks

The moral right of the author has been asserted.

All rights reserved.
No part of this publication may be reproduced, stored in a retrieval system, or transmitted, in any form or by any means, without the prior permission in writing of the publisher, nor be otherwise circulated in any form of binding or cover other than that in which it is published and without a similar condition including this condition being imposed on the subsequent purchaser.

Published by [Penman House Publishing]

ISBN: 978-0-9908764-1-0

Typesetting services by BOOKOW.COM

In Memoriam
A friend to us all on Saturday afternoons.
Tom Magliozzi, better known as the elder half of the
"Tappet brothers" of NPR's Car Talk, brought
enlightenment, enjoyment and loads of laughs to millions.
You will live as long as we remember and few of us will
forget.
Rest in peace, old friend.
KFR

PREFACE

Disclaimer

This is a work of fiction and not a factual account of any actual events. Names, characters, places, and incidents are the products of the author's imagination or are used fictitiously. Any resemblance to actual events, locales, or persons, living or dead, is entirely coincidental.

Acknowledgments

Acknowledgements

The mechanical process of writing is, for many, a solitary undertaking. Armed with the knowledge of your craft, you must confront the daunting blank piece of paper alone.

However, the creative development that comes before and after are, for me, loaded with some of the most important people I know.

There are those who supply a word, a phrase, a gesture at exactly the right moment. There are some who are perfect sounding boards. Some provide and some inspire, some motivate, some encourage and some can be depended on to deliver a swift kick.

Christopher Clarke has helped immeasurably in ways he could never imagine and he can imagine a lot.

Aaron Aalborg*, Michael Crump* and Kelly Danforth, fellow authors and friends, have provided insight no one else could or would. The entire Penman House Publishing* crew has stayed the course from first to last on this project.

Alexandre Rito* has, once again, proved when it comes to cover design, he is a mind reader. He was able to take insane ramblings and turn them into art.

Steve Passiouras at Bookow*, only knows how to do things the right way. Heâ??s worked his magic again.

Courtney Harrington, a beta reader without peer, canâ??t be thanked enough. Her careful reading provided insights that couldnâ??t be found elsewhere.

Justin Ray gets a special note of appreciation. Without his assistance, those things that needed doing wouldnâ??t have gotten done. His minions miss him.

A debt of gratitude is owed to the indomitable Roxann. She made this book happen by doing the heavy lifting when I couldnâ??t.

She believed when I didnâ??t. She heard the echoes, long before anyone else.

Links

Aaron Aalborg, author of:

â?¢ They Deserved It

â?¢ Revolution

â?¢ Terminated

Michael Crump, author of:

â?¢ Candymanâ??s War

www.stillpointfiction.com

Penman House Publishing

penman-house-publishing.blogspot.com.tr/

Alexandre Rito

www.designbookcover.pt

rito@designproject.pt

Bookow

http://bookow.com/

steve@bookow.com

CONTENTS

CHAPTER ONE

He was pushed roughly into a chair and the hood removed from his head. Julian Blessing sat separated from his host by a large, heavily carved, mahogany desk. His eyes adjusted from the total darkness of the hood to the soft, pale yellow, subdued lighting in the room. Night had gathered outside. Julian's nostrils flared as he took in the faint smell of incense that floated on the light currents of breeze. A fire murmured in a fireplace.

The large man, who brought Julian to this place, stood in respectful silence. On the desk, a clock provided counterpoint to the silence.

Julian's host sat studying a leather portfolio on his desk; a pen was poised in his right hand. He read the papers, nodded once and signed. The man straightened in his chair, looked past Julian, and a young priest silently rushed forward, accepted the portfolio, turned quickly and left without looking either left or right. If he were ever asked, he could truthfully say he never laid eyes on the American, Julian Blessing.

His host sat back and openly studied Julian, then looked at the guard who nodded and left. The host's cassock was black and simple. The drape of the garment, over his shoulders and down the sleeves, spoke of rich fabric and impeccable tailoring. Julian took all of this in, and more.

The scarlet piping, buttons, and wide sash were badges of political rank. The pectoral cross attested to his spiritual authority, but none of it hinted at the tremendous power Julian could feel emanating from this man.

"Mr. Blessing, thank you for coming." The voice was relaxed, cultured, perfectly modulated and did not hint at the irony in what he said. The man's Italian accent gave his English a lyrical quality and he spoke only slightly above a whisper.

"Are you enjoying your time in Rome? It is truly a remarkable city in so many ways, would you not agree? But look at me; I am a poor host it would seem. I am Antonio Cardinal Luciano, Archbishop of, well, that doesn't matter I suppose."

Julian considered for a moment, then said, "Indeed, it seems it is a remarkable city if one wants to be abducted." He smiled an easy smile he did not feel. "I must say, I have never been kidnapped in a finer place. The Eternal City is remarkable if only for that."

Cardinal Luciano appeared placid and his smile indulgent. The placidity and the smile never reached his eyes. Steel gray eyes without remorse or kindness looked at, and into, Julian.

For over a year, with the help of his teachers, Julian had been honing a paranormal ability to read people. Not their thoughts, but he could get a sense of them, feel them. It was a talent that had come in handy more than once.

He tried to read the cardinal, but the man was impenetrable. He had a wall around his thoughts and he had no intention of issuing Julian an invitation. The cardinal did smile more broadly and shake his head slowly at Julian's attempts.

Julian said, "These are not my usual business hours, but there are always exceptions for princes of the Church. Why am I here, your Eminence?"

"I have been following your career, Mr. Blessing," the cardinal said. "In New York, you had your first indications of your special talents. You left the reality you knew for one you had only glimpsed. That takes courage.

"At the behest of your mentor, Mrs. Bragonier, you traveled to Ireland. Your teachers there showed you what is real, and what is possible, and what can be accomplished with your gifts. With persistence, you learned your lessons well. That takes dedication.

"And that brings you to Rome and to me." Cardinal Luciano thought for a moment and continued.

"I must say, with little training, your exploits in Ireland were impressive." The cardinal's voice turned hard and sinister. "You, however, are now on a much larger stage. The risks here are high and the consequences of failure are often fatal. The rewards are, of course," the cardinal paused, "proportional."

The older man stood and walked toward one of the towering windows. His slight limp was hardly noticeable.

The thick Persian carpet absorbed his footfalls. His words felt deep, slow and resonant in Julian's mind. He was becoming accustomed to speaking without spoken words and hearing the thoughts projected by others.

"Mr. Blessing, you are here because you feel it. You have felt it your entire life even though you did not understand. Fortunately, there were those of us who took you in, nurtured you and continue to do so even now.

"There is something wrong in the world," the cardinal thought. *"That feeling is strong and getting stronger. It grows as it festers and feeds.*

"The wool has been pulled over mankind's eyes for a very long time. It is meant to blind man to the truth." Julian felt the cardinal's words more powerfully than he had felt any before.

"You and I, and those like us, all hear the echoes. They are echoes from a different time with a different truth. The truth you and I know about the nature of reality is not a truth reserved for us alone. We use knowledge and talents that are available to everyone."

"Your Eminence, I am..." Without turning from the window, the cardinal raised his hand and silenced his guest. The man's heavy ecclesiastical ring glowed a dull gold in the failing light.

"As I am sure you know, people are easily led. It is something they want and need at a fundamental level. They need someone or something to blame, to be afraid of and to believe in.

"Although led to believe the exact opposite, mankind is limitless in its ability and capacity. However, taking hold of the potential, as those like us have done, presents a difficulty. In doing so, there would be no one to blame but one's self for any and all failings.

"Because of this, man, individually and collectively, wants to be led even if he is wrongly led – even if he knows it is wrong. Still, being led is uncomplicated. The truth is very complicated, don't you agree?" It was a question that was not.

The cardinal gazed out the window at the dome of St. Peter's Basilica, silhouetted by the last of the fading sunset. He turned, and with his forehead mirroring his concentration, returned to his desk.

The man thought, and Julian felt, *"Mankind has been enslaved for millennia. It was knowingly at first, but in time, as with many things, it became a habit and no further thought was given to the reason."* The cardinal rounded his desk and sat. His smile was easy and relaxed and wasn't a smile at all.

"This kind of slavery is not particularly unpleasant for most. It isn't expensive because when one does not know the value of what one is giving up, there is no way to calculate the cost."

"Let me guess," Julian said aloud. "The solution to mankind's ills is known only to you," he stated with a boldness that was fast eroding. "Eminence, with all respect, unless you get some new material, you will soon become a cliché."

The cardinal regarded Julian, smiled, and switching back to spoken words said, "Known only to me? Not at all, Mr. Blessing, you know it every bit as well as I do.

"We are tasked with helping to guide mankind. We are a lamp in the darkness. We attract many to us, but we shine a light for all. To date, our task has been to allow people to find their own way in the dark.

"Ours, however, is not some weak esoteric belief. We practice a sort of muscular ideology. We are sometimes called on to fight for the truths we hold, to die in some cases. Soldiers of reason, if you will," the cardinal said.

"Soldiers of reason, Eminence?" Julian mused. "Poetic."

The cardinal smiled, but glossed over the sarcasm and continued. "You were drawn to the tasks you perform now. You are compelled to follow a truer sense. Many have talents, but few wield talents such as yours and fewer still take to them so quickly or so thoroughly. Your use of them is still infantile, but you improve daily. You, of course, know all of these things," the cardinal said.

"There are, however, things you do not yet understand, things your teachers have not taught you. You were told humanity is taken in by its own slavery. What they did not teach you is the situation is far more dire. There is a noose around mankind's neck, Mr. Blessing. That noose is being tightened. What I know, and you do not, is who holds the other end of that rope."

"Eminence, I'm sorry, but I really don't know where you are going with this," Julian said.

"I will speak plainly to you, Mr. Blessing." Julian knew this would be anything but plain. "There are those who wish to wrest the end of that rope away and free mankind from slavery. A laudable cause, no?" the cardinal said and Julian inclined his head slightly. "But it cannot be done without people like you and me.

"Something you do not yet understand is the value of your talents or the value others would assign to them. In New York, you were a financier, a man who understands how fortunes are won and lost. But fortunes are nothing when compared to real wealth.

"Power, Mr. Blessing, is the only wealth worth having. There is a group that would freely give you that type of wealth for, what shall we say, a consideration? What is it Americans say? Yes, 'Doing well by doing good'."

The cardinal had traveled a circuitous path, but Julian recognized the point of the trip. "A consideration, Eminence?" Julian said. His lips held a cold, hard line.

"A consideration, Mr. Blessing. The members of the group, of which I speak, want you to join them to help knock off the shackles and to loosen the noose. The power that comes from leadership is yours in exchange for your loyalty and your assistance."

"And this group," Julian said. "What is its motivation? What's in it for them?"

"That is a fair question and the answer an easy one - profit. It is the motivation for all commerce, all of life, no? Can you imagine all of mankind equipped as you and I are? The world would change very much for the better. The poorest of the poor economies would find parity with the richest of the rich. Productivity and innovation would soar. The change would be irrevocable and to the benefit of all.

"This group is poised to free mankind and to harvest the rewards proportionate to its investment," the cardinal said. "It has been preparing the ground for a very long time and now is the time. Its risk has been enormous. Should not the return be enormous?"

"And our part in this, Eminence?"

"People like us have existed since time out of mind. Our mission has remained constant. As I said, we guide. Perhaps we have reached a point in human development where our mission needs to change, but only slightly. Rather than simply guide, we need to lead. We can propel society as a whole into a bright future, Mr. Blessing.

"Change is coming. You can feel it, hear it. The echoes you hear are echoes that have reverberated through the world for thousands of years. They are louder now, more resonant in our modern world," the cardinal said.

"We stand at the epicenter of change. You can place yourself on the right side of that change or the wrong side. The choice, and the consequences of that choice, are yours entirely."

Julian assessed the cardinal as he felt the man attempt to penetrate his thoughts. This interview wasn't quite over. Julian could feel it, sense it.

"Oh, Mr. Blessing," the cardinal said almost as an afterthought, a well rehearsed afterthought. Julian smiled slightly, but the smile faded quickly.

"You brought enemies from your life in the United States, no? One such enemy is here in Rome and so has come to my attention. I mention this only because I am concerned for your continued wellbeing and that of your dear friend, the lovely Dr. Dwyer. She is conveniently here in Rome on a hospital fellowship, no? How very nice for both of you. Love is a magnificent thing," the cardinal said pleasantly.

"Dr. Dwyer." Julian said the name without inflection. It was neither a question nor an answer.

The cardinal's face turned somber, his tone was contemplative. "I know the doctor's safety is always uppermost in your mind. I am only warning you. Your enemies may try to get to you through her.

"You and I have much in common," the cardinal continued. "You scoff at this, I know, but do not judge hastily. The distance between you and me is measured in mere degrees. For now, what concerns you, concerns me. I shall warn you if I hear of any plots involving you or the doctor. Rome is a small village really. I hear everything sooner or later."

The cardinal smiled pleasantly. "You have much to think about so I will delay you no further, Mr. Blessing. The man who brought you here will convey you back in safety. Rome can be a dangerous place as well as a delightful one. We will talk again and soon."

The air went electric when Julian said in a whisper, "Eminence." He drew the word out. "Your fault, my fault, nobody's fault, everybody's fault – if the doctor is harmed, the price will be very high. You do not know what I am capable of. I wish you a good evening. I will make my own way back to my hotel if that is all right with you."

"Of course, I understand completely." The cardinal's smile looked to Julian like more of a snarl. "If you have no need of my driver," the cardinal's face went dark and his mouth twisted to an ugly slash before he said, "then neither do I."

The scream that cut through the quiet was drenched in pain and pleading and terror. It seemed to come from every corner of the cardinal's mansion at once. It echoed, clawed at the air, begged for mercy and then was gone.

Julian's gaze never left the cardinal's face. The man's expression turned pleasant, but his eyes were gray and deathly cold, knowing and unknowable.

He smiled kindly and said, "You see, Mr. Blessing, I know what you are capable of. To a very high probability, I know what you will do, what you will not do and how far you will go.

"It is you who does not know what I am capable of doing." The smile was gone as quickly as it appeared. The cardinal cocked an eyebrow. "We will speak again. Good night and go with God."

Julian turned slowly to leave, but was arrested by the cardinal's thought. *"Oh, Mr. Blessing, I write my own 'material', as you call, it and you needn't fear. I don't think I'll be turning into a cliché anytime soon, do you?"*

A young priest, shaken and pale, fidgeted outside the cardinal's study and wordlessly escorted Julian to the front door of the residence. The staircase leading from the front entrance swept gracefully down to the street. Julian descended, stepped off the sidewalk, looked up at the building and shivered. He could feel the malice, the power, and the smell of death that clung to the occupant.

* * *

Julian's steps were heavy and slow. His chest expanded to take in a breath. What he got instead was some of Rome's famously polluted air. Within steps, he felt a presence behind him. It was someone with an abnormal interest in him. Julian picked up his pace slightly, then turned abruptly into a side street and waited in the shadows.

The steps he heard were light. He knew it was a woman and he knew she was following him, but she made no attempt at stealth.

When she passed him moving at a leisurely pace, Julian stepped from the shadows. The woman stopped but did not turn around. Slowly, she took her hands out of her jacket pockets and let her arms hang easily at her sides.

Her voice was as relaxed as her stance and her English had an Italian accent and cadence. "Paying your respects to one of the princes of the Church, signore Blessing? I would not have thought Cardinal Luciano would be receiving so late at night. You must be a very special visitor, no?"

"Who are you and what do you want?" Julian's voice was brittle. "And please, don't turn around."

"Ah, yes, we have not yet been introduced. My name is Belladonna Saviano. I, of course, know who you are, but to better answer your question, I am Ispettore Saviano from the Guardia di Finanza. If you will allow me, I can show you my identification card. It is here in my pocket."

"No, why don't you just keep your hands where I can see them. I'm having some difficulty believing the finance police are following me. Did I fail to pay a VAT somewhere? Who are you really?"

Two Vespa scooters passed on the next street and Julian could feel the riders. He sensed the woman several floors above the street before she looked out from her tiny balcony. He felt the woman before him. No other presence was nearby.

"What, signore Blessing, am I to do? You have asked who I am. I have told you. I have offered to show you my identification, but you are unwilling to allow me to do that. What would you have me do?" the woman asked. Her voice was light and easy and Julian felt she was smiling. His eyes were pinched in concentration as all of his senses went to the highest state of alert.

"Wait – I know how we can solve this little problem and demonstrate that you can trust me. You can look at the identification card of my Assistente Capo, what you would call a sergeant."

"You watch entirely too many old movies. I have to say that is not very original, but I will play along. Where is this imaginary sergeant of yours? From what I can tell, you and I are..." Julian had no doubt the pressure behind his right ear was from the barrel of a handgun. A large hand appeared over his left shoulder holding a police identification card in the name of Enrico Marino, Asst. Capo, Guardia di Finanza.

Julian had worked hard to hone the talent of sensing people, of feeling their proximity and intentions. Each individual had what he called a signature. Still, he could not sense the man directly behind him who so clearly had a weapon pressed against Julian's skull.

"Is your curiosity satisfied?" the woman said. "Are your fears put to rest? Grazie mille, Enrico. Say, 'thank you', signore Blessing.

Enrico is a, how do you say, a stickler for form. The word is 'Grazie,'" the woman said as she turned. The barrel of the gun was pushed a fraction of an inch and Julian's head canted to one side.

"Grazie, signore Marino," Julian said. The weapon was withdrawn, as was the identification card. Julian started to turn, but had his direction reversed abruptly by the sergeant.

"How marvelous. Did you hear that Enrico? Signore Blessing is trying to speak Italian. True, his accent leaves much to be desired, but he is trying and that is good. Walk with us, signore."

The woman was of medium height, lean and athletic. Even in the subdued glow from a distant street light, Julian could see she was in her early thirties, attractive, and her eyes and smile left Julian feeling he would not underestimate her again. That still left the man behind him. Julian could not understand how the man could have no signature, no presence at all.

The inspector and Julian walked side by side while her assistant remained a few paces behind them.

"So why are the Finance Police following me? What makes me so interesting?" Julian said flatly.

"We follow people who follow people sometimes. We do this especially when the people doing the following are bad and the people being followed are tourists and therefore good. All tourists are good, no? You are a tourist, are you not, signore Blessing?"

"That's right, I'm a good tourist," Julian said.

"Do you hear that Enrico? The signore says he is a good tourist, but he does not mention he is a terrible liar." Julian heard the man behind him snort and his inspector smirked.

"If we are to be friends, signore, you must not lie to me. What you are really doing in Rome, I do not know, but I will in time."

Julian walked beside the inspector in silence.

"Why don't we sit here and talk for a moment?" She indicated a small, tired cafe with tables outside. Their umbrellas were furled awaiting closing time.

From behind, Julian was pushed to a table. The sergeant sat at another table across from him. Enrico Marino was a large man, not tall but broad shouldered and he exuded an unblinking lethality. For all of his physical presence, still the man had no discernible signature. The inspector sat to Julian's right and ordered for all of them.

To Julian, the inspector's signature was a maze of facts, figures and strategies. Her calm exterior belied an active mind alive with calculations and intuition.

"Your English is perfect, Inspector," Julian said.

"I studied at American University here in Rome where I learned English and other bad habits. If we are done with the small talk, I will ask you a question. Please do not waste my time by making more false statements. If you do, we are done and you can go on your way. " Julian understood the unspoken, 'But you will regret it.' Julian nodded.

"Good," the inspector said. "Do you know any Russians? Specifically, do you know any Russian gangsters?"

"I do," Julian said without hesitation. "I caused some a bit of trouble in New York. I got in the way of their business and cost them a lot of money. It would seem they were very attached to that money. They were unhappy and offered to kill me. I declined the offer and left New York."

The inspector's gaze was penetrating, trying to jackhammer her way into Julian's head. "Enrico, should we believe this man?" Her assistant didn't look away from Julian's face. The big man nodded his head once, but made no other movement.

"Well, that's settled. We believe you." The women smiled. "Now, I will tell you what we know. We have been following some Russian gangsters. They are establishing a money laundering operation here in Rome. If left unchecked, they will control much of Italy in a year or so.

"We would stop them, but in time they will run into the Mafia and many on each side will die. In the long run, this is good. There will be fewer to arrest and so, less paperwork." The inspector smiled broadly.

"Still, in the short term, we do our job to cut down on civilian casualties. While we were following one of these Russians, I looked across the street and the man we had been following the day before was doing a poor job of following you, do you see?

"We decided following someone who was following someone would be far more interesting than what we were doing. We ended up at your hotel.

"Having completed his task, your stalker lost interest and went away. Enrico followed the man back to a set of offices we have under surveillance in the Via del Pellegrino. I don't think there is any doubt, but your location was carried back to his bosses, do you?" Julian acknowledged that.

"While Enrico was busy, I waited at your hotel. You are staying in one of our best hotels. Not pricy, but very good. They have a wonderful cafe and better biscotti. Well, imagine how surprised I was. Who should appear, but Cardinal Luciano's driver who serves also as the cardinal's bodyguard. The man has a criminal record and I do not like him. I would not like him if he didn't have a record. I am like that sometimes." Her conversation was light and breezy, but she watched the impact every word had on Julian. She looked for his reactions. She got none.

"This man went in and both of you came out," the inspector said. "In the company of the bodyguard, you looked unhappy. Without ceremony, or even much politeness, you were pushed into the back seat of the cardinal's car and the driver put a bag on your head. This, of course, was not necessary, but I suppose it added to the sense of theater.

"The rest you know far better than I, is that not true?"

Julian nodded and thought this woman spent a lot of time asking questions that weren't questions.

"What was the purpose of your visit to the cardinal tonight?" the inspector asked.

"I have been asking myself that question too."

"Well," the inspector asked, "if you will not discuss generalities with me, what am I to do with you? What, of value, can or will you tell me?"

"I believe the cardinal's driver is dead."

The inspector's eyes got hard as she watched Julian more carefully. "And you would know this, how exactly?" Her smile was overly polite and overly insincere.

"Inspector, take my word for it. Even if you never find a body – and you won't – that man is dead."

"You were a witness, then. You were standing nearby when the man fell over and died. Is that it?" the inspector asked. "I can tell you, I have no intention of taking your word of anything. You will have to do better, I am afraid."

"I can only tell you what I know. If you don't like my answers, perhaps you should ask someone else. I don't know if you will get better answers, but they will be different," Julian said with a shrug.

The inspector ignored the remark and held up her hand to stop her assistant from chastising Julian's bad manners. "I will look into this. Sadly, I cannot look too far. The Vatican protects its own and doors will be closed to me if I begin asking too many questions. Still, I will attempt to verify your story."

The three sat in silence as bored waiters stood against the walls waiting to lock up and go home.

CHAPTER TWO

Doctor Ailís Dwyer's eyes narrowed as she examined the body of a 73-year-old woman. The woman lay motionless and terrified in a hospital bed in Rome's premier hospital. Her breathing was fast and shallow and she cringed when she looked at the men and women in white coats who ringed her bed.

Identical stethoscopes draped around their necks, they had identical medical charts in their hands. They looked on unmoved and were unmoving. Some were interns, others were residents, a few were experienced doctors like Ailís, taking advantage of medical fellowships in Rome.

One man stood out in spite of there being nothing remarkable about him aside from his short stature and advanced age. He was the only one who wasn't looking at the patient. He was watching Ailís' every move, every flicker and twitch of expression.

A resident read from the patient's case notes. Symptoms, followed by history, followed by blood test results, and all in an annoying drone.

Ailís moved to the patient's bedside and reached for the woman's hand. Taking it firmly in hers, she looked into the old woman's face and smiled with warmth. The patient smiled back uneasily, but with gratitude, at the sight of any friendly face.

Ailís spoke softly, and an intern interpreted from English to Italian, "'Tis a lovely morning. Please, ignore all of these people.

They all want to help you, but for now there is only you and me. Do you understand?"

The woman nodded with exaggerated slowness.

"It's help I need right now. Will you help me?" Ailís' eyes never left the woman's face. The patient nodded once.

"You live in the mountains, don't you?" Ailís asked. The patient nodded enthusiastically.

"I'm a country doctor in Ireland and my practice is in the mountains, although we have a lot of farmland too. I love the country," Ailís said in a conspiratorial whisper and made a face. "It is much better than the city." The patient smiled more broadly and nodded.

Ailís leaned in and the translator had to do the same. "You told them you were tired, but not how tired, or for how long." It wasn't a question and was delivered with kindness. The woman looked guilty and broke eye contact as she kneaded the bed sheets. She shook her head. No.

"Your memory - you didn't tell them about losing your memory and not being able to concentrate." The patient looked away again.

"Well, that will be enough of that," Ailís scolded, but smiled. "Why didn't you tell them?"

"I'm old," the patient said. "Old people lose their memory sometimes. I didn't think it was important because everybody knows about old people."

"May I?" Ailís asked as she rolled the patient onto her side and looked at the sores on her back. Rolling the patient back she said, "Thank you. You have been very kind to help me. You can help me further and yourself." The patient looked puzzled.

"You must always tell your doctor everything. We study in the big cities sometimes and we forget what is important and what 'tisn't. We depend on our patients to remind us." The patient nodded her gratitude.

Ailís took the woman's hand again and squeezed. "We will have you home to your mountains in no time." Her smile matched her patient's. Ailís walked to the sink in the corner and washed her hands.

She turned as she dried her hands and addressed the small old man whose gaze never wavered. "Lyme Disease. Lyme Borreliosis, specifically. Third stage. Treat with large doses of amoxicillin, or cefuroxime axetil. It is very possible she has a neurological form of the disease, in which case she will require IV treatment with either ceftriaxone or penicillin." It was matter of fact and she smiled while her fellow doctors looked skeptical.

"Well, Dottoressassa." The old man looked grave. "You are correct, of course. None of the blood work would have shown that. Knowing about the memory loss would have helped." The man chuckled and said, "On to the next patient, signore e signori."

The doctors shuffled out murmuring and making notes. Ailís turned and winked at the old woman in the bed as a nurse pulled the sheets up. The old man stayed behind and linked his arm with Ailís'.

"The diagnosis was excellent, but the way you interacted with the patient, that was what mattered," the old man said. "She became your patient the moment you touched her. She knew it and you knew it."

"Dr. Stefani, I am only a country doctor," Ailís said and smiled. She is a woman from the country, from the land," Ailís smiled at her patient. "Her heart is good and her life is hard. Kindness goes a long way. I've seen enough of that disease not to know it. You gave me the one you knew I would get right. You may fool them," she nodded toward the other doctors, "but you don't fool me."

"Perhaps, but I wanted those idiote to see. We have all forgotten what medicine is about. We think our profession is about illness and disease states. It is about people. They will never understand." He pointed to the herd of doctors who gathered around the next patient. "I don't know why I bother, but bother I must." The man's English was Italian inspired and carried a soft chuckle.

"You will be out with your young man tonight, of course," the doctor stated.

"My young man, is it? He isn't anything of the sort. Mr. Blessing and I are friends. Nothing more," Ailís said maintaining the fiction of their relationship for no reason that was apparent.

"Based on a friendship we enjoyed when I was on a fellowship in Dublin, you force a fellowship out of me so you can be in Rome at the same time as your," the doctor added air quotes, "your friend.

"If he is just a friend, run away with me. We will go to Paris where they understand love."

Ailís smiled. "And wouldn't your poor wife be objectin'?" Ailís laughed and the lines at the corners of her eyes showed that she laughed often.

"Only if she finds out," Dr. Stefani said and his laugh lines were an older version of Ailís'.

* * *

The restaurant was dark, quiet and intimate. Julian sat with Ailís Dwyer at a corner table. A single, elegant, red candle cast shadows that allowed Julian to study his lover's face.

She looked up from her menu and smiled as she found herself looking into his soft gray eyes.

"And what, Mr. Blessing, is it you find so fascinating that you would be staring at me like that? Doubtless, you've further intentions to steal my virtue," she said with a wide smile. The rhythm of her Irish-accented English brought back so many rich, warm memories for him.

"My darling, I find everything about you fascinating and am only too happy to do anything you would like me to with your virtue. That and I love looking at you. I have from the moment I met you," he said. His smile was warm and adoring.

"Go on with ya," she said and smiled more broadly. "I'm sure you tell that to all the women in Rome when I'm not around to protect you from yourself. Besides, I've been working all day; I've worn all my makeup off and my hair looks like straw.

"Add to that, Italians use garlic in everything. I swear they would put it in their coffee if they could. No doubt they've tried. That accounts for a dreadful case of dragon breath that no amount of mints and brushing will banish," she said and waited for what had better be the correct response.

Julian continued to smile and study her. "Ailís, you are one of those women who look perfect without makeup. It could never hope to enhance perfection."

She pursed her lips. He was doing well. So far.

"As for your hair," he continued, "it is tousled, wild even. It gives you that devil-may-care look people find fascinating, fashionable and undeniably sexy."

She smiled, tilted her head to best advantage, and pretended to examine her menu.

"You do have dragon breath and I meant to mention it to you." He reached across the table with a package of mints. "'Never turn down a breath mint.' I think Oscar Wilde said that."

Her eyes filled with fire and her mouth was twisted with outrage. "You animal. You are nothing but a hateful animal and will be punished for your impudence and your ignorance," she hissed.

"Ignorance? Do you mean it wasn't Oscar Wilde?" Julian said and raised his eyebrows with the mock surprise and the expectation that she would explode at any moment.

She was still sputtering some minutes later when the waiter arrived to take their order. The man smiled, quickly turned and left, but not before he heard Ailís spit, "Isn't it men who are the worst of creatures and you are the worst man in the world."

The waiter had been a waiter long enough to know when his presence somewhere might prove hazardous to his health. He expected a crater to develop at table seven and he didn't want to be collateral damage.

* * *

Ailís woke the next morning in a much mollified frame of mind. She showered, dressed and smiled at Julian as he lay sleeping. "I do rather love him," she said to herself. Her smile was extravagant.

She studied the planes of his face, a face she had come to know so well. She looked at his hair, going a distinguished gray at the temples. She examined the scar on his cheek. "You brought that on yourself trying to save the village," she whispered. "You should have died from that beating, but you're too stubborn."

Her smile was soft, but the corners of her mouth turned down and she closed her eyes. "And I nearly lost you that time. I won't give you up so easily again."

She opened her eyes and the smile returned as she watched Julian turn onto his side. "I stitched that gash up and did a very fine job of it too. I don't know whether you look more delicious with or without it. With, I think," she mused.

She leaned over, brushed his hair aside and kissed his forehead. Ailís turned and left, closing the door softly behind her.

* * *

The front desk clerk called to her as she passed. The man rushed around the counter.

"Dottoressa Dwyer, this arrived moments ago for signore Blessing. Should I give it to him or would you accept it?" The man inclined his head and smiled his eagerness. Doctors regularly stayed in the hotel but female doctors, and one as beautiful as this Irish doctor, were rare and needed to be savored, preferably at close range. The clerk was Roman and so understood such things.

Ailís took the offered note. It was a delivery notice from an international overnight delivery company. It gave an address on Via Venit Settembre. She recognized it as being near the hospital.

"It is a gentleman you are," Ailís said and smiled. "I'll take it and pick up the package after I finish at the hospital. No need to bother Mr. Blessing."

The clerk beamed, took her hand and kissed it lightly. Ailís decided she liked Romans.

* * *

Bernini's magnificent fountain sculpture of the Four Rivers, topped by the Obelisk of Domitian, sat unappreciated as two police officers walked by, captives to their own thoughts.

The piazza was an amalgamation of restaurants, bars, tourist shops and covered stalls for artists, selling everything from poor quality da Vinci knock-offs to caricatures of Barack Obama. Usually full of tourists, it was populated by office workers returning from lunch and street vendors visiting with each other.

Inspector Saviano paid little attention to the catcalls that came her way from a group of four men in their late twenties, seated on cement benches that fronted the fountain. It was a normal, if unpleasant, part of Italian life. Her assessment had been incisive and decisive. Businessmen recovering from a too large and too liquid lunch judging by their fashionable suits, expensive ties and slurred speech.

The inspector left the calls in her wake, but heard them rise again with entirely too much enthusiasm. She stopped and turned. Her partner sighed heavily and shook his head.

An attractive, slim, and shy young woman, an intern perhaps, had become the latest target of admiration from the men on the benches.

The inspector walked back and intercepted the young woman as she came forward. Taking her by the arm the inspector whispered, "Come with me."

Both women stopped in front of the men. The youngest, with a licentious grin and a cock-sure attitude, stood and approached. "Sit," the inspector said. The man grinned more broadly and Enrico Marino crossed his arms and awaited the fireworks.

"Ah, cucciola mia." He said it in the same way one would speak an endearment to a puppy.

Enrico's expression was pained, but he couldn't look away. His partner took her identification card out of her jacket pocket. It was for form. She had to identify herself. Bella held it uncomfortably near the man's face.

"I am supposed to be afraid of that? It makes me want you all the more, my pretty one." His comrades laughed. The young girl tried to slip away, but Bella captured her arm again and brought her back.

The inspector put her warrant card away. She smiled up at the man and said, "A big man like you, afraid of my police ID card?"

Enrico groaned.

"No, you should be afraid of this," Bella said and drove the knuckle of her index finger hard and fast into the man's sternum.

It wasn't a punch, it was a press and she followed the man using his own imbalance against him. He stumbled backwards falling heavily into his friends. A lot of expensive suits ended up on the ground.

"Stay where you are," the inspector barked as the men scrambled out from under each other. "Let me explain something to you." She sat on the bench and brought her companion along. "I am all about options.

"This is the first option. There are four of you. I will hurt two of you and arrest two of you. I haven't decided for what, but I will think of something career-ending for you. You can decide who gets what." Bella smiled sweetly. "My friend and I will wait." She smiled again at the young women beside her and patted her hand. A snarl followed as the inspector dared the men to get up.

After a few moments of surly looks and hushed obscenities, the inspector said, "I am heartbroken you do not like my first option. I was looking forward to it. Still, I will offer another. She turned to her young companion.

"Cara, do you pass by here every day?" the inspector asked and the woman nodded and looked embarrassed.

"And do these fools verbally assault you every day?" The woman nodded hesitantly and looked at the ground.

"It isn't assault. It's a compliment," the first man down said with heat.

"Is it a compliment if I come over there and kick the balls right off of you? Shut up before I give you a compliment that will deny your momma any grandchildren. As if!" Bella spat.

"You!" the inspector pointed at the largest of the four. "Come here."

The man scrambled to his feet. "Sit. Give this nice young woman your business card," Bella said. The man looked confused. The inspector grabbed the man's tie and pulled. "Business card. Now! And write your cell number on the back."

He reached into his coat pocket, fished out his wallet and wrote his number as instructed. Bella gave the man's card, and one of her own, to the young woman.

"Good. Here is the second option. This is more complex. I know none of you are very smart, so follow along." She turned her attention to the young woman. "Cara, going or coming from wherever you go or come from, you are to call this clownish sort of man." Bella pointed so everyone understood who the players were. "He will escort you." The man opened his mouth, but self-preservation closed it for him.

"You," she turned her frightening attention to the man. "You will escort this young lady. Should she encounter any name calling, or whistling, or abuse of any sort you will beat whoever commits such sins. You must do this with vigor, capisci?"

"If his performance is poor, call me," the inspector said to the girl. "At that time, we will return to my favorite option."

Bella stood and whispered to the woman, "He isn't bad looking and he has a nice ass, no?" The young woman blushed and nodded. With vigor.

The inspector returned to her partner and they continued on their way. "Enrico, amore mio," she said, "are you the only man worth knowing?"

The big sergeant thought a moment and said, "For you, Bella? Most definitely, I am the only one."

CHAPTER THREE

The accent on the telephone was distinctive and the phrasing one -of-a-kind. "Professor, thank you for calling. It's good to hear your voice," Julian said. Professor Reginald Bragonier, professor of history at Trinity College Dublin, was the British husband of Julian's mentor, Bridget.

"Julian, old son, this is ugly business. It likes me not that our Ailís is missing. What hear you from the authorities?" the professor asked.

"Nothing has come from the police other than they are doing everything they can to find her."

Julian continued with the sequence of events. "She finished her shift at the hospital and we were to meet for dinner as usual. I talked with the Chief of Staff at the hospital. He confirmed she was coming to meet me. It seems strange though."

"Strange in what way, my boy?" the professor asked.

"Ailís told Dr. Stefani she had to go pick up a package. But that was all. The front desk clerk said he gave her a package delivery notice. The police will be running that down, but I plan on following up as well. She never mentioned a package to me and I talked with her on the phone this afternoon. It may have slipped her mind, but she is always so detailed," Julian said.

"Ah, well, that is…" the professor burbled and stalled before coming out with it. "That would be my fault I'm afraid. You see, I sent you some documents by overnight express," the professor finished in a rush.

"What express service? The clerk couldn't remember the carrier so I've been checking with all of them. I have just two to go. Which carrier, professor? And documents? What kind of documents?"

"I will look through my papers for the carrier as we talk. As to the other, I ran across an obscure reference to the Roman coins you found here in Ireland. Like any historian, I went to work digging deeper. I found a gold mine. I felt some of my research findings were highly volatile politically. I don't mean historically, but today."

"Volatile in what way and would they be volatile enough for someone to take Ailís?" Julian demanded as his heart thundered and his focus narrowed.

"Let's say religiously and politically explosive. Events in the Vatican, and elsewhere today, can trace their lineage directly to the documents I unearthed. The papers would be volatile from any point of view. At least, that's where the evidence points.

"Julian, I've not nailed it down yet, but I'm on to something important and very likely dangerous," the professor ruminated. "Could it have lead to this sort of thing? I have to answer, it is possible.

"Copies were sent to a colleague of mine in the antiquities department at Sapienza University there in Rome, for further study. He has access to local resources I do not," the professor said and then continued.

"You were correct. I never doubted you by the way. The treasure you unearthed here was only half of what it should have been. The other half never left Rome."

"Literally, ancient history, professor. I still don't understand. How could it still be dangerous two thousand years after the fact?" Julian asked.

"Well, my young friend," the professor said trying to lighten a darkening mood, "be careful how you use the word ancient. I've been called that and I'm still dangerous enough. As for the how of it, I will leave my colleague to explain."

"I will contact him. But tell me, how is Bridget?"

"Yes, well, when confronted by one's own ignorance of the ways of history, it is always best to change the subject," the professor said and, moved by the force of the professor's snort, Julian smiled in spite of himself.

"My Bridget is doing swimmingly. The woman positively blossoms when in my presence. Wait, I better not say that aloud. She nearly destroyed me the last time."

Julian heard the professor's chuckle and couldn't help but smile again. The professor supplied the name of the overnight service and the waybill number, and the name of his fellow professor in Rome.

"Thank you for calling me back professor. When I know more I will let you know," Julian said.

"Before you ring off, I have something more," the professor said and Julian remained silent.

"We are all concerned Julian - Bridget, Moira and the rest. Concerned for our Ailís of course, but concerned for you as well. Have a care son. We live in a wicked world."

"I'll be careful professor," Julian said and hung up the phone. He lay on his bed and stared at the ceiling trying to see into the past, trying to connect with Ailís.

Past viewing was a talent he had exhibited early on and his teacher, Moira Hagan, had encouraged and helped him to develop it. Julian felt he wasn't very good at it because he couldn't control the visions.

While others could see into the future, Julian was able to see past events as if watching reruns on television. Sometimes, he would see pieces of the very distant past while at other times, he was able to clearly watch events unfold near the present. He could not control what he saw or when.

He fell into an exhausted sleep seeing another of former Prime Minister Silvio Berlusconi's fraud trials. For Berlusconi, the past, the present and the future looked pretty much the same.

* * *

"Inspector Saviano, I really don't need any help. I just want to ask a few questions," Julian said as they hurried down Via Sasilina and closed in on the express delivery service.

"Signore Blessing, although you make a valiant attempt at speaking Italian, it is not sufficient to find out the time of day. Secondly, the businesses in Italy do not like it when foreigners burst into their offices and start demanding answers. I, however, am the police and charming so they always make an exception for me.

"Am I not charming, signore Blessing?" Her partner, Asst. Capo Enrico Marino, rolled his eyes and looked bored.

"Sorry, I was thinking. What did you say?" Julian said, his thoughts miles away.

"I see my charm is lost on you, signore," the inspector answered with derision dripping from her lips.

Once inside, the sergeant found the district manager. They spoke for a moment and Marino returned with a slip of paper and whispered something to his inspector.

"Enrico, you are a treasure. Bring these men to me one at a time," the inspector said and Marino disappeared into the labyrinth of cartons and package carts.

"Here, we will use this conference room. Enrico says he has the names of the men who were working when your package arrived. Enrico is very valuable. He has many cousins. In this case the manager is his third cousin. Because of this sort of thing, he and I are able to accomplish much," the inspector said.

"I am taking your word for the importance of this package. Perhaps one of these men will have something of value to tell us. This, you may notice, makes these men far more valuable than you since you have failed to provide anything of substance about yourself or your true business in Rome," the inspector said.

"I am a tourist," Julian began. "I am looking for a package that was sent to me from Ireland. A package that has gone missing. The person who picked it up has gone missing also. You are being kind enough to assist me. What else is there to say?" Julian replied.

With a sigh and a shake of her head, Inspector Saviano made a face and said, "Tourists are not often thrown into the back of limousines and taken to secret meetings with one of the most powerful men in the Vatican. I speak, of course, of Cardinal Luciano. Members of the Russian mafia are also not following random tourists. So, you don't mind if I doubt your tourist story."

"Your sergeant is coming with some people. I can tell you, not one of these men knows anything," Julian said.

Enrico Marino opened the door and roughly shoved a small, balding, bespectacled man into the room.

The inspector said, "Sit," and her assistant forcefully introduced the man to a chair.

The questioning began and Julian again said, "He knows nothing," but the inspector fixed him with a glare. Julian left to, as he said, 'wander.' He walked through a canyon of cartons, containers, packages, boxes of all shapes and sizes and rooms of machinery. The building seemed never-ending. Individual packages lost their shape as they formed heaps on the backs of overburdened carts.

Julian stopped, and tried to quiet his thoughts and focus his attention as his teacher had instructed. After a few moments, he felt calmer. He was back in control of himself and could better control the elements of his search, but still, he knew nothing of substance.

He rounded a corner and could feel, immediately, the signature of someone who did know things, things of substance. He was a man who kept secrets in exchange for money.

Julian returned to the conference room and attracted Enrico Marino's attention. Together, they tracked through the facility again and eventually found the keeper of secrets. Marino recognized the man as being wanted for burglary and assault on a police officer.

The burly sergeant grabbed the man and pushed him against a nearby wall. Handcuffs were placed on wrists and the suspect was led away to the makeshift interrogation room and Inspector Saviano.

Julian knocked once then looked inside saying, "Having any luck?"

The inspector said, "Signore Blessing, you are beginning to annoy me. Do you have this effect on everyone?"

"Only those who like me," Julian said.

"Then I must be falling in love. None of these men knows anything. This may be difficult for you to believe, but this man," she pointed to the man sitting across the table from her, "actually knows less about anything than you say you do," the inspector said.

She turned to the man and said in Italian, "Thank you, now go away."

"I have someone for you to talk with who does know something," Julian said. He felt he had made progress and his face wore an eager look.

Enrico Marino pushed a large man into the room and shoved him into a chair. Marino said two words as an introduction, "Antonio Califano."

The inspector said in Italian, "You have been a busy burglar. I am with the finance police, so burglary does not concern me. Still, I keep up on things. You struck a policeman. That does not concern me either, but Enrico takes that sort of thing personally. The policeman was his cousin.

"My associates believe you know something. I say they are wrong. You are too stupid looking to know anything of value. Which of us is right?" She smiled pleasantly.

"I don't talk to whores like you," the man drawled.

Switching to English, the inspector said, "That's it? That is as original as a clown like you gets? I am a prostitute? That's it? Enrico, punish this man for being unoriginal."

Her assistant stepped behind the prisoner and pushed Califano forward, bouncing his head off the table.

After thirty minutes of questioning, the inspector sat back in her chair with no more information than when she started. The air was nearly blue with profanity, most of it lost on Julian.

"Yet another man who knows nothing. I am shocked," the inspector snarled.

"May I ask him a question?" Julian asked.

"Why not?" the inspector sneered.

"Parli inglese?" Julian asked and the man shook his head, no.

"Madonna mia! Is this what we've come to Enrico? What is next, signore Blessing? Are you going to ask him if he would go to the bakery with you? How much more grammar school Italian must we endure? Enrico, we bounced the wrong man's head off the table!" the inspector cried out in frustration.

"You ask if he speaks English and he tells you no. In fact, he does; he just doesn't speak it to you. The man is an idiot, but he speaks English. If you have something of value to add, add it now before I become unhappy with you." She glared at all three men and said, "All of you."

Julian smiled at her and pulled his chair closer to the table. "This will only take a moment," he said.

Califano sat in brooding silence with his face twisted in a sneer of disgust.

Julian let his shoulders drop and his eyes became hooded as he stared into the man. The thought he sent Califano hit the man with enough force to push him back in his chair.

"I do not want to repeat myself," Julian thought. *"You will tell me everything you know about the package and the woman who came to collect it. You know what package and what woman so don't bother with that excuse."*

The man could feel Julian's words as clearly as if they had been shouted at him, but Julian sat placidly looking into the man's face. Califano, his eyes wide with a mixture of fear and hatred, spat at

Julian and missed. Enrico moved up behind the man, but Julian raised his hand to stop the sergeant.

"Please, take this man's handcuffs off." Marino shot a questioning look to his inspector who nodded imperceptibly. With a pinched look of concentration, she watched Julian's every move, listened to his every breath.

The man was rubbing his wrists when Julian's next thought struck hard. *"I am having to repeat myself. Let me give you something you can remember so this doesn't happen again."*

The man screamed as the fingers of his right hand began to twist in a paroxysm of excruciating pain. Enrico Marino moved a step and his inspector shook her head bringing her assistant to a halt. Although Califano tried to stop it, his hand twisted into a claw and the spasm began to work its way up his arm. He shrieked again and swore. Julian sat back in his chair, then released the man.

"Let's start over again. What happened to the package and the woman? Lie to me and you will feel something far worse than a muscle spasm. Oh, and I'll leave you that way for the rest of your life. Capisci?" Julian thought.

The prisoner nodded once, his eyes wide with terror.

"Please, tell the inspector everything you know and do it in English," Julian instructed.

For fifteen minutes, a frightened, confused, and angry Antonio Califano told his story.

He had been alerted to a package by a friend, a man he was in prison with. The friend wanted Califano to locate a specific package and then take it home. He was assured the reward for performing this task would be substantial.

Califano located the package. It was awaiting a signature for pickup. He stashed it away. The prisoner said, "This woman came in. Una bella fica. She asked for the package. Nobody could find it. Two men came in, said something to her and she ran out to get into their car. One man was tall, the other short. Both in black suits with guns under their jackets."

"And that is all you know?" Julian thought. Califano nodded once. He felt Julian's message. *"Two mistakes. Both bad.*

"Your first mistake is that isn't quite all, am I right? I said I wanted the whole story and I don't have time to waste. Your second error? 'Una bella fica' – a nice piece of ass? See, I know some Italian, but not much. Doesn't matter; it was a bad thing to say. In most circumstances it might have proved very bad, but you may yet save yourself. That is, after you receive a reminder."

Julian smiled indulgently as the prisoner fell from his chair, howling, while he clutched his groin. Neither police officer paid attention to their prisoner's suffering, although Enrico winced slightly. Both the inspector and the sergeant were more interested in how this was happening.

Califano crawled back onto his chair panting heavily and his story began to spill out faster.

The waiting car had diplomatic plates. Vatican license plates, Califano thought, but he couldn't be sure. The man who arranged Califano's participation was driving the car. They nodded to each other. When asked, the prisoner begrudgingly supplied the driver's name.

The story continued. That same night, the driver appeared at Califano's door and gave him a thousand euros for the package and another eight hundred to forget what he saw. The man left in a different car but also with diplomatic plates. The prisoner supplied the plate number.

"Enrico," the inspector said in a mild voice, "please call dispatch to send a car to take this fool away." Her assistant nodded, handcuffing Califano again.

The man's struggles were useless. He looked at the inspector. "You bitch! You said you didn't care about the burglaries and that thing with the cop!"

The inspector was inspecting Julian, before she shifted her gaze to Califano. "I lied. I do that sometimes." She smiled and wrinkled her nose. "But thank you for your information and for cooperating with the police like a good citizen."

"Daughter of a thousand bitches!" the prisoner spat. Enrico pushed him out the door and they were gone.

The room was quiet for a moment. "What the hell was that!" the inspector screamed at Julian. "I don't even know how or where to begin with you. What was that? Who are you? What were you doing? How do you do what you did?"

The inspector was nose to nose with Julian and he could feel her breath on his face. "Listen to me. I don't have any amulets or charms to protect me from the evil eye," she said while making the corna, the sign of the horns, at Julian with her hand. "But if you try any of that shit with me, I swear by the Madonna, I will shoot you in your stupid face! Blessing, I am waiting, so you better start telling me what I want to know."

"My friends call me Julian. I was thinking we might be friends," he said and smiled his hopefulness. The smile never reached beyond the corners of his mouth.

Inspector Belladonna Saviano threw her head back and bellowed, "ENRICO!"

Her assistant entered the room looking as taciturn and unhurried as usual. "Enrico," his inspector said in rapid fire Italian, "is witchcraft a crime? I know it's a sin and that's good enough, so please, kill this man. The Church will forgive and protect you. We'll put his body in a barrel and I know you have cousins who know people who will take the barrel out to sea. Please, Enrico, do this one little thing for me," she pleaded.

With a nearly imperceptible shake of his head, her assistant looked at Julian and made the sign of the horns. Julian smiled having no idea his disposal was under discussion.

The inspector hung her head and switched back to English, "Why is there never an inquisition going on when you need one? Blessing, I'm sure the church would be delighted to burn you as a witch, wizard, sorcerer, magician or whatever the hell you are. I'll even bring the matches."

"I really don't know what you're talking about, but none of that matters," Julian said. "We have a lead. So, now we go find this driver. The hell with the package but this could lead to the doctor, right?"

The inspector's brow furrowed, as she looked at Julian as if he was mad. "We are not going anywhere. Nothing Enrico and I are going to do in any way includes you. You are to go back to your hotel, or go sightseeing, or go to a nice restaurant or, oh, wait, I know, you could leave the country. That would make me very happy. Ultimately, it would make the Italian government happy. They do not know that yet because they have not had the pleasure of your company.

"Under no circumstances are you to get involved in this investigation. Capisci, signore Blessing?"

"You can call me Julian." Julian despised playing the fool. This time doing so got him what he wanted. He sat and smiled foolishly.

* * *

Inspector Saviano and her partner put Julian into a taxi and instructed the driver to deliver him to his hotel and nowhere else. The inspector was emphatic each of the three times she repeated, "Nowhere else."

Julian waved goodbye through the taxi's rear window. His grin left the inspector and her assistant on the curb shaking their heads.

He turned around in his seat and the too-broad grin devolved into a thin, tight line and there was fury behind his eyes. The change did not go unnoticed. The driver had looked in his rearview mirror and what he saw chilled his bones.

Half a mile away, Julian pushed a crisp, orange fifty euro note into the front seat and quietly said, "Città del Vaticano, per favore." At the next intersection the driver had a decision to make - risk the ire of the police or follow the dictates of free enterprise.

A second crisp, orange fifty euro note floated into the front seat to join its brother. The driver looked again into his rearview mirror. In the years to come, he would tell of the time he had a fare who could see right into your soul.

Some decisions are easier to make than others. The driver turned his taxi toward Vatican City and drove.

CHAPTER FOUR

The taxi delivered Julian to the mouth of St. Peter's Square. Ten euros more and Julian had exact directions to the Vatican garage and carpool. He started off on foot to find the St. Anne Gate, the working entrance to the Vatican.

* * *

The Corpo della Gendarmeria, who manned this entrance, were the picture of vigilance, checking and rechecking employees as they entered and turning away Hawaiian shirted tourists who demanded to see the Pope.

The entrance stood next to the Gendarmeria barracks. The area was alive with fit young men in dark blue uniforms with foreign legion caps in blue. Julian read the signatures of many of the men. To him, each had mastered the art of looking relaxed while being perpetually alert and mindful of where they worked and why.

Julian approached the checkpoint prepared to be either denied entrance outright, or, at the worst, arrested. Still, he had to try and trying the easy way first was always preferable to the other option.

He had experienced the phenomenon of stepping out of linear time to appear elsewhere. This was a new talent he had tried only a few times. He had told his teacher, Moira Hagan, he was 'inexpert' in his use of it. Her response had been a less than reassuring, 'What a load of bollocks. You're awful, ya eejet.'

These semantic disagreements were a frequent part of their student/teacher relationship.

He took a breath and calmed his thoughts. His paranormal talents were newly discovered, raw, and occasionally he wielded them badly. He had asked his mentor what his gifts were for, what greater agenda he was advancing.

The professor's wife, Bridget Bragonier, responded, "What we do is shine a light into the darkness. We scatter the shadows. If we do it correctly, we are able to make the seemingly impossible happen." That seemed like so long ago to him. He had seen and learned and done so much since those early days.

"Well, let's make the impossible happen," he whispered to himself. At his approach, the two officers eyed him carefully, then looked away. He walked past them and was thunderstruck. Bridget had been right.

Following his taxi driver's directions, Julian followed Via Rusticucci, inside Vatican City, as the street jogged to the right. He passed the plain, brown sandstone Vatican post office, turned right and could see the Apostolic Library on his left. The driver said the garage and motor pool would be on his right.

He had gotten by the Vatican police. On reflection, that had not been so much impossible as improbable. Two hundred feet ahead of him stood the impossible.

The slightly built and highly volatile Inspector Belladonna Saviano was talking with two men in dark suits. Explaining himself to the inspector would be unwise, he knew. Julian felt his best course would be to station himself nearby and wait for the inspector to leave.

Turning away from the impossible, Julian walked directly into the immovable – the inspector's sergeant.

"Signore Marino," Julian said and tried to look pleased. "What a surprise." He meant every word of that. The man said nothing. He looked at Julian without blinking or moving.

"How long have you been following…" There was no reason to complete his sentence. Suddenly the truth became exposed to glaring daylight. Julian made it past the Vatican police because the sergeant, who had been following him, waved them away.

"Well, gosh, nice chatting with you. It seems I must be going."

"Going so soon, signore Blessing?" Julian closed his eyes and turned. He had been intent on getting away from Marino and never felt the inspector walk up behind him. This, he swore to himself, he would work on. Unless the inspector killed him.

"I gave you a set of instructions, signore, did I not?" Her tone was pleasantly derisive.

"My thoughts exactly, Inspector. You told me to do some sight-seeing, and as you can see, I am. You told me to leave Italy and I have removed myself – by the way, to a place where you have no jurisdict…" Julian could sense the signature of two men who were now standing behind him with Marino. Both the newcomers had a keen interest in him and both had plenty of jurisdiction.

"I'm sorry, I believe you were about to say something about my authority within Vatican City?" the inspector said. Her eyebrows were raised, her brown eyes opened large and she looked expectant.

"Me?" Julian attempted. He sensed two more men joining the group that was now forming behind him. He didn't enjoying being the center of attention.

* * *

Julian sat handcuffed and seated in the back of the inspector's car. She sat beside him and her sergeant drove. "What am I to do with you, signore?" the inspector asked. "You have caused Enrico and me far more trouble than you are worth. I agree, that was not difficult because you have proved to be worth almost nothing.

"We try to assist you and for our efforts, you obstruct our every move, you lie to us, you meddle where you are not wanted, and now you defy me by refusing to follow my instructions. Please, answer me, signore Blessing. I am absolutely dying to hear what new bundle of lies you have manufactured for Enrico and me." Julian opened his mouth, but closed it when she continued.

"I say this only because you have, as yet, failed to tell even one truth to us, although I am enthralled by many of your half-truths. Am I wrong? Please tell me, signore." She looked at Julian as though he might answer with something truthful or even plausible.

He sat in silence and examined the buttons on his shirt as Rome flew past the car's windows.

"Oh, you have no answers for me. I am crushed. Tonight, I shall go home and cry into my pillow," the inspector said in a voice that dripped condescension. "Enrico, can you not see that I am crushed?" Her assistant looked briefly into the rear view mirror, then nodded his head.

Belladonna Saviano turned to her prisoner and leaned in close. Again, Julian could feel her breath on his face. This woman was not a respecter of personal space.

She didn't speak above a whisper, but her voice was pure acid. "Listen to me carefully, wizard or magician or whatever you are. If you disobey me once more, you will be on the next airplane out of Italy. I am not a witch, signore, but I am a bitch and if you cross me again, I will make you suffer as few have ever suffered.

"Enrico," the inspector snapped, looking over her shoulder. "Am I not a bitch? Tell signore Blessing. I do not want him to be confused on this point."

Her assistant drove, looked neither right nor left and said nothing. The inspector stared at Julian and waited a full minute before she said, "Enrico, you are a very wise man and Julian Blessing is a sciocco!"

Enrico Marino looked pained and began to shake his head slowly when he heard the fool, Julian Blessing, say, "What's a sciocco?"

* * *

Marino drove up Via Nazionale and double parked in front of the Hotel Quirinale Roma to a symphony of car horns and shouted curses. The two police officers marched a handcuffed Julian Blessing through the lobby, removing his handcuffs only when they were in Julian's room.

Inspector Saviano's order left Julian no room to maneuver. "Remain in your room," she said. "If you are hungry, call for room service. If you are bored, look out the window. If you are lonely, read a book. If you are horny, read a book. If you are tired, go to sleep, but do not go out of this room until we come to get you. Capisci? And none of your sorcery, signore stregone!"

"What's a stregone?" Julian, the wizard, asked.

* * *

"Dominic, if it weren't for people, the world would be a far better place, no?" Cardinal Luciano said to his assistant. The young priest suppressed a smile and answered, "Yes, Eminence."

"I can hear the cogs in your head at work. You believe I am making a small joke. I assure you, Dominic, I most assuredly am not," the cardinal said.

"Eminence, without people the world would be lonely for you. Without people, what would be the point of winning? There would be no need to struggle except to survive," Fr. Dominic Giglio said.

The cardinal smiled. "A finance expert and a philosopher? How is it I am so blessed? You are right of course, but still, allow me to hope and dream of a world without people."

* * *

As the inspector and her assistant walked down the thickly carpeted hallway toward the hotel elevator, Enrico asked, "Bella, what do you think?"

The inspector stitched her eyebrows together and considered for a moment before saying, "Enrico, I honestly don't know. You know what they say, 'When the game is over, the king and the pawn go into the same box,' no? This Blessing is not the king, but he is not a pawn. And there are others. I can feel it. We have not yet identified all the pieces. Il amore mio, we must find out where he, and the rest, fit on the chessboard and do it well before the game is over."

Enrico asked, "Do you think he is a stregone, a wizard or sorcerer or whatever?"

His inspector only shrugged. "He is something. We will discover what before we are done," she said.

* * *

Unpleasant, unattractive, and unhappy, Bogdan Sokolov ruminated on things that made him even more unpleasant, unattractive and unhappy. In his office on Via del Pellegrino, in the Campo de' Fiori district of Rome, the focus of his displeasure was Julian Blessing.

Sokolov had been following the out-of-sight-out-of-mind policy regarding Julian. Now, he was in plain sight and so never far from Sokolov's thoughts. Julian had cost Sokolov a lot of money in New York. Mobsters, Russian and otherwise, do not like this.

"Now, this Amerikanskaya is in Rome. Following me?" Sokolov thought. "Nobody could be that big a beelyat!" Bogdan Sokolov had not yet gauged Julian's nearly unlimited ability to be an accidental idiot. The Russian would live to regret underestimating accidental idiots. They had a habit of being unpredictable and therefore dangerous.

* * *

Rome, at midday, was fully alive. Sounds, sights and smells mingled and merged into a chaotic orchestral arrangement.

A black car with heavily tinted windows sped through Rome's hyperactive thoroughfares, turned up cobbled streets and down broad avenues. Once inside the gates of Vatican City, the vehicle negotiated the narrow streets and glided gently to a stop in front of a building whose only designation was I.O.R. above the unimpressive entrance. Istituto per le Opere di Religione.

A young priest hurried down the front steps and opened the vehicle's back door. Julian stepped out as the priest welcomed him to the Vatican Bank.

Once inside, Julian was ushered into a large, richly appointed office. The priest said, "Eminence, Mr. Blessing has arrived."

A portly man in his late sixties with sharp features, green eyes and a head of slate gray hair turned from his office window, smiled, and with a slight gesture, dismissed Julian's guide.

"Please come in, Mr. Blessing, and thank you for agreeing to meet with me today." The Irish accent was not thick, but it was unmistakable. "I am sorry I was unable to provide you with more notice.

"I hope you've not eaten. I've arranged for lunch to be served in half an hour." The cardinal smiled his welcome and his voice was jovial with just a touch of irony.

The cardinal extended his hand and said, "Terrance Cardinal Patrick Manning. When I say it like that it makes me sound grand – something a poor boy from county Mayo could never be."

Julian knew it all for the lie is was and the cardinal knew he knew. The man's accent was like Ailís', clearly well educated Dublin, not Mayo. Julian had been in Ireland too long not to recognize that the man was from the upper reaches of Irish society. He felt the cardinal might have read about poverty, but that was as close as he got. He was not so much pretentious as powerful beyond words and Julian could sense it easily.

"Your Eminence, it is a pleasure to meet you. How can I be of assistance?"

The cardinal took Julian by the arm and led him to a seating area that overlooked the Papal gardens. "Son, it isn't what you can do for me, but what I can do for you. Please, sit here. It's a lovely view and one that few get to see from this angle."

Julian had learned from the Irish. Cardinal Manning would get to the point of the interview in his own time and in his own way. The path would be littered with clues and hints. What was said, and what was subtly not said, and what was pointedly avoided would each have value. There was nothing for it but to listen with care and wait.

* * *

Cardinal Manning and Julian sat and admired the papal gardens. Both men chatted amiably about Ireland and Julian's impressions of rural Irish life. They discussed the pros and cons of life in New York and New York's similarities to Rome.

As the cardinal spoke, Julian pursued his own internal dialogue.

To Julian, the cardinal's signature presented a pleasant, crafty, and unbelievably complex man whose agendas had agendas of their own. The man's intellect and experience were the basis of his personal power and his sense of humor allowed him to appear charming without necessarily being so. Still, for Julian, there was something out of place. This cardinal had something askew, something off.

Julian felt he was talking with the cardinal, but there was an echo to the man's personality. A fraction of a second after the cardinal spoke, Julian heard a resonance. Something shadowed Cardinal Manning and Julian didn't know what. He told himself he would revisit that later. Now was the time to listen with great care.

A bell rang once somewhere in the cardinal's suite of offices. The older man took a deep breath, savored the sight of the gardens before him, and sighed. He rose from his chair and led Julian into an adjacent dining room.

The dining room was small enough to be intimate and was tastefully understated to impress. The table was laid for what promised to be a lunch that would eliminate the need for dinner.

"Please, Mr. Blessing, sit and prepare to be amazed. My chef is a wizard." The cardinal winked and smiled more broadly than was warranted. "Before our meal arrives though, let us take a private moment, shall we, to reflect and be grateful. Sure it is that you have many things for which to be grateful." Again, the cardinal smiled and again, Julian heard the echo.

A full minute passed before the cardinal looked up, rang a small bell on the table, and a liveried steward arrived and served lunch.

"Mr. Blessing, do you mind if I call you Julian? It 'tisn't formalities we need to stand on, now is it?" the cardinal said. Julian enjoyed the Irish English sentence structure and the way the cardinal employed it not to charm but to disarm. Julian nodded knowing this relaxation of formalities was a one-way street.

"Julian, I told you when you arrived, it was my good self who meant to be of assistance to you," the cardinal said. "Well, help you I shall. I'm afraid my authority is, however, strictly spiritual so the assistance I can offer is only my advice. I may be able to call in a small favor here and there to aid you though.

"You have come to my attention for several reasons. This is the Vatican and we all have our tasks to perform. In addition to overseeing the Vatican Bank, one of my duties is to watch over all things Irish. I am the resident Irishman and so the resident expert. At least my betters say that. I've always suspected I'm it because no one else would take the job of dealing with the Irish." The cardinal's smile was as practiced as his speech had been.

"Your friend, Dr. Dwyer, is missing." The cardinal said it flatly, a statement of fact, but he looked grave. "This is a vital concern to me and to others.

"You are deeply tied to the Irish Republic, Julian. I understand you've applied for residency. Even without that, with your many ties to Ireland, you are now one of my flock. What concerns you, concerns me deeply.

"To that end, let me tell you this. Have a care, my son. You are swimming in a shark tank. I know many of the sharks personally and know how dangerous they can be. In my early days in Rome, I was bitten many times."

Julian drifted into his own Irish accented English. "Ach, wouldn't your Eminence be talkin' about a time before he started biting back?" The cardinal eyed Julian carefully, smiled broadly and nodded his head.

"You have been to see Cardinal Luciano." The cardinal held up a hand. "No need to say anything. Rome is still a very small town really and the Vatican is smaller still.

"Tread lightly around the Cardinal Archbishop. He is a man who is not only powerful, but he can be deadly. I know some who have suffered at his hands. I can say they are not the men they once were because of the exchange. I will not ask you about your conversation. I do not need to know the contents. Still, I can tell you that nothing said or done will be to your benefit."

Julian nodded his understanding and asked, "Eminence, what would be the best way to protect myself?"

Cardinal Manning thought for a moment before saying, "Julian, my advice is to stay away from his Eminence, Cardinal Luciano. However, I know this is not advice you will follow – I'm not sure it is advice you will be allowed to follow. The cardinal has what is probably an unholy interest in you and he is unlikely to let you slip away so easily.

"I do have a resource you can use to help you with this, but we can speak of that later."

Julian nodded.

"I know who you are, of course." The cardinal smiled, toyed with his butter knife and let the sentence hang in the air, his green eyes alive with mischief.

After a mouthful of crab salad, Julian said, "Eminence, I can't tell you how delighted I am to hear that. I frequently don't know who I am, so it is good to find someone who does."

"Yes, well perhaps I stated that incorrectly," the cardinal chuckled. "Let us say, I know what you are – approximately. I know the life you live, although I'm ignorant of the how of it all. I'm familiar with your activities in Ireland, to a large extent, and your life in the United States before that. This is a subject upon which

I have dedicated much study. It may seem odd to you, but I know many who are like you.

"You are acquainted with Mrs. Bridget Bragonier, of course," the cardinal said. "She is probably the most intelligent, charming and terrifyingly formidable woman I have ever met. I knew her in her younger days. She was captivating then and has become more so with time, although it has been donkey years since I've seen her." Julian said nothing and the cardinal continued.

"The Church has known of the group to which you, and she, and the others belong for a very long time. I will remind you, the Church calculates time in terms of centuries so very long is very long indeed.

"Careful study has been made of the works all of you do and those who came before you. I can tell you, scores of theologians and philosophers have debated, to exhaustion, the relative value most people like you have brought and continue to bring to the table. That value has been proven to be substantial.

"Holy Mother Church has dealt in the spheres of the corporeal and the incorporeal, the realms of the physical and the metaphysical, for millennia," the cardinal smiled, "with successes and failures on both sides of that coin. The natural and the supernatural are well known to us and so you are perhaps better understood than you think.

"I am authorized to tell you, the abilities you and many of your associates wield, as well as your activities to date, present no obstacle to the Church.

"I cannot tell you that you have our support or blessing, but I can say we will not stop you or work against you. That, in itself, is an endorsement of sorts and one not without value."

"You said, 'Most people like me,' Eminence, but not all?" Julian said. "You mean we are not universally prized?" He smiled.

The cardinal smiled back and looked thoughtful. "I like you Julian. You are an honorable man, from what I can tell, and you try to do good work.

"For this reason and for your protection, I will tell you, there are those who share your gifts, but whose intentions are not your intentions." The smile left the cardinal's face and he looked stern and unyielding.

"Their motivation is purely one of self-interest. The results of their actions are often reflected in the haunted eyes of those they have harmed.

"Trust that men without honor, such as these, are well known to us and their activities are closely monitored. Still, they are dangerous," the cardinal said.

Julian said, "Our earlier discussion about one of your brother cardinals and the discussion we are having now is, of course, related. Am I right, Eminence?"

Cardinal Manning smiled broadly and with his Irish accented English fully engaged again said, "Ach, sure it is, Mr. Julian; it stands like this wi' me. Although your honor is free to say such a thing with confidence, a humble Irishman and a poor priest besides, would never dare to speculate."

Julian and the cardinal shared a chuckle and the remainder of their meal was passed in pleasant conversation. Still the myriad of threats facing Julian were serious and, if possible, he wouldn't leave without addressing them.

After lunch, Cardinal Manning walked with Julian to the front door of the Vatican Bank – a rare honor and not one lost on Julian. The cardinal became serious as they approached the security checkpoint.

"Julian, I mentioned I would suggest a way you might protect yourself."

"I thought to remind you," Julian said, "but knew you would circle back to it in your own time. I have, your Eminence, been among the Irish too long to think it would be otherwise."

The cardinal smiled, reached into the wide scarlet sash of his cassock and handed Julian a piece of paper. "This is the name and address of," Cardinal Manning hesitated searching for the right nuanced expression, "a friend. He is someone who will understand you, someone who is like you. In a way, he knows you better than you may know yourself and perhaps better than you wish he did.

"This man is knowledgeable in the ways of Rome, the workings of the Vatican and the mind of someone from whom you need to protect yourself.

"My son, make seeing this man your first order of business. He can help you in ways and in areas where no one else can. You can trust him with your life. One day, you may have to."

"I understand completely, your Eminence. Thank you for taking time from your busy schedule to talk with me today. Still, there is something that is troubling me," Julian said and the cardinal nodded and looked suitably concerned.

"Dr. Dwyer," Julian said.

"Yes," the cardinal said and his eyebrows moved closer together. "As I said, the doctor has been on my mind since I heard of it. I realize she is incredibly important to you and I understand the full impact of how important.

"I have contacted the authorities, of course, and have used my influence as best I can. Do not think they are handling this as anything but a case with the highest priority. As yet, I know nothing. I will continue to make inquiries of my own and to lean on the various police agencies. Please, know both you and the doctor shall be in my prayers. Go with God, Julian."

* * *

Needing time to think, Julian declined the offer of a ride back to his hotel. He walked into the sunshine of a perfect Roman afternoon. He was deep in thought, considering the things the cardinal said and the things left unsaid. He was not so distracted that he did not sense the presence of someone who was a jumble of overheated emotions. He stopped before reaching the bottom step. Julian closed his eyes, hung his head and held out both wrists in front of him.

"Stregone – in the car now!" Inspector Belladonna Saviano barked.

The inspector and Julian were rocketed into the back seat as Enrico Marino, sped away from the curb. The car careened down narrow streets, disappeared into even narrower alleys, only to reappear on a broad thoroughfare. The vehicle shot through the gates of the Vatican and vanished into the heart of Rome.

"We have a problem," the inspector said to Julian. "A very large problem and this time it isn't you."

CHAPTER FIVE

Bogdan Sokolov didn't so much shout into the telephone, he breathed fire. "You asshole! I give a fool like you a simple problem to solve. You were to bring me that dick, Blessing.

"'Bogdan, of course you can trust your brother-in-law to do this simple thing for you.' That is what I say to myself and what do you do instead? You send some other idiots who are now in jail! I say to myself, 'I should just kill you', but my sister would have to go find a new husband and next time he may be a bigger asshole than you! Is possible, but I do not see how."

Bogdan Sokolov was unhappy and would soon get a lot unhappier.

* * *

The sedan sat in an underground parking garage. Belladonna, Enrico and Julian sat in the dark silence. No movement. No sound. The busy streets of Rome swarmed with cars, motorbikes and pedestrians. But for the three, the only sound was their breathing.

"There are people who want to kill you," the inspector said. "We came to collect you this morning. I told you to stay in your room, so, of course, you had to go out. You do that a lot. Neither Enrico nor I like this habit of yours. The next time we will take stronger measures to keep you where we leave you.

"On this occasion, however, your disobedience probably saved your life. We, as I say, arrived to pick you up, but instead of you, stregone, we discover two Russians. Imagine our surprise.

"They were not happy about being arrested. It happens sometimes. My report will read that during the arrest, the suspects resisted and some small damage was done to the hotel room before they could be restrained. In fact, your room was destroyed," the inspector said and smiled and shrugged.

"The hotel's management was initially most unhappy and wanted you arrested too, but..." Julian cut in. "The hotel wanted me arrested? Russians in my room?"

"Oh, stregone." She was at her most condescending.

"Now, follow along wizard. The Russians were there to kidnap you, after which I'm sure they would kill you. At least that is what they said after Enrico asked them. You know how polite Enrico can be – he has a way with people. We will explain all of this to you later.

"As for the hotel, well, they assigned one of their rooms to you and it became ruined. You must learn to take responsibility for things entrusted to you, no? Do not worry yourself though. The hotel's manager is Enrico's second cousin, so you will not be arrested."

"Well, that's something, I suppose," Julian said.

"Yes, all was forgiven once he told them you had fled the country leaving your room bill unpaid. Enrico reminded his cousin that you had left a credit card on file with them. The room charges and all repairs will be in your next billing. You should thank Enrico for being so clever," the Inspector said."

"Like hell!" Julian shouted. "You two wreck my room and blame it on me. I have to pay for the damages and you tell the manager I fled the country. Do I have any of this right?"

"See Enrico, I told you he would understand. He is not so big a fool as you say he is," the inspector said and her sergeant snorted.

"Well, I need to get my things."

"No need," the sergeant grunted.

"Enrico is a man of very few words; you may have noticed." The inspector smiled. "He means, no need to go back because all of your things are in the boot of the car. I might add, you are very well organized, very neat in your habits. We threw it all in a plastic bag and brought it with us. You had some luggage, but it was bulky so we left it. Besides we were in a hurry."

"My things are in a garbage bag? Jesus!" Julian hung his head in defeat and said, "Would you mind giving me a ride to another hotel? After all your 'help,'" he put air quotes around it, "I think you'll agree I need another place to stay."

Enrico snorted again, shook his head and looked bored.

"You see, stregone," the inspector said, "we are the police. It is our business to discover things. For instance, we have discovered you aren't very good at this thinking business, so we have done all the thinking for you.

"We have managed to find you a charming little place where they will accept a man who uses a plastic bag, instead of luggage, and they will ask few questions. Not all of our hotels in Rome would." The inspector smiled more broadly this time.

* * *

On the Piazza della Pilotta in the center of Rome, a man spoke in a voice just above a whisper. "Yes, Eminence. I understand completely." He hung up the phone and leaned back in his desk chair. He steepled his fingers, and said softly, simply, "Good." The word summed up his outlook for the future. "And now begins the end."

✳ ✳ ✳

"It's a whorehouse!" Julian whispered his shout. Whispering, he didn't sound as outraged as he was. However, his facial contortions made it very clear.

"Is it? Are you sure? You are far more familiar with such places than am I, it seems. I have no need to frequent such places," the inspector said with a sadistic smile. "I will ask the proprietress if what you say is the case.

"Signore Blessing, may I present your hostess, signorina Joselina Conaletti," the Inspector said. "Signorina, signore Blessing believes your establishment is a house of prostitution. Is this true? Surely, it cannot be."

The old woman looked up at Julian with, if not madness, severe eccentricity in her eyes. She walked around Julian and his garbage bag of earthly possessions. Reaching out she squeezed his left bicep. She poked a finger into his stomach in a way that made it turn.

Julian tried to read this woman, but her signature was a muddle of emotions and avarice.

Signorina Conaletti smiled a licentious smile and cackled. Julian shivered. She did not look at him so much as examine him as one would a bug. She grabbed his right thigh and he jumped. She sniggered.

The old woman addressed the inspector in Italian, "Bella, where did you find such a pretty one? What is wrong with him that you would give him to us? No matter, for you, he can stay."

The signorina addressed Julian in heavily accented English. "Signore, I am the owner of Casa Felicità. We do not provide whores. We bring joy to men in need of it. Belladonna can tell you of our good works."

"Oh, many good works and all very legal. Several members of the government have been regulars for years. Apparently they are in need of much joy, no?" The women smiled at each other and the inspector called to her assistant. "Enrico, leave the whores alone. We are going."

She continued to Julian, "Signorina Joselina says you can stay, but you must behave or you will have to leave." The inspector added, to watch Julian squirm, "Of course, some of what you charge your customers will have to go to signorina Conaletti."

"What!"

* * *

A man in his late sixties with sharp features and slate gray hair looked into the distance. His green eyes were hooded in thought.

A younger man in a conservative, perfectly tailored black suit asked a question and looked wary. "This newcomer, this Julian Blessing, will he will be trouble, do you think?"

"Nothing you need worry yourself about. Leave him to me. He will prove useful," the cardinal said. His smile was thin and shrewd and Cardinal Manning's Irish accent showed not at all.

* * *

Julian left the House of Joy, entered a taxi and gave an address to the driver. Ten minutes of insane driving left him breathing hard and standing in front of Sapienza University.

Bridget's husband, Professor Bragonier, had given Julian a name and address for the chair of the antiquities department at Sapienza, Professor Agostini. Agostini was in possession of a copy of the papers Ailís had attempted to pick up from the express service.

Julian felt there might be some clue to her disappearance and doing something was always better than doing nothing.

No matter where he looked on the campus, he encountered block after block of purpose built architectural madness. The university was a mash up of styles. As he walked, he was treated to an absurd smorgasbord of collegiate gothic, Doric, baroque, neoclassical, modern and, what Julian thought of as just plain ugly buildings. Finding the antiquities department would be a miracle.

It appeared in the form of Giovanni Silvestri. The young man was in his very early twenties with fashionably long hair, tight jeans and a tee shirt that read 'New Mexico ~ the Land of Enchantment.'

Julian stopped and turned when he felt Giovanni's signature. 'A young man with an uncommon interest in you,' is what it said to Julian. The student stopped abruptly ten feet short and his face broke into a smile that disarmed coeds and charmed their mothers.

"I'm sorry, sir. You look like an American and a lost one at that. I need to practice my English and I am lost only half the time. We could help each other, no?" Giovanni said.

"You're right. I am an American, but I've not yet begun to be lost. That, I suppose, will come in an hour or so of wandering around. I would appreciate some help.

"As for your English, I can tell you I have worked with Americans who didn't speak the language as well as you."

Giovanni smiled more broadly and extended his hand for an introduction. "Gio Silvestri. A humble student at the college of economics and business. How can I help?" A wild pack of young women passed on the sidewalk and flirted outrageously with the young man. He ignored them.

"I'm Julian Blessing and I am looking for the antiquities department." Gio brightened. "Specifically," Julian continued, "for Professor Agostini." Gio paled.

"You wish to see professore Agostini? Agostini the Terrible? Agostini the Destroyer of Students? Agostini, the Embodiment of Evil and the Slayer of Academic Careers? Are you in need of a doctor? Are you ill? Only a madman would seek out that creature.

"Signore, a thousand apologies." Gio looked contrite as he tried to collect himself. "I am sure you know what you are doing and have important business with the professore. I will happily lead you to the department. I will point out his office. I cannot get too near though."

"Gio, your reticence to drop in on the professor is based on some personal experience?" Julian asked chuckling at the answer he knew would follow.

"We can walk in this direction." Julian's guide pointed the way. "My story is a short one. It is different from those whom the professore shriveled slowly." Gio shivered violently.

"I was to major in history. I have always loved the subject and lived to be a teacher of history upon graduation.

"I had Professor Agostini as a tutor. At the end of our first session, he said he would kill me if I did not change my major. Economics and business was as far away from the professore as I could get." Giovanni took a deep breath and let it out slowly.

"As bad as all that?" Julian said.

"That bad and worse. The man is a horror. He is a fiend sent from hell to torment students. Many believe he drinks the blood of those who fail his courses. He is well stocked since nearly everyone fails. It is true," Gio said and crossed himself.

Julian laughed, something he had not done in days. The sun was warm, the company was amiable and the walk a pleasantly slow one. It would be easy to lose oneself in such circumstances but there were other circumstances that sat heavily upon him.

They talked of America and Italy, New York and Rome. Gio was fascinated to learn Julian had been a broker on Wall Street and Julian was impressed his guide spoke five other languages.

Giovanni consulted a bulletin board to see if the professor was in class or would be in his office. They walked a bit further and Gio abruptly stopped at an archway that led to a brick, late gothic revival building.

"We have arrived, Mr. Blessing. That is you have arrived. I am just leaving. You will find the Professore From Hell on the second floor, room 250. This building only has two floors. If there were more, the professore would be found in room 666." Gio made the sign of the horns in the general direction of room 250.

"Gio, you have been very kind. Please give me an email address. There are some contacts I can send you, along with a letter of introduction. I still have associates in New York. No one there has friends," Julian said. "That is a thing you should remember."

Giovanni rooted through his backpack for pen and paper. He wrote out his address and phone number and shook Julian's hand vigorously. Julian watched as the young student walked up behind an especially attractive coed and draped his arm around her. She was not displeased.

Julian turned to look for the office and then stopped. Something was wrong. Something was out of place. What, he could not tell. That it was there, he had no doubt. Not a signature, but a presence, a darkness.

He knocked lightly on the door to the professor's office. The signature of the man on the other side of this door caused Julian to smile. He knew a man like the occupant of this room – Professor Bragonier. "One professor is much like another," Julian thought.

"Enter and state your business," a man's voice said in Italian. The voice was firm and brooked no disagreement. This was not a request, but a command and Julian understood the intent if not the words.

"Professore Agostini? Mi chiamo," Julian began.

The professor held up his hand and interrupted. "Before you murder the language further, you are Mr. Blessing. Professor Bragonier told me to expect you. I have information for you and you are here to learn. That puts you in the top one percent of people on this campus. Students, Mr. Blessing, are a curse, but one with which we must live." The man's voice had softened. The accent was heavy, but the professor's use of English was precise.

He indicated a chair and Julian sat in front of a badly battered desk. Stacks of papers stood ready for grading. Books on well-ordered shelves lined two walls of the small office. Prints of long ago battles hung on the walls. This was a room both timely and timeless.

The professor rose and walked to a locked file cabinet. Julian saw a small man with a huge presence. His signature was vital and strong. In his late sixties with a gray fringe of hair, he sported a goatee that gave him a carefully constructed demonic look.

With a large envelope in hand, the professor returned to his desk and withdrew a sizable stack of papers. The pages were edged with annotations. Footnotes supported the text from the bottom of each page.

Professor Agostini's notes were plentiful. It was plain to see he had spent time with these documents. If he hadn't learned anything from them, it would only be because there was nothing to learn.

"You are searching for coins, Mr. Blessing?"

"Professor, I am searching, if not for the truth, for a signpost pointing the way to it." Julian smiled and inclined his head slightly.

"Then, sir, we will get along famously. Of coins, I have none, but truths, of a sort, I have them in abundance." The professor, eyes alight with mischief, had a class of one. He was now in his element.

"I will begin by setting the stage slightly and correcting a misconception under which you labor. At the outset, and not without good reason, Professor Bragonier and I agreed with you. We were all of us wrong.

"The Roman coins you found in Ireland we first believed to be half of a larger treasury. In fact the evidence supports the opposite. What you found in Ireland is only a tiny fraction of the whole.

"Where to begin?" The professor laid both palms down on the papers. "Let me tell you a story," he said.

For two hours the professor spun out a chronicle of court intrigues, the illegitimate children of popes and petty kings, of greedy prelates, murder, larceny and betrayal, the rich and the powerful, the famous, the infamous, and the unknown powers behind the throne of St. Peter. It was a story of money – what it could buy, who it could enrich and who it could destroy. And the innocent. Always the innocent and always it was they who suffered.

The professor traced a course that took the story from ancient Rome to the ends of the modern world. One fact had led to another. One rumor led to another fact. On and on throughout history, innuendo led to rumor, led to fact, led inexorably to a darker truth.

The older man looked off into the distance as he spoke. He had done the research. He knew the story by heart and had no need to consult notes or look for validation or even acknowledgement from Julian.

"And that is the present state of my research. Sadly, there is far more I do not know than I do. I can tell you, I do not like this. There are parts of the story I have had to fill in based on a stew made up of facts, fables and insinuation. I like this even less. To me this is a puzzle and now it has taken hold so I must solve it. The pieces are here. I have yet to draw it all together. There is something missing.

"So, Mr. Blessing, what have you to say?" The professor smiled as he came back into himself. He was a professional realist. He was resigned that the past created the present and that the present created future histories. He was happy in history and saddened by the present and despaired for the future.

Julian thought for a moment. "A question, a clarification really."

The professor's eyebrows shot up and he leaned forward. "There was something about which I was unclear? I have made some error?" It wasn't a question, but a statement of incredulity.

"Not at all," Julian said. "It is not your ability to teach, but my in-ability to understand. Rather my not wanting to believe. Nothing more."

Mollified, the professor snorted, "In that case, please ask your question."

"Are you saying the Roman coins, the ones that never left Rome, were the seed money for an organization still in existence today? To believe that, changes the world. Professor, it is my sincere hope you will tell me how wrong I am." Julian's face was tight and his gray eyes sharp and penetrating.

The professor nodded his head slightly and only once. "I can only tell you what the research shows. Although we wish to believe otherwise, the study of history is not a science. Still, we do our best and follow the evidence where it takes us," the professor said.

"I can say," he continued, "we don't always follow willingly. Some historical facts lead me to conclusions that are simply awkward. Some are nearly impossible to accept. By its nature, much of my research contradicts what we have previously known. In this case, you have stated the case accurately.

"If this has answered your question, please tell me what you have learned." The professor sat back in his chair, watched Julian carefully and waited. The look said he was prepared to wait a very long time.

Julian sighed deeply before answering. "Well, in a way, what we have is the most complex money laundering and organized crime operation in the history of, well, history."

The professor's smile was a challenge. "And that is all?"

"There is an secret organization operating today that has been in existence at least as long as the Catholic church and perhaps longer." Brows laced together, mouth set, eyes cold and hard, Julian let out a noisy breath.

"You are a good student, Mr. Blessing. You are willing to accept as possible what you are unwilling to believe is true," the professor said. "In this, you are a better student than I am an historian.

"I did not want to believe," the professor said. "I discounted out of hand the idea an organization could operate unseen for millennia. I rejected the idea even though all of the evidence pointed to that being the case.

"I went so far as to speculate the treasure was used to fund the fledgling church. That seemed like a reasonable conclusion when compared to where the trail of evidence was leading."

The professor continued. "An organization operating in parallel, whose rise to power mirrored that of the Catholic Church, was a thing I could not credit. That it could be more secretive than the Church was a thing unbelievable. In the end though, I was forced to accept what I tried so desperately to reject.

"You, Mr. Blessing, have shamed an eminent professor." Agostini smiled and inclined his head in acknowledgement. "Bravo."

"Professor, please understand, I am not shackled by the research. You presented the evidence your research validated. I jumped ahead. Nothing more," Julian said.

"A further question, if I may," Julian said and the professor nodded and looked interested. "Throughout, you have not really mentioned Professor Bragonier." Julian left the rest unsaid.

Julian's host arched an eyebrow, thought, then said, "Because you are an excellent student and come to me recommended by my friend, I will take no offense.

"In fact, you are correct. I have made little mention of my colleague. We approached this subject in as scientific a manner as possible. He provided me with the sources of his research, but not with his conclusions. I have done the same.

"We will be meeting in Paris next week to, rather literally, compare notes. For now, he knows the early history of this while I took it from that point forward. Until next week, neither of us knows the inner thoughts of the other," the professor concluded and threw a questioning look at Julian.

"Now it is time for you to educate me about something you said. I have of course, heard the term money laundering. I have heard the term 'speed of light' in the same way. The first is decidedly bad while the other is decidedly interesting if not always good. Beyond that, I confess my ignorance," the professor concluded.

Julian relaxed slightly. His face said he needed to gain control of emotions and thoughts in full riot. "Well, professor, that is a lecture best given over lunch. Would you join me? I know of a perfect trattoria only a quick cab ride away." Julian dangled the bait.

"Hmmmm," the professor intoned. "Perhaps it is a subject best suited for such a place. We must be in haste though. I have another class in three hours." He said it as though a three-hour meal was a bare minimum requirement.

The men locked the professor's office and proceeded to the street where Julian hailed a cab. He tried at least. All of them darted by without paying any attention.

"Allow me, Mr. Blessing. This is Rome and so a subtle Roman touch is required." The professor stepped two feet into the street and locked his eyes on the face of the next cab coming up the broad avenue. The professor snarled and the driver stood on his brakes and slid to a stop.

"Professore, good to see you," the driver said, leaning across the front seat as Agostini slid in.

"It is nothing of the sort, Lorenzini. You despise seeing me as much as I loathe seeing you. This is what you do with the antiquities degree I gave you? You certainly didn't earn it," the professor said and the driver sputtered an explanation.

Julian could feel a familiar signature. He turned and greeted Gio Silvestri. Julian asked the young man to join them for lunch. Gio was genuinely pleased. Free food for a student was proof of the existence of God. And there may be wine. Evidence that God is good.

"That would be perfect, Mr. Blessing. Again I will have the chance to practice my," the words died on his lips and he visibly paled and Julian smiled a mischievous smile.

"Oh, signore, I had forgotten. I have a class starting in a few moments and…" Gio stammered.

"Oh, this lunch promises to be more educational than any class you might have. Please, you can ride in front," Julian said.

He stepped closer. "Signore, please. That is Agostini the Terrible in the back seat," Gio whispered. "You are only inviting me because wherever you are going doesn't have students on the menu. Sir, he eats undergraduates. Don't you understand?"

"In you go," Julian said and opened the front door. The professor was already comfortably situated and looking forward to lunch.

The taxi set off. Although it was a mild day, the driver and his front seat passenger perspired heavily.

"Giovanni Silvestri." The professor said the name as though it was foulest thing he could think of to say to another human being. Gio did not move.

"I am talking to you, Silvestri. Is all that hair getting in the way of your hearing?" the professor sneered.

Gio turned in his seat and did a valiant job of looking surprised. "Professore, how good it is to see you again."

"You see what we have to work with, Mr. Blessing? A graduate and one who prays to graduate and neither can tell a lie to save themselves. What good is a university education without learning that?" the professor scoffed.

"I hope you are giving a ride to this Silvestri creature out of pity," the professor said.

"In fact, I would like Gio to join us for lunch. He is a business major and our topic will be business," Julian said. The professor shook his head, sad, but resigned.

"What is it you Americans say? 'There is no such thing as a free lunch?'" the professor snorted.

CHAPTER SIX

Julian, the professor and Gio found a table at Armando's, a family run trattoria a few hundred yards from the Pantheon. Small and intimate, the restaurant's wainscoting formed a stage for family photos and bad paintings of Roman scenes. White tablecloths covered green table covers while wall sconces washed diners in soft, yellow light.

The crowd was a mixture of tourists, both foreign and non-Roman Italians. All were drawn by the warm setting, the excellent service and dependable fare. An older waiter in starched white shirt and black full-length apron remained nearby Julian's table. All of the other waiters made sure they were elsewhere. Agostini the Terrible, that was reason enough.

"A question, if I might, professor?" Julian asked. The man nodded.

"We have a waiter nearby, while no one else will come near our table," Julian said and the old man chuckled. "What makes this waiter brave enough to risk having the soul sucked out of him or whatever it is you are said to do?"

"That is Marco Malzone. Not too long ago, he was Professor Malzone. He knows I'm not going to absorb his soul or drink his blood," the professor said. "You see, he was a professor and not a filthy student." The older man looked pointedly at Gio.

"Professor Malzone, but no longer?" Julian asked.

Julian's tablemate smiled and raised his eyebrows as if the answer was obvious. "Being a waiter pays far better than being a university professor. And he has the chance to interact with people and not students who are not people at all." Gio seemed to be absorbed in reading his menu, but winced at the way the professor said 'students'.

They ordered and Julian began his lecture.

"Professor, thank you for allowing me to invite Gio to join us. As I say, he is a business major and the bit of business we are going to discuss is not what he would ever learn in school.

"Gio, today's topic is money laundering. It is a painfully simple concept, but it's execution is anything but simple," Julian began.

"On the simple side, the object is to turn dirty money into clean money. The money is dirty because it was the result of a criminal enterprise. Clean money is that which is able to enter circulation freely and return untraceably to the criminal over time. So far, so good?"

Both the professor and the student nodded. Agostini's nod was guarded while Gio's was enthusiastic.

The waiter arrived with a bottle of wine and Julian poured.

"For the sake of argument, we will say Gio is the criminal in this case," Julian said.

"Ah," the professor said and toyed with a breadstick. "Type casting. I like this already. Do carry on."

Julian chuckled and continued. "Gio's criminal enterprise has brought in a lot of cash. Cash that will attract the attention of the authorities if he tries to spend it. To clean his dirty money, he must do a couple of things first.

"The stages are placement, layering and integration. Regardless of circumstances, era, level of criminality or societal differences, those stages never change.

"The object is to put as much distance as possible between the proceeds of crime and Gio. For that, he might use underground banking, a la India and parts of the Far East. He could clean his money by way of cyber attack on banking institutions. For our example though, we will stay with legitimate banks as a first step.

"All bad guys, according to the movies, have a flock of evil minions. So, let's say twenty-five of Gio's minions each have twenty-five accounts at twenty-five different banks around the country," Julian said. "This is the placement stage."

"Wait," the professor said. "Why must the money be placed into so many banks in so many different accounts?"

"Ah, yes," Julian answered. "Governments have tightened up on what they deem to be suspicious activities.

"No single transaction can exceed certain limits or reports must be filed with the authorities and that draws unwanted attention," Julian answered.

"I see," the professor said and took off his glasses to clean them. "Go on, this may yet be fascinating."

"Absolutely. Fascinating," Gio said before being frozen by the professor.

"Next, we have to layer the money," Julian continued. Our purpose is to play a shell game, moving the money from one place to another, often pointlessly.

"Each layer, each move, buries the source of the money, and thus obscures Gio's involvement further. The more Gio is being watched by one or more governments, the deeper the money has to go. It is being scrubbed with each move. So far so good?" Julian asked and his students nodded.

"Remember, Gio has minions to assist, so each is busy buying and selling things. Taking loans out against money on deposit might be one method of doing this for larger items – cars, houses and such.

"They are buying cars and houses, artwork and jewelry and investing in stocks and bonds. They may lend the money at an overly attractive rate to a legitimate business that is strapped for cash. They may form a partnership so, obliquely, Gio is now the recipient of dividends.

"Now, it is time for Gio to collect his laundry, so we are entering the integration stage. The items bought are sold slowly over time, generating clean money by circulating through the system.

"A minion bought into a carwash, let's just say. That thing is spinning off a $100,000 a year profit. Another bought into a struggling, but very viable, chain of local pizzerias and took it nationwide. No matter what is bought in the layering phase, it is time to either sell it or start collecting dividends in the form of a proportional share of the profits. Simple, no?" Julian concluded his lecture.

"In a word, no," the professor said tilting his head to the side as if looking at the world that way might help any of this make any sense.

"It would seem, as the money moves around, some of it is being lost. I buy something and for quick sale, sell it at a reduced price. Loan money at full face value and collect on the discounted loan. The money can't be cleaned all that quickly, so our little criminal, Giovanni, is out the money until it returns," the professor concluded and he squinted in concentration bordering on consternation.

"Exactly," Julian exclaimed. "Money is lost, although not much and it often averages out. Money is lost here and made there, but mostly Gio can count on getting eighty percent of his money back. This is the cost of doing business. Remember, Gio has a minimal investment in his crime.

"Secondly, Gio will have his money back in hand in two to three years, a period of time in which the money is distancing itself from him. But keep in mind, dirty money is constantly entering the system and returning nice and clean, so there is a steady cash flow."

Julian could sense that both of his students understood. Nearly understood. Not yet and not completely, but they were almost there.

"Okay, maybe another example would help," Julian said. He winked at the professor and the man inclined his head slightly.

The waiter brought their food, another bottle of wine, filled water glasses, and was gone.

"For the professor, we will take it out of the present and cast ourselves back into history. We are in ancient Rome. A Roman senator finds himself in possession of a great deal of money. A very great deal of very dirty money. He knows if he begins to live lavishly and well beyond his known means, suspicion will be raised and ugly questions will be asked.

The professor didn't move, but Gio nodded and his eyes brightened further.

"For the most part, things are greatly different in the past. There are no reporting regulations and no banks. Still the principles of money laundering must be followed if we expect to make dirty money clean," Julian said.

Gio piped up and for the first time didn't care what the professor said or thought. This was education. "Placement, layering and integration."

"Exactly, Gio. Some things never change," Julian said and then asked, "So, professor, where do we place the money?"

The professor knitted his eyebrows together. He had the pieces; he just didn't know where they fit. "It is the center of the Empire we are talking about. Rome and a Roman senator. He can trust few and must protect himself from the rest. That is, those he doesn't murder outright. Dead enemies are the best kind to have."

The professor continued to think aloud. "His political allies are not his friends. His friends are not his friends. That leaves family and certainly not all of them."

"So, gentlemen," Julian said. "Our man spreads the wealth with trusted family members. Not too many, but enough so the spread is thin on the ground. No one person has enough to cause too much trouble, but everyone feels enriched. Now what? Your turn Gio," Julian said.

Gio, without much thought, launched. "Well, he assigns each family member an area so they don't get in each others way. One is tasked with buying and selling ships and cargos. Another is charged with accumulating wealth by way of investments in legitimate businesses. The senator would have inside information on the empire's plans for expansion, so construction seems like a good business to be in.

"Another might take on the slave trade. Rare goods, luxury items would be another area. Hey, those things could be smuggled on the ships and people would pay big for that stuff." Gio was on fire.

"One thing is missing," the professor said. His companions looked at him. Gio's was one of extreme interest and Julian's was one of contentment. He knew exactly where the professor would go.

"Influence," the professor said and Julian nodded.

"By the Madonna, that's right," Gio said. "Huge amounts of cash would move around and there would be no trail. Another senator is tipped off by our senator of a big score. The first senator can get that tip only if he delivers some political favor or a percentage of the profits. Christ, this could go on forever." Gio nearly glowed and the food sat untouched on his plate.

"Let's go forward a century or two. Now what?" Julian asked.

"Lots of people are very rich or very beholden to those who are very rich. Influence buys power and power buys more power," the professor said. "But," he looked thoughtful, "how is all of this held in place. To work, it depends on following a rather exact plan under strong leadership. Each player must trust his fellows. How would that be maintained for such a long period of time without breaking down? Even La Cosa Nostra has been unable to make it work."

Julian watched his companion, sipped his wine and knew who had the answer. It was bubbling to the surface in five, four, three, two…

"Cabal," Gio exploded with an exalted look of triumph with an infectious grin. He rushed ahead. "Yes, a secret economic, political, criminal, hell, even religious organization. The first example of truly organized crime. Still, something had to hold it all together, beyond family or leadership or even threats of death. The professor is right." Gio looked around and lowered his voice, "La Cosa Nostra leaks like the Italian treasury."

Julian smiled and looked into his wine glass. Gio had taken a slight detour and Julian was fine with that. "Well, that is a discussion for another time," Julian said, but he knew the answer. He had heard the echoes, he had seen into the mist of antiquity. He knew, although he did not fully understand. The past without intervention would be the future.

The professor, with excruciating slowness, lowered his head and looked over his glasses at Gio. "A student who can think." The professor turned his over-the-glasses gaze to Julian. "What will be next? Students who actually learn things? The world will spin off its axis and we will all tumble into space."

Their meals had gone cold, but none of the three diners noticed as they finished their food in silence. Julian paid the check. Gio excused himself.

"I'm in this study group not far from here. I'll just leave you and go on my…" Gio began before the professor interrupted.

"Silvestri, do not bore us with your sad excuses to mask the squalid half hearted sexual escapades of yours. Be in my office day after tomorrow ten o'clock. I need not say be on time. I may let you back into the antiquities department. And I may, yet, not kill you."

* * *

The professor and Julian got into a cab for the ride back to the university.

"You have a question, Mr. Blessing? I have been doing what I do for long enough to know a question on the cusp," the professor said and smiled at his turn of phrase, a phrase he had used often with good effect.

"We know where we began. We know where we have been. What remains, professor?" Julian asked.

The professor's smile was smug but without conceit. Deep lines gathered at the corners of his eyes and mouth. "Professor Bragonier said I would not be disappointed with you."

"Then both of you professors are too kind," Julian said.

"The question you ask is the only one worth asking and, to a degree, you know the answer," the professor said. "What we do in the present, having made discoveries from the past, allows us to rectify the future."

CHAPTER SEVEN

Julian stood on the Piazza della Pilotta in the heart of Rome at the edge of Quirinale hill. The building he faced couldn't be more different from Sapienza University .

This was an imposing gumbo of neoclassical architecture. The simplicity of lines combined with the sheer majesty of the building's scale. The entire edifice was crowned with soaring columns that threatened the sky and spoke of a time long past.

Julian climbed the steps of the Pontifical Gregorian University. His appointment was for five o'clock and he was early.

A researcher on the first floor looked shaken when Julian mentioned the name of the man he was to meet. The way was pointed out and Julian took his time climbing the main staircase and walking down the long, broad hallway. He savored the smell of old books and dust as he followed the office numbers and the names in brass plaques beside each door. His appointment would be with a man in a corner office at the end of the hall.

Julian could feel the intensity well before he reached the door and the plaque that read Fr. Marek Soski, S.J. Before he knocked, Julian's fingers began to tingle and he felt, rather than heard, the words. Soft, warm, intimate, welcoming, the words rang in his mind. *"Come in, Mr. Blessing."*

The room was large, and from what Julian could see, unadorned. One wingback chair fronted a large desk. Tall, heavily curtained windows ran the length and width of the room, and the office was swathed in darkness. Sunlight did its best to work through the curtains as they moved in a gentle breeze.

"Thank you for seeing me, Father. There are times," Julian said as he approached the desk, "when places veiled in darkness were meant to intimidate. Is this such a time?" He smiled.

The voice that answered was a whisper and Julian could feel the smile in it. "Are you intimidated, Mr. Blessing?"

"More curious than anything, but I'm sure you knew that, and many other things, when I arrived," Julian said. He felt the priest's answer. *"Well before you arrived, actually,"* the priest thought.

Julian sat and his host swiveled slowly in his desk chair to face his guest. The priest said, "Cardinal Manning has sent you to see me. Why would he do such a thing?" Soski still didn't speak above a whisper and even that appeared to tax him.

Julian answered, "The cardinal said you are someone I could rely on. He said we had much in common and that you can help me." The priest's signature was there, but well protected. This was a man who was giving nothing away.

"May I ask a favor?" Soski said and Julian nodded. "I speak with difficulty as you have noted. Would you mind if I dispensed with…" He was choosing his words with care and Julian helped.

"Dispense with words? Of course." Julian had become accustomed to projecting and receiving thoughts. When first he began, he lacked the discipline and control necessary. His initial attempts were the paranormal equivalent of Tourette syndrome with his unguarded thoughts coming out at the most inappropriate times. Those days seemed long ago to Julian, but not so very long ago.

Julian could make out the silhouette of the man behind the desk. As light invaded, and was pushed back by the curtains, he saw glints of white hair and a lean silhouette, but nothing more.

"Thank you for that kindness. An injury left me in a condition where it is difficult to speak. I am fortunate I have this alternative, but it is not one I can use at the corner market," the priest thought and Julian could feel the man's smile again. *"Now, please tell me how I can be of assistance."*

"Father, there are Russian gangsters who want me dead. They feel they have good reason for that. I, of course, don't agree. There is also a man who wants to make use of my abilities. I have said no, but he is not a man who will take that for my final answer. I feel safe in saying he will not stop until he gets everything he wants.

"There may be other suspects, but my feeling is one of these two have kidnapped someone important to me. The purpose is either to lure me out or to suck me in. In either case, I do not care if it will secure the release of my friend. As you can see, I am in need of an ally. I would be grateful for any assistance you could give," Julian said, then waited for his host's considered response.

"Mr. Blessing, for the struggles you are facing, I don't know if there will ever be enough allies of the type you seek. Let me state the obvious for both our benefits. Circumstances, it seems, have not conspired to thwart you. They have set out to destroy you. At least that is the way it would appear."

"Oh, and here I was thinking the situation was hopeless," Julian said and felt his host smirk.

Soski's thoughts whispered the same way the priest whispered when he spoke aloud. *"You have been careful not to mention names, so let me state them for you. It has taken no divining on my part. None of the talents you and I would usually employ need be utilized in this case. Doubtless, you have heard it before and you will hear it again. Rome is really a very small village. Gossip and gossips abound. Eventually I hear most things that are of importance.*

"Bogdan Sokolov is the Russian with an unhealthy interest in you. If gangsters are a blight, Mr. Blessing, Russian gangsters are a pestilence and Bogdan Sokolov is the plague.

"His Eminence, Antonio Cardinal Archbishop Luciano is the prelate who wishes to make use of your unique gifts. Doubtless, you sense the cardinal's intentions are not entirely pure. So, the use he would make of you would not be for the benefit of any other than the cardinal. Dr. Dwyer is missing. She is very dear to you and her safe return is of the utmost importance and, as is said, speed is of the essence.

"You have demonstrated an extraordinary control, both of your actions since she was taken and your thoughts and emotions right now. I mention this because your self-discipline is remarkable. I will return to the topic though.

"You are correct, of course. It is a near certainty either the Russian or the cardinal is holding her.

"Mr. Blessing, this is not easy for me to say and it will be harder for you to hear. It will be harder still for you to do. It is imperative that you do what you must do rather than what you want to do. You have followed that path so far, but you are becoming frustrated. You must stay the course. For now at least," the priest said.

Julian followed the priest's thoughts with great care. More was at risk than he had ever bargained for. He needed information and as much and as quickly as possible.

Soski continued. *"Finding the doctor is of paramount importance to you. You must not allow her disappearance, or her wellbeing, to cloud your thinking. She will not be harmed because, while her value to you is beyond all measure, to the ones who took her, she is valuable only if alive and well.*

"You want to act, but you need to be ready to act. What brought you to Rome is not the reason you are here. I am a clever man. Some use the word brilliant, but they do not know me at all if that is what they think. I have, over the years, developed my talents so that now they are substantial. Still, as a clever man, I know the talents you have accessed press against the boundaries of what any of us have known heretofore.

"This is not flattery, believe me. You are a person who has been under much scrutiny, discussion and debate. Your talents are considerable. It is important for you to understand this. However, as yet, your ability to use your talents is insufficient for the tasks at hand. This you do understand, although you wish it were otherwise.

"Mr. Blessing, your potential is unlimited. No one has gotten where you are so quickly. You have an original mind and your approach to things is, let us just say, unique. This heightens exponentially the effectiveness of your gifts.

"I believe you are approaching your current dilemma incorrectly. When you stop seeing your talents as adjunctive to your life and start seeing them as your life, then you will begin to understand. Your understanding will lead you to what you must do."

"Understand what, Father?" Julian asked.

"According to your teachers, what is it that we do? What is our responsibility?"

"We shine a light into the darkness. We push back the mist and listen to the echoes of a truer reality. In this way, we strengthen our own understanding and help others see that there is another, better way of life."

"Exactly. Sokolov wants to kill you. Luciano wants to use you. One or the other has taken your doctor in order to get to you. Thus far, your response has been to hide, to run, to chase clues, and to gather allies and information. You are seeing this as a physical threat and so are preparing to take physical action.

"Understand this; do not give credence to what you know to be false. The reality the gangster and the cardinal are presenting to you is their reality, not yours. You, sir, have been playing their game. It is time they played yours and yours exists on a metaphysical plane, not a physical one. You want desperately to act. I am advising you to wait, continue to gather your resources, enhance your gifts and be ready to act correctly when the time is right. You will know when that time is.

"That said," the priest continued. *"I wish to warn you of something and I want there to be no confusion in your mind on this. You will, in all likelihood, be called upon to do things that go against your moral code. I speak of things of which you think yourself incapable. Believe me, we are all capable of a great deal more than we would like.*

"You may be given no choice but to use whatever means necessary to protect yourself, the doctor and others from imminent harm. You may have to resort to force, Mr. Blessing. Extreme force. You must be prepared for that."

Julian nodded slowly.

"There are teachers who can help you," Fr. Soski said. *"I am not one of them, but I can help you in my own way."*

The priest opened his center desk drawer and took out a leather bound volume. The curtains moved and Julian watched his host's long, thin, fingers caress the book lovingly. With a sigh, he set it on his desk. The priest folded his hands in his lap and the book began to move toward Julian. It stopped half way across the desk.

"What is this?" Julian said and Soski answered immediately.

"It is called the Jesuit Book. It is what you have been told does not exist. You were told, as was I, there is no textbook for what we do. Our teachers did not mean to deceive. They told us what they had been told.

"The book has been compiled in secret over many hundreds of years. That is a lot of people keeping a secret for a very long time. We Jesuits have a habit of documenting what we have been told not to and keeping secrets forever if necessary.

"In this case, the book will help you unlock mysteries that have plagued you and reveal concepts that will reshape the world around you in ways you could have never thought possible. It will allow you to progress further and faster than ever you thought possible. It will give you the tools necessary to push back the darkness in your current situation and every situation thereafter.

"The echoes you hear," the priest continued, "the ones we all hear, will become stronger and the message will be unmistakable using what you find between the covers of this book. No teacher could do so much.

"Not my original teacher, but a man who taught me some of what I know, gave up his life to safeguard that book. I, too, have made sacrifices to keep it safe. Many others, before us, have suffered and died in order to protect it. There are those who would use the book to undo everything that has been done by the group to which you and I belong. Cardinal Luciano is one such man.

"Take the book if you are willing to benefit from it and willing to safeguard it with your life.

"If this is a burden you do not wish to take up, leave the book on the desk. That reaction would be perfectly reasonable for any man. I realize, however, my words are of little use to you because you are neither perfectly reasonable nor any man," Soski said.

Julian closed his eyes for a moment. He opened them, then let his hand hover over the desk. The book began to move slowly toward him. He controlled his breathing and centered his thoughts. Julian's next action would be life altering and he knew it.

He picked the Jesuit Book up when it rested under his hand.

With that action, he stepped off the edge and, for once, did not worry about the fall. He pledged his life without knowing the price involved and with only a vague idea of the risks.

Julian had no choice but to trust the reality he now knew and discounted the one he had known all his life.

* * *

Julian left the Gregorian University lost in thought. He questioned whether he would be able to keep the book safe. Soski told him to take the book only if he was willing to protect it with his life. "What if I am unable to protect it?" His blue gray eyes mirrored his turmoil.

Although consumed by the ideas that raced through his brain, Julian was not so lost that he didn't register the light colored Mercedes that pulled away from the curb behind him. He smiled and shook his head as a nondescript sedan pulled away behind the Mercedes.

* * *

"Please, signore Julian. Do just this one small thing for poor Joselina. The Conaletti family has never been very healthy. The Lord may take me at any moment and then what would become of my daughters? They would be out on the street like common whores. My daughters are not common."

Julian found himself doing a lot of headshaking since his arrival at Casa Felicità. "Signora Joselina, of course they are not common. It is only…"

"Signorina," the madam interrupted.

"Pardon me?" Julian asked.

"I have sadly never been married. I am signorina Joselina. It sounds so poetic when I say it, no? The family of Conaletti may not be healthy, but we are proud, so signorina if you please."

"Yes," Julian said. "Of course. Per favore, accetti le mie scuse, signorina. My apologies. Still, I doubt very seriously God will be taking you away from us anytime soon. Judging by the flow of traffic, Casa Felicita is on an unbelievably firm financial footing, so there is no worry there, either. And to answer your question for what seems like the fiftieth time, no I cannot turn your plaster statue into gold."

"But signore Julian, my poor girls – think of the hardship you are causing."

"I am not causing anything. Listen, marble was good enough for Michelangelo when he carved the Madonna and Child, so learn to live with your plaster copy. Besides, I don't know where you got all of this, but I can't turn things into gold," Julian tried to explain. "I'm pretty sure no one can."

"But you are a stregone, a sorcerer, you know a wizard. My Belladonna said so and she is with the police. She is not allowed to lie," Julian's landlady cried.

"I am not a wizard!"

"Okay, wizard," the old woman turned a hard eye on Julian. "Business is business. You do this one little thing for Joselina and I will send Lisa to your room for a week. Hey, she is very popular with Americano tourists. They call her Mona Lisa. The Americani say it is because she is so noisy, but I don't get what that has to do with the painting. Who can understand Americani? As for my Lisa, she is new, but she makes up for it with enthusiasm. She is very vigorous."

Julian hung his still shaking head and said, "For the fifty-first time, I am not a wizard and do not send anyone to my room."

"So! My lovely daughters aren't good enough for the big shot wizard!"

"Okay! Fine! I'm a wizard! There, are you satisfied?" Julian fired back. "However, wizards don't turn things into gold. Never have to my knowledge. That is for alchemists. That is their line of work, not mine!"

"Ah ha, God has answered Joselina's prayer by sending her a wizard. Listen, I checked with a priest I know. He said God created wizards, too, so that means it is okay to do business with you. So, do you know any of these, what did you say, academics?" Her excitement was building.

"Alchemists, not academics," Julian said and his voice showed his weariness.

"Whatever. Same deal with Lisa if you can put me on to one of those guys and you'll get a cut. Small cut. Okay, okay – two weeks, but no more. Time is money."

* * *

Everything about the Jesuit Book made sense to Julian while it made no sense at all. It was not a large book and not highly detailed. Einstein said, "If you can't explain it simply, you don't know it well enough." The creators of the Jesuit Book understood the subject completely.

The book's true value, its elegance, lay in rendering complex concepts in concise, deceptively simple terms. The trick was not to over think, jump ahead, or try to out-guess the book and its principles.

Julian consumed and was consumed by the book. As each point came into focus, it wasn't imprinted on his memory. The principle fused with his mind, his soul.

Each reading seemed to shine a light on a different aspect of metaphysical study. Some areas he had investigated, experimented with and dismissed when his experiments failed. Now he could see the reasons for his failures. His errors in thinking stood out in stark relief once seen in the light of the Jesuit Book.

With each reading, a new talent would appear. He wielded none with precision. In Ireland, he managed to nearly set his room on fire by mistake at one point. But talents he worked with previously now came to him easily, naturally and far more potently.

Without looking up from his book he said, "Come in, Inspector."

Belladonna Saviano pushed the door to Julian's room open and let her eyes adjust to the dim light. "Joselina tells me you cracked under her intense interrogation. She says you confessed to being a stregone, a sorcerer, a wizard, whatever. She did say you aren't much of a wizard in her opinion."

Julian turned from his book and answered, "She wanted me to turn plaster into gold. I refused and it left her despondent. For someone who runs the House of Joy, she doesn't seem especially joyful. But how can I help you, Inspector?"

The inspector sat on Julian's bed and he turned in his desk chair and waited. The more he concentrated, the more he could feel her emotions. Her thoughts eluded him, or came to him half formed, but he knew she was frustrated and trying to cover it with light conversation.

"Inspector, did you have any luck following the car that was following me from the Gregorian University?" Julian asked.

"I don't know what you are talking about. Were you at the Gregorian? I thought we agreed you would stay here. Why should I think you would listen to me though – you haven't so far," she said.

Julian closed his eyes for a moment. When he opened them, he felt he had gone into a kind of auto pilot state. He had no reason to say what he was about to say or to know what he could not know. His voice was hushed and his cadence slow. The inspector had to strain to hear him.

"I am sorry your investigation has stalled. Your superiors are unhappy with you because of it. They don't know how hard you are working. They also don't know you are making progress. Slow progress, but progress all the same.

"The Russian, Sokolov – you have drawn together a number of threads and you are very near learning what sets his organization apart from dozens of money laundering operations in Italy."

Julian took a deep breath and returned to himself. He smiled and said, "Why don't you tell me about that? Perhaps you know more than you think."

Inspector Saviano remained still for a full minute, then another, before she said, "I am of two minds, stregone. Part of me says I should use what you know and what you can do. Another part of me thinks I should arrest you for some fabricated violation of the law just to keep you out of my way. I feel sure you can tell the future. Is that not one of your magic tricks, wizard? Please, tell me what I am going to do with you?"

Julian smiled. "Inspector, you are as stubborn as signorina Joselina. I am not a wizard. I do not do magic. I do not foretell the future. I do not read minds and I do not turn plaster into gold.

"I am just a tourist. True, there are some unpleasant things swirling about me right now, but for the most part, I am simply a..."

"Yes, yes, you are a tourist," the inspector said. "You are a tourist who can cripple people without moving a muscle, a tourist who can terrify lifetime criminals. You know things you can't and you do things you shouldn't be able to.

She warmed to her topic. "You are a tourist who feels free to defy orders from the police. Russian gangsters try to kidnap you, your lady friend has already been kidnapped, you make late night visits to high ranking Vatican bank officials, you dine with other high ranking Vatican bank officials. You've been visiting the Gregorian and have met with the Ghost.

"The list just keeps growing, but I will stop now only because I am about to become angry and when I become angry, even wizards need to hide."

"Before we move along with Sokolov, you mentioned 'the Ghost?'" Julian asked.

"Fr. Soski is called the Ghost. Wizards and ghosts – at one time, my life held such promise." The inspector looked despondent.

"Inspector, please, it is important. Tell me what you know of Soski."

"Are you blind? Have you not seen him? Madonna, you're merely frightening. That man invented terrifying.

"What, why are you looking at me like that? Oh, alright, but if you tell him I told you I will carry out every threat I have ever made against you. Hai capito?"

"Yes, I understand. This stays between you and me, but I must know all of it," Julian said and the inspector believed him and began her story.

"The Ghost worked for Luciano. He was the cardinal's right hand man. That is all that is known. It is all anyone knows for certain, anyway. He worked for the cardinal and now he doesn't. What he did, no one knows. What happened, no one knows.

"The back street whispers give more detail, but it is impossible to say, with certainty, what is truth and what is fiction. After distilling it all, what I will tell you is the most plausible version," the inspector said.

"It is said the cardinal wanted something Soski had. He would not give it up. An altercation of some sort followed. I stress 'some sort', wizard, but don't think I've forgotten about you and your tricks, so we can surmise what kind of altercation, no?" The inspector looked at Julian pointedly.

"Soski crawled away nearly dead, but the cardinal didn't get off lightly. You noticed Luciano's limp? He didn't get that from too much dancing.

"Months later, I was promoted to inspector. My partner in the Finance unit became curious about the nature of this whole business.

"He suspected money was involved somehow. He made very discreet enquiries. Forty-eight hours later he was directing traffic far away from the Vatican.

"I didn't know him in his days with the cardinal, but they say Soski was handsome, charismatic, a genius and sexy, too. He was away from Rome for over a year. I met him briefly not long after his return. The man was a ruin in the same way the coliseum is a ruin. His eyes were dead, his skin unnaturally pale and he had burn scars on his face and hands. His hair had turned dull silver and he could hardly speak.

"He seldom goes out of the Gregorian and when he does, he is bundled up like he's going to the Alps," the inspector said and looked disturbed.

"And?" Julian prompted.

"I said he seldom goes out. The fact is, no one has ever seen him go anywhere. He is one place and a moment later he is gone only to appear elsewhere. And so he is called the Ghost. I think that part is told only to frighten the children, but I have seen his eyes. I tell you stregone, I looked into those eyes and terror touched my soul."

They were silent for a while, each a prisoner of their thoughts.

"Sokolov?" Julian looked expectant and less cheerful than he appeared.

The inspector closed her eyes and she let out a long breath. "He is attempting to get a man inside the Vatican Bank.

"I don't know how far along he is with that project and I don't know what is being planned. I know, since it is Sokolov, it is about money laundering. His plan obviously involves the Vatican Bank, so hundreds of millions of euros are involved.

"My superiors and the state's prosecutors listened to me and they have read my reports. Their conclusion is I know exactly nothing because I can prove nothing." The inspector let out another long sigh that ended with a grunt of pure frustration.

"Inspector, let's go find some proof, shall we?" Julian said as though that was a reasonable thing to say.

CHAPTER EIGHT

Cardinal Luciano's assistant, Fr. Dominic Giglio, entered the cardinal's study and stood in a respectful silence. The cardinal smiled and invited his assistant to sit down.

The day started in bright sunlight, but had devolved into an afternoon dark with threatening rain. The cardinal closed the portfolio on his desk and pushed back to listen to his assistant's report.

"Dominic," the cardinal said. "You really must do something to protect your thoughts. You are the definition of transparent. You have good news for me on a number of fronts, so tell me of them."

"Your Eminence is of course correct. I am transparent and I do have encouraging news stemming from many sources," Fr. Giglio said.

The priest continued. "As a trial run, the companies in Switzerland have successfully transferred a sum of money to your joint stock corporation in Florence in exchange for goods that the Swiss know will never be delivered.

"Our man at the Florentine bank made a few adjustments and the money appeared as a credit to your archdiocesan special account at the Vatican Bank. A number of intervening transactions occurred, but are of little consequence.

"The total time the funds were in your corporation was under eight seconds. That was important for the purposes of the test, but it doesn't really matter since none of your accounts can be traced back to you."

The young priest continued. "As you know, your Eminence's archdiocesan special account exists to fund the building of the orphanage. There is, of course, no orphanage. The contractor for the building project requires a substantial deposit, so this afternoon's credit will be transferred to the contractor in," Fr. Dominic stopped and looked at his wristwatch, "in approximately twenty three minutes.

"Your Eminence is, indirectly of course, the general contractor, although that, too, would be impossible to prove. Checks will be drawn up tomorrow to pay for labor and material being supplied by eleven wholly fictitious companies, all of which we control."

Fr. Dominic continued. "In turn, those companies…"

"Dominic?" the cardinal interrupted.

"Yes, Eminence?"

"Dominic, the details of these various operations are inconsequential for my purposes," the cardinal said. "Your report, please, without the chapter and verse this time."

"I am sorry, Eminence. Please forgive me. The Vatican Bank credited your account for," the young priest consulted a file folder, "seven hundred fifty-three thousand euros today," the priest said.

"There, that wasn't so hard, was it?" the cardinal said. "What other news do you have for me?"

Fr. Dominic Giglio looked through another folder and scanned a piece of paper before he began. "Mr. Blessing has been extremely active, but is no nearer his goal than when he started. He has two police officers helping him, but they have yet to develop a lead on Dr. Dwyer's location."

"Good," the cardinal said. "Let's hope it stays that way for awhile. Having Mr. Blessing unfocused suits my purpose right now."

"Eminence, Mr. Blessing has, however, met with two people who are worrying to me," Fr. Dominic said. "He had a rather long lunch with his Eminence Cardinal Manning. The following day, Mr. Blessing spent time at the Pontifical Gregorian University," the priest said.

"So, he has been to see my old assistant, Marek Soski," the cardinal said. "I wouldn't worry myself with Fr. Soski if I were you. Although formidable at one time, he is a spent force today. I am afraid our last encounter, before he left my service, left him a bit worse for wear.

"Still, Blessing in the company of one of my brother cardinals from the Vatican Bank, that I find interesting in the extreme.

"You've done well, Dominic. Again, I wouldn't worry about Soski. He isn't likely to want his old job back. You have filled his shoes rather well," Cardinal Luciano said.

Fr. Dominic Giglio shivered when he saw the cardinal smile.

* * *

An inconspicuous door led from the House of Joy to the private garden. On the discreet door was a discreet sign, neatly lettered and bearing a delicate decorative border. The sign was in Italian and signed by the proprietress of Casa Felicità . Julian was able to work out the somewhat less than discreet meaning - "ENTER AND DIE."

Joselina was unhappy. Julian had spotted the garden and asked to rent it. The madam felt Julian had taken unfair advantage of her.

"Mamma," one of Joselina's working daughters said as she tried to bring comfort to her employer, "what did the Americano do that would cause you to give up your beautiful little garden?"

"Il mio bambina, you are a good daughter to ask after your old mother's heartache. The man is not a man at all. He is a devil – maybe even The Devil. One or the other. I'm not sure yet." Joselina made the sign of the cross, then made the sign of the horns and pointed them in Julian's general direction.

"But Mamma, what has he done? Tell me, how did he make this happen? Throwing you out of your own garden wasn't nice."

"Daughter, I tell you the man nearly crushed me with the pressure he applied. He used the worst, filthiest, most underhanded thing ever used in the history of filthy, underhanded things! At first, I believed my Belladonna when she said that…that…. that creature was a wizard. She told me to beware or he would do some of his wizard shit. But I tell you, he is no wizard.

"Would that God and all His saints would send me a mere wizard. No, God wants me to suffer, so He sends me a devil, for only a devil would do such a thing." Joselina dabbed at her eyes with a handkerchief, then made the sign of the horns again just to be on the safe side.

"But Momma, tell me what he did! What could be so bad that it would upset you so and cause you to give up your precious garden!"

"I named a stupidly high price, he doubled it and paid in cash and in advance."

"The bastard!" the girl hissed.

"All devils are bastards! I learned that the hard way from Fr. Alfonso who comes to see Adelina on Thursday afternoons between two and two fifteen – stingy bastard won't even pay for a half hour and he never pays for overtime AND he wants a clergy discount! The world is full of bastards!" Joselina said.

"Momma, the Americano is a bastard, a devil and a wizard! Why do you allow him under your roof?"

The proprietress closed her eyes tightly. She opened them and said, "ARE YOU DEAF, YOU STUPID COW? HE PAYS IN CASH! IN ADVANCE!" Joselina's voice spoke of heartache. And avarice.

* * *

Julian stood in his rented garden. He held the Jesuit Book in one hand and stared at the discreet door. He could feel Joselina and one of her employees on the other side of the door. He couldn't feel their thoughts, but he could feel the emotions behind them. He extended his right hand toward the door and focused. The heavy oak door began to shudder, then groan, with the force he applied.

He heard the two women let loose a string of profanity and prayers as they retreated deeper into the house. In the world of metaphysics, physically extending his hand was a useless motion. It did help him focus though. He had practiced without the gesture, but the brickwork within a meter around the door on every side had paid the price. Besides, he felt it gave him a wizardly air and that caused him to smile.

He sat down on a bench in the shade of an ancient olive tree, rested his back against its gnarled trunk, and returned to his studies.

* * *

Inspector Belladonna Saviano sat under a similar olive tree in a park near the headquarters of the Guardia di Finanza. She had just received a one-hour dressing down by her colonel. Her lack of progress regarding the Russian money laundering operation was glaring. The State's prosecutor's office was asking the colonel questions. The colonel was now asking the inspector the same questions. She had no answer beyond, 'Progress is being made slowly. We can afford no mistakes.'

Before ordering her out of his office, the colonel suggested Belladonna might not be cut out for the Organized Crime Investigation Group. "Perhaps," he said, "your talents might be better put to use in data processing."

Belladonna sat beneath her tree and pulled grass out by the handfuls.

"Bella," her assistant greeted her as he sat down on the grass.

"Ah, Enrico, they have been talking to you too. I can tell because you are smiling."

"That bastardo Leonardi from Internal Affairs brought me in for questioning. Imagine that. Me. What has the world turned into, Bella?" Enrico asked.

"It has turned into shit from where I am sitting. What did he want and what did you tell him?"

"That fool asked me if I enjoyed taking bribes from the Russians. I told him I did not, but I enjoyed his mother last night – twice. He went away unhappy," Enrico said with a smirk.

"Enrico, the world is filled with unhappiness and now you have added to it by upsetting that merda Leonardi. Did you really do his mother?" Belladonna asked.

"Mi Bella, you know you are the only woman for me."

"You are sweet Enrico. Was she any good?"

"Non cattivo." Enrico shrugged.

"Non cattivo – not bad. You are a pig," Belladonna said not unkindly.

Enrico Marino, Asst. Cappo with the Guardia di Finanza, shrugged.

* * *

"Terrance, Il Convivio de Troiani is, I believe, the perfect place for a meal. I am surprised you were able to get us in," Cardinal Luciano said, unable to read his brother cardinal beyond the superficial. This was a concern to him, but he had greater concerns right then.

"I've known the Troiani brothers for, well, I won't mention the number of years. They occasionally feel they need to extend me a small courtesy. I must say though, Angelo has outdone himself this time. The oxtail with celeriac is really superb they say. The wine list is rather extensive, but also rather expensive. I hope you don't mind the house wine," Cardinal Manning said smiling, knowing Luciano would mind very much.

Sitting in the old section of Rome, the restaurant had taken up residence in an ancient Renaissance palace. It was known for its elegant rooms, beautiful tableware, uncompromising service and absolute discretion. The menu was a mixture of the old and new of Roman cuisine.

Each cardinal wore a simple black suit with a Roman collar. Both faced each other across a small table in a quiet corner. Each man knew the other well and each knew what ordinance the other brought to the field. A single tall, slender taper cast a warm glow over the battlefield.

"Terrance, I heard some disturbing news recently. I understand you had a visitor, an American. I know of this man and must warn you against placing too much faith in him. He was, I believe, involved in some dealings with the Russian mafia in New York. Now, it seems, he is here in Rome.

"You are blessed with a spotless reputation. I would hate to see that blemished in any way. There are rumors you may be our next pope. We have had Italians, Poles, Germans and, most recently, an Argentinean – an Irish Pope might not be such a bad thing. I tell you all of this as one friend tells another," Cardinal Luciano said and smiled warmly. The warmth never reached beyond the corners of his mouth.

"Ah, Antonio, Antonio, I am afraid you have been listening to the wrong sorts of people. A poor Irish priest as Pope? That will never happen. And it never happening is a good thing," Cardinal Manning said as his face took on a furrowed, contrived thoughtfulness.

"I have been fortunate, Antonio, blessed I might even say. I've risen far higher than I ever dreamed possible. I am content to spend my remaining days right where I am. I entered the seminary with every intention of serving the Church. I wish only to end my life in Her service."

The cardinal's smile was a reflection of Cardinal Luciano's. It was a smile without sincerity. It did not speak of friendship or offer sympathy or understanding. It spoke of cunning, trickery and a ravenous deceit. It was a smile on the face of artifice.

"Still," Cardinal Manning continued. "I do appreciate your words of advice as I appreciate your friendship." With terrifying cordiality, both men smiled and enjoyed their dinner.

* * *

He could almost see it. Julian had a talent for seeing into the past – sometime the recent past and sometimes the ancient past. His work with the Jesuit Book had given him the clues necessary to control how far back he could go.

This time, he was almost there. He watched as two men approached Ailís at the express package counter. It unfolded as Califano said. Julian cursed himself. He was rooted to one spot and couldn't get another angle on the car, the men or Ailís. Califano said Ailís went with the men willingly, but what Julian saw was different. The men approached, said something to her and she fled the express counter, but not from the men – with them. To Julian she almost seemed to be urging them to hurry.

It was nearly time Julian had determined. He had been marking time as Fr. Soski had said, running, hiding, following clues. The time for gathering information was almost over.

* * *

The day was bright as the inspector and her assistant walked side by side down the broad steps of the Palace of Justice. They risked their lives crossing the Piaza dei Tribunali and gained the entrance of the Ponte Umberto, all in one piece with no drastic spikes in blood pressure. Rome's traffic was being kind today. The bridge over the Tiber River wasn't especially crowded for noontime. A few businessmen, a couple of students and, judging by the Hawaiian shirts, some American tourists were all that were out in the Roman sunshine.

The two police officers took their time and admired the tall trees and the sludge brown Tiber as it twitched along, too bored to do anything more energetic.

"Enrico," his inspector began. "If you weren't a policeman, what would you be?" She looked into the distance as she considered her own options.

"Well," Enrico said, "I would be an opera singer."

"What? An opera singer? We have been drunk together a few times and I've heard you sing. You are awful."

"I am a policeman. Anything else would be a dream and if I am going to dream, I will dream big. Put me down for an opera singer."

Belladonna laughed and Enrico smiled just before the corners of his mouth turned down. She said, "I would like to be a fashion designer. It is the furthest thing there is from being in the police, no, Enrico? Enrico? Enrico?"

Her partner was no longer beside her. She found him fifteen feet behind her holding Julian Blessing by the throat, pushed up against a light standard. The way Enrico was standing told the inspector her assistant's weapon was drawn and probably pressed against Julian's chest.

She took her time, knowing Enrico would have some useful words of advice for the American.

Enrico Marino's eyes were like obsidian – hard, black, angry and merciless. "Do wizards die from gunshot wounds?" he hissed into Julian's face. The barrel of the sergeant's Beretta 9mm pressed painfully into Julian's sternum.

Julian's voice was pinched and he was breathing rapidly. "Pretty sure they do," were the only words he could choke out.

Julian's reading and rereading of the Jesuit Book had given him scores of metaphysical responses. The only countermeasure he could manage for this situation was to try to get oxygen into his lungs the old fashioned way.

A chill passed through Julian as he watched the policeman say, "Let's find out for sure, wizard."

"Enrico, please let signore Blessing breathe, but don't let him go. And put your weapon away. You know how I hate loud noises and the tourists are staring," the inspector said.

"Signore, what is it about following two well trained and heavily armed police officers that made you think doing such a thing was a good idea?" The Inspector let a full thirty seconds pass before she said, "That's right, nothing made it a good idea. What are you doing following us?"

"I went by your headquarters and asked for you," Julian said still gasping.

"And you found someone there who just said, 'Oh thank you for asking, signore. Bella and Enrico are at the Palace of Justice. Can we give you a lift over there?' Is that what happened?" the young woman asked.

Julian struggled to break Enrico's grip on his throat. "I came away with that impression, yes – except for the lift part." The grip tightened a fraction.

"Enrico, please let the signore go," the inspector said. Reluctantly, her assistant reholstered his firearm and let Julian breathe.

"Now, signore, what is it that you wanted that would cause you to track us down and risk your life?"

"Califano was wrong." Julian was bent over with his hands on his knees still gasping. The police officers exchanged looks.

"Wrong in what way?" the inspector asked pleasantly.

"The car that drove the doctor away from the airport wasn't from the Vatican. C08004 – diplomatic plates. Assigned to the Ukrainian embassy," Julian gasped and began to cough. "At least, that series is assigned to them."

"Enrico, stand our new friend upright. He is going to take us to the other side of the bridge, buy us some gelato, and tell us how he knows what he shouldn't – again," the inspector said with a pointed grimace.

* * *

"Shit, shit and shit," the inspector said as she returned to her seat in the outdoor café and pocketed her cell phone. She looked down into her cup of melted gelato. "And shit," she added.

Enrico looked at Julian and jerked his thumb in the direction of the bar. Julian left to find some gelato that wasn't melted.

With her treat restored, the inspector said, "There is no C08004 and certainly not at the Vatican. The Ukrainian embassy has a C08001, 02, 08 and 11, but no 04. Somebody is going to a lot of trouble to put this at Bogdan Sokolov's door or Bogdan Sokolov is that stupid."

"Well, that's enough for me," Julian said quietly.

"What's enough for you?" the inspector turned to Julian and asked.

"I'm tired of screwing around. I'm going to see Sokolov," Julian looked up and said.

Enrico rubbed the center of his forehead to dispel an ice cream headache while his partner looked dumbfounded.

"So you are going to go see the man who wants you dead. Is that right?" the inspector asked.

"What Mr. Sokolov wants and what he gets may be two different things. I've been sitting on my hands for too long. I'm going to find the doctor, then we are leaving Rome," Julian said. "Want to tell me where Sokolov is?"

"Enrico, is he serious?" Her assistant looked into Julian's eyes and what he saw there disturbed him. He nodded his head once.

"I am afraid my government wouldn't like it if I stood around while a tourist committed suicide. They become cranky because they have no sense of humor. Sadly, we cannot allow you to do this thing."

Julian pushed back from the table slowly. He looked relaxed, his face serene and his manner tranquil. "Inspector, Sergeant," Julian looked to each in turn. "I realize you have the best intentions, but I'm afraid this is something I have to do. You can't go knock on the Russian's door and sit down for a chat. I can.

"Inspector, you said, you can't allow me to do this. In fact you must allow it, because you have no choice." Julian spoke softly and slowly, without pretense or bravado. He looked almost apologetic. His eyelids were heavy.

"Both of you, I promise I will report back everything I learn," Julian said and smiled.

"No," the inspector was emphatic. Enrico leaned forward slightly in case the American moved further than his inspector wanted him to.

"I'm sorry," Julian said. He took a slow deep breath and closed his eyes. When he opened them, all movement around him appeared to have stopped. He had developed the ability to step outside of linear time while working with his teacher in Ireland. The Jesuit Book helped, but he still couldn't maintain it for long. But in a few minutes he would be a block away and the police officers would be questioning their sanity.

CHAPTER NINE

"Very nicely done, Mr. Blessing. Bravo."

Julian had stepped back into the normal flow of time directly into the path of Cardinal Antonio Luciano. "Your Eminence does get around," Julian said.

"My car is right here. Perhaps I can offer you a ride?" The cardinal posed it as a question, but it wasn't.

"Thank you, but walking is good exercise and I don't do enough of it. I see you found a new driver, Eminence. Does he understand how temporary his job can be?" Julian asked.

The cardinal smiled and shrugged. "It was my hope you and I could have a talk, signore Blessing. May I call you Julian? A pleasant drive around Rome is conducive to conversation, I find."

"It is a funny thing. The more you insist I get into your car, the more I am disinclined to do so. Why do you think that is? As for the whole name thing, let's just leave it the way it is right for now."

"Ah, I see. My car makes you uncomfortable. Perhaps we could walk together? I suppose only your friends call you Julian and I, as yet, have not earned your friendship. Do you have many friends? I am fortunate; I have many friends from all walks of life. I would be honored if you would consider me your friend.

"As a show of good faith and friendship, let me pass along a word of warning," the cardinal continued. "You are newly arrived in Rome and so have no idea of whom you can and cannot trust. Currently, you count the Jesuit priest, Fr. Marek Soski, as an acquaintance, perhaps even a friend. I would not be much of a friend myself if I did not warn you. Soski is not a man to be trusted."

"But Eminence, Fr. Soski is one of us. Are you saying not all of us are to be trusted?" The sarcasm in Julian's voice did not faze the cardinal at all.

"Sadly, Mr. Blessing, it is true. Nearly all of us can be trusted. We share certain core values and desire only to enrich mankind. Soski has no such values and is interested in enriching himself only."

"What would cause you to come to that conclusion?" Julian asked. He was beginning to ache from the effort to protect his thoughts from the cardinal. Although Julian's barbs were not lost on Cardinal Luciano, the man wanted to know what Julian knew and everything he had ever known. If that meant Julian's mind would be destroyed in the process, well, to Luciano, that was the cost of doing business. The two walked past dun colored shops that managed to put on display a colorful sameness.

"Fr. Soski is a thief. He stole something from his employer and when confronted, he refused to confess or return the item. Despicable is what I call it. The man has no honor," the cardinal said and his mouth twisted in disgust.

"But that isn't true, Eminence." The cardinal spun too quickly and overbalanced, nearly falling into the priest who addressed him. In a clerical suit and roman collar, the man wore a black overcoat on a pleasant Roman afternoon. A broad brimmed fedora and dark glasses completed the wraith that stood before Julian and the cardinal.

The priest's dry rasping whisper brought a smile to Julian's face and caused the cardinal to recoil with only one hissed response, "Soski."

"Mr. Blessing," Fr. Soski said. "It is a terrible world indeed when princes of the Church make free with the reputations of others."

"The eighth commandment, Eminence?" Soski goaded. "I know you are a bit out of touch with that sort of religious thing, but you remember – that's the one about bearing false witness. There is another one about murder, but I forget the number." The priest looked expectant while the cardinal looked rabid. "I would be delighted to hear your confession," Soski added.

"Do not tempt me, Soski. Reason dictated I should have finished what I started with you." The cardinal spat the words.

"Oh, Eminence, you would have. If you could have. You were distracted. I understand completely. How is your limp? I've been meaning to ask." Fr. Soski smiled an evil smile and continued.

"Speaking of reason, Mr. Blessing, has the good cardinal regaled you with his 'Soldiers of Reason' speech. It is one of his best. You really should ask him to recite it to you. Although many find it laughable, I believe you would be more restrained and respectful. The cardinal demands respect, although he may not command it." Soski was enjoying goading Luciano.

"Father," Julian said, "his Eminence did use that phrase when we first met. I must say, I had never thought of us in those terms."

The cardinal's car was parked at the curb on the far side of the street. The driver left the vehicle on a run when he saw the exchange between his employer and the two men.

As he approached, Julian saw the man reach under his suit coat. Julian's response was instinctual and blistering. He concentrated and extended his hand slightly. The driver stumbled, slowed and stumbled again, then a look of horror crossed his face and he began vomiting. He fell to his knees and the revolver he had been reaching for dropped from his hand and skittered, vomit encrusted, to the gutter.

Julian returned to the conversation to find the cardinal and Soski looking at him. "Cardinal," Julian said, "your driver seems to be ill. Maybe some bad antipasto, huh? Want me to get you a taxi?"

The cardinal smiled a narrow smile and said, "Have a care for the company you keep, Mr. Blessing. As I said to you before, I can use a man like you and your efforts would be," the cardinal paused, "appreciated."

"Eminence, friends don't use their friends, do they?" Julian said.

"As I said, choose your friends wisely," the cardinal said and Julian could feel Luciano probing his mind.

"Indeed, Mr. Blessing," Fr. Soski said as he deflected some of the cardinal's intense scrutiny. "If you choose your friends wisely, it makes it so much easier and enjoyable to murder them later."

The cardinal left his attack on Julian, turned and walked to his car. He got behind the wheel and merged into traffic easily, leaving his driver retching in the gutter.

"Shall we?" Julian asked and Fr. Soski nodded. Together, they both made their way through a small portico into a smaller piazza crowded with parked cars. Soski walked slowly, painfully, and Julian slowed his pace to match the priest's.

"That was nicely done with the driver. Luciano was impressed or shocked. I don't know which. Can I assume the Book is helping then?" Soski asked.

"It is helping. However, that whole driver thing, well, I was trying to trip him. I have no idea what I did to make him start throwing up like that. Looked painful," Julian answered and winced at the memory.

"I wouldn't worry about it. Once, in the early days, I was learning to calm my thoughts sufficiently to be able to move a large tree branch out of the road. My teacher told me progress comes slowly. I can hear him saying that even today."

"Did you get the branch to move?" Julian asked.

"No, I set my teacher's house on fire instead. Not the whole house. Just a small shed that then set the rest of the house alight. Not the outcome I was hoping for actually," Fr. Soski said.

Contemplating the nature of personal growth, and the part the multilayered web of maladroitness and bold stupidity have to play in it, both men walked up the broad steps and into the cool, dark embrace of the Basilica di Sant' Agostino.

Julian and Fr. Soski walked down the wide center aisle of the Basilica. The priest had removed his fedora. The hair Julian took to be silver, when seen in the dim light of Soski's office, was a dull white. The skin on the man's face was dry and withered. A network of deep lines extended from under the priest's dark glasses along with signs of old scarring.

The church was small, but took every opportunity to increase its grandeur. Heavily veined marble pillars ascended to towering frescoed arches. Stained glass windows grew from the arches and bathed the interior of the church in blue and red sapphire, wispy purple and ghostly white. Six naves set deeply into the outside walls hinted at treasures without lifting their veils.

Rather than genuflect, Fr. Soski stopped next to the first pew and bowed his head. Julian watched the man and reflected this priest would bow before his god, but to no other.

The men sat in the pew and enjoyed a companionable silence absorbing the church's smell of pungent incense and dust.

Julian was the first to break the stillness. "Following me Father?"

"Why would I be interested enough in your activities to follow you? Conceit is the original sin, Mr. Blessing."

"I will bow to your superior knowledge of the Bible, Father and confess my sin."

"Bible? Oh, no, I got that from a bit of Japanese anime I saw once," the priest said and smiled. "Besides, I'm not as agile as I once was and I seem to lack the ability to be inconspicuous. This overcoat is not part of a clever disguise. I am susceptible to the cold and so wear this topcoat year round. So, following people is out of the realm of possibility for me.

"The Holy Father leaves Rome in July because it is too hot," the priest said, "and here is Fr. Soski with his overcoat." Again, the priest smiled. He chuckled, but that soon spiraled into a painful sounding cough. With difficulty, he cleared his throat. Speaking, Julian knew, was taking its toll.

"Father, why don't you rest your voice. We might need it if we have to order in a restaurant later, no?" Julian said.

Soski acknowledged the kindness and accepted Julian's invitation. *This is a church I visit with some regularity. It is intimate and usually empty as it is now.*

My eyesight isn't what it was so I come here to sit up close to the altar and admire the talent of those who made something so plain, so beautiful." Julian could feel each hushed word the priest thought.

Now, Luciano, he was following you. His interest in you is unholy and unhealthy. Take care my friend," Soski said. *My earlier question was a serious one. Did you enjoy the cardinal's 'Soldiers of Reason' monologue? He has given it many times, although not in the way I originally wrote it. He relies on others for his originality. It doesn't matter though.*"

"Father, call me Julian if you wouldn't mind," Julian said and then continued. "I have a problem."

"Dr. Dwyer - yes I know. Julian, I have given this a great deal of attention. It hasn't done me any good, but you need to know neither you nor the doctor have been far from my thoughts. There are many of us who are trying to find her. There seems to be a screen around all of that which has not yet been penetrated," Soski said.

"Father…"

The priest touched Julian's sleeve and said, *"Please, Marek is preferable to Father Soski."*

"Marek, anyone could have her, although the Russians and Luciano are first on the list of suspects. For all I know, Cardinal Manning could have her. I don't know anything about Manning. Can he be trusted? Are the police doing all they can? Might the police be somehow complicit?" Julian asked.

"Cardinal Manning is a cardinal, and as such, he is a political animal. He can be trusted as much as one can trust any dangerous wild animal. However, I believe he is rather tame in comparison to many of his brother cardinals. I doubt he has the doctor. What advantage would he gain by taking her? He seems to want nothing from you, but time will enlighten us."

Fr. Soski continued, *"I have been on to the police. You may trust they are doing all they can. That is not nearly enough for you. I know this. As I've said, I admire the restraint you have continued to show thus far. I doubt I would have done so well in your place. Please, believe, if I could put your mind at rest, know I would.*

"All of that is, however, an aside. You have a plan. You are a man who is never far from a plan. This one, I think, renders cardinals, gangsters and the police irrelevant. I could be mistaken, but I doubt it."

"I'm going to see the Russian, Sokolov. I have sat around long enough," Julian said. "I have no idea where he is but, I'm sure if I stand around, one of his men will find me."

"Rather than that, let's make an appointment with him, shall we? I want you to do something, not for me, but for you. Are you willing?" Soski said and Julian nodded.

"Sit back and look at the doorway to the right of the altar. Look at the door and then into it. Tell me when you can see the individual grains in the wood," Soski whispered in the sepulchral silence of the church.

Julian's eyes became heavy. Through half hooded slits, his vision began to narrow.

The door to the right of the altar and the sculptures above the door.

The door and frame.

The door.

It took some minutes, but Julian narrowed his focus further to the wood on the door and nothing else. He sent the thought – *"Now."*

"Good. You are as fast a study as they said. Julian, on the other side of a door, not unlike that one, is your Russian. See him. Watch him. Feel him. It is necessary that you know this man well before you meet him.

"I know you think this is impossible. How could you locate one man out of so many? Remember, we shine a light into the darkness. This man is using that darkness to his advantage, but his dark little corner festers and reeks from his crimes and his sins. Use the light to your advantage and know we make the impossible happen."

A minute, then two passed. Soski watched Julian. *"The building he is in, I can see it. I see the office, his men. Got it – I see him,"* Julian thought.

"Julian, watch him for a bit and then let Sokolov know that you want him to make himself available for you tomorrow. Take your time.

When you are sure you have his attention, give him your message. Watch him and make sure he understands."

Julian sat in transfixed silence. The old church gave voice to its age as its timbers creaked and a whispered breeze moved the flowers on the altar. Julian closed his eyes and smiled. Soski knew it was done.

"And?"

"It was difficult to get his attention. He is a man not easily distracted. I believe my message came through with some clarity though. I just hope I got the right guy."

"You will not have long to wait," Soski said. *He will react while you continue to act. You are now ahead in this game.*

"Keep something in mind, Julian. You are juggling many balls and all of them are important, but not equally so. You must assign them their priorities, and you must not lose your focus. You must never underestimate either the cardinal or the Russian. You must learn to master yourself and your gifts quickly, but well. You must find the doctor and neutralize the many threats that surround you and her," Fr. Soski said.

Julian looked to the high altar. *"Can I do it, Marek?"*

Fr. Marek Soski followed Julian's gaze. What the priest saw caused him to close his eyes, sigh deeply and rest his chin on his chest. What he saw, just for a moment, was the future.

* * *

In an office on Via del Pellegrino, in the Campo de' Fiori, a man dabbed gingerly at the scalding coffee that had spilled into his lap.

Bogdan Sokolov was really looking forward to that cup of coffee. Instead, what he got was a message, a niggling thought, a recent recollection, a dull tingling inside his head. It made his skin crawl. *"Soon, Sokolov, very soon. Tomorrow in fact."* He had no way of knowing the message's origin, but he knew on some primal level all the same.

Sokolov waved one of his men into his office and said, "Blessing. Find him now and bring him to me."

* * *

In a church on the other side of Rome, Fr. Soski smiled and nodded once to his companion. "He got the message," the priest said.

CHAPTER TEN

"Eminence, we noticed an irregularity during an audit today," a small officious looking man with thick glasses said.

Cardinal Manning looked up from the paperwork neatly arranged on his desk. He nodded and the small man continued.

"A transaction took place - that did not. As a result, the Vatican Bank has endured a loss that is not insignificant. That is cryptic I know, so allow me to explain," the small man said and continued to detail a fraudulent transaction of mind-bending complexity.

Wire transfers, missing account information and bogus remittances followed exploited security weaknesses, simultaneous debits and credits and cascading deposits made to multiple nonexistent accounts at foreign banks. Cardinal Manning sat in emotionless silence absorbing a litany of tortuously circuitous deceits.

"The amount involved?" the cardinal asked

"Seven hundred fifty-three thousand euros, Eminence."

The little man said nothing further. Cardinal Manning walked to his window overlooking the Papal gardens. "Signore," Cardinal Manning continued, "seven hundred fifty-three thousand euros has gone astray. I should think it would be missed. Please, tell me when we are going to recover the misplaced funds."

"Eminence, after an extensive search, we have no idea where they went."

The cardinal asked, "You have your suspicions, do you not?"

"My suspicions are not evidence, Eminence. The audit of our funds transfer system was decided at the last moment. No one, aside from the auditors, knew an audit would take place.

"I can say with certainty, had an audit not been in progress, this fraud would have gone unnoticed anywhere from days to upwards of a week. Had that happened, we would, I feel sure, have sustained further losses." The little man stood in respectful silence.

"And, signore? Give me the rest, please," the cardinal said.

"The methods employed in this attack, Eminence, lead us to two disturbing facts. Seven hundred and fifty-three thousand euros is not insignificant to be sure. However, an attack of this complexity could have easily netted the thieves seven and a half million. This, Eminence, was a test. There will be more attacks and I fear they will be costlier."

"Signore, you said there were two facts. Why are you keeping the second one from me?"

The small man removed his spectacles, cleaned the lenses with a handkerchief and never lost eye contact with the cardinal. "Eminence, someone within the Vatican Bank has betrayed us."

✳ ✳ ✳

"Marek," Julian said, "there is something that puzzles me. There are actually many things, but for now, let's consider just one."

The two men walked down a narrow cobbled street away from Sant' Agostino. The air was cool for a summer day in Rome and graced the Roman evening with an easy breeze and nostalgic feeling of calm.

Julian's companion smiled.

"When you approached the cardinal and me this afternoon, I saw you coming. I didn't know who you were – I've actually only seen you in the shadows of your office, but I couldn't really sense you. You had only a slight signature. How is that possible?"

"Through hard work, I assure you," the priest thought. *"You will see a brief mention of it in the book, but I researched the subject and talked with people who had the ability. It was a talent I thought would prove to be useful and it has, as you saw today. The cardinal never felt me either. Surprising him is something I enjoy – perhaps too much, but there you have it. Simple pleasures for a simple man."*

"Something else," Julian said. "There is a man, a policeman. I know he isn't one of us, but he doesn't have the slightest bit of signature. I've had him follow me, stand right behind me in fact and I never felt a thing. The question is the same, how?"

"I, too, have run into this phenomenon on two occasions. I was so intrigued that I spent a year doing research on the subject. I pestered everyone I knew. All of them had run into occurrences of this, but not one had an explanation. In the end I was left to draw my own conclusions," the priest looked thoughtful.

"You are one for the dramatic pause. I'll bite, what did you conclude, Marek?" Julian teased and prompted.

"Again, simple things. There are people, how many I don't know. A percentage of the population perhaps." The priest drew a deep breath and began a painful cough. *"Pardon me, my lungs were burned in my accident and it bothers me sometimes even when I'm not talking. Anyway, what you are describing is what I've come to call spiritual transmogrification."*

"Marek, please don't take this the wrong way, but you do know that is a word only a Jesuit would choose," Julian said and Fr. Marek began to laugh which devolved into a racking cough, causing Julian to wince.

"Well, I stand guilty. It is a rather grand word to be sure, but it is really the best word for the job and you may trust, I tried many others. I didn't want anyone accusing me of being a Jesuit." The priest smiled.

"I believe it happens when an individual becomes so fixated he gives himself over to something. He does it so completely he transforms into something between himself and the object of his obsession.

"That might be a cult, a political movement, a philosophy, a leader, country, or cause, or anything really that has the power to captivate the person so utterly that the individual lives for the object of his particular mania." Fr. Marek concluded, *"Does that fit?"*

"I'm sure it does, I just don't know where. The man I'm thinking of is a good policeman I think, dedicated and seemingly honest, but I don't know if his commitment rises to the level of mania," Julian said and wondered. "Perhaps though."

* * *

Signorina Joselina Conaletti stood at the front door with her daughters backing her up. It was after closing and even if it wasn't, the two very large, very ugly, very dangerous men at the door would not be coming in.

"Perhaps you are deaf as well as stupid looking. What am I to do with you my little Russian friends? I will only say it once more. Go. Away," Signorina Joselina said and smiled an evil smile as she looked up into the faces of the men towering over her as she closed the door.

The larger of the two Russians put out his hand and stopped the heavy wooden door from closing. "We leave when we have Blessing."

"Well, if that's all it takes, you have my blessing to leave." The madam attempted to close the door again and this time, in a murderous rage, the Russian pushed it open throwing the woman back into her employees.

"We search, we find Blessing, we go. Now get out of our way, whore."

"Provaci ancora!" said a handsome, fiercely muscular, singularly lethal Italian man with a bald head and a huge semiautomatic pistol. He had the muzzle of his weapon wedged firmly in the ear of an unhappy Russian. He seemed to be sighting directly through this Russian's head and into that of the other Russian.

"Oh, I'm sorry," signorina Joselina said righting herself and straightening her housecoat. "You have not been formally introduced. My little Russian friends, this is signore Giuseppe Sarro. He is our night watchman, our protector and our friend." Behind their employer, the girls nodded and smiled enthusiastically.

"In case you need a translation, he says 'Try again.' I believe he is inviting you to give him a reason to put a bullet in each of your heads. It looks like he has decided one bullet will do. Bullets are expensive, no?" Joselina said.

"It is like this my friends. Giuseppe is a man of few words, but I can tell you, the dome of St. Peter's could be filled with all the shits he doesn't give for whether he kills you or not."

Magician like, signorina Joselina produced an even larger handgun trained on the face of the second Russian just before he started to move. "We've had a good month," she said. "A few extra bullets won't matter." At Casa Felicità, the Russians were finding no joy whatsoever.

Signorina Joselina looked beyond the Russians, her eyes narrowed and she shook her head imperceptibly.

Julian stood on the curb at the rear bumper of the Russian's car, nodded his head and smiled broadly. The thought he transmitted struck Joselina Conaletti and Giuseppe Sarro simultaneously.

"Please, lower your weapons. There is going to be a very loud explosion soon and I don't want any guns going off by mistake. Fingers off those triggers, boys and girls."

Sarro, shrewd and mistrustful, shifted his gaze to his employer and she nodded and lowered her weapon. Her enforcer did the same and the Russians looked confused. Momentarily.

"Gentlemen," Julian announced as he climbed the stairs toward the front door of the whorehouse. The Russians turned to find their prey standing five steps below them, hands in pockets looking at them with a smile. He stood absolutely still and looked into the two men in front and above him.

"Now, I realize your Mr. Sokolov is impatient to meet me," Julian began. "However, you must make your boss understand something. I have granted him an appointment, but it is not until tomorrow and he will have to content himself with that."

The large men stood bunching their fists, impatient to beat Julian senseless and then beat him some more.

Julian said, "Now off you go and tell Mr. Sokolov, he needn't send people to find me. I know right where to find him. The Russians shifted uneasily and Sarro caressed the trigger guard, anxious to put his pistol to work.

The big men descended toward the still stationary Julian Blessing. Their plan was simple and painfully evident.

When they were three steps above him, the smile on his face turned to a cruel line, "Gentlemen, do not be stupid. Tell Mr. Sokolov I will be at his office at eleven and that it will go badly for him if he keeps me waiting."

The rear curbside tire of the Russian's car exploded. Every car alarm within three blocks went off simultaneously. Every dog not sensible enough to take cover was barking. People looked out windows, shouted curses and enthusiastically made rude gestures.

The ground was littered with Russians and prostitutes. Three people remained standing - Joselina Conaletti, Giuseppe Sarro and Julian Blessing.

Julian said, "You two." The Russians looked up at him with murder in their eyes. Those looks evaporated when they felt the words. *"Don't call on me unless you are invited and never bother my friends again."* With that, the front curbside tire blew and the neighborhood again erupted in shouts, curses and spirited gesticulating.

Julian stepped around the Russians and entered the whorehouse saying to the proprietress, "That is just so cool. I'll never get tired of that." He began to chuckle and Joselina Conaletti made the sign of the horns after she was sure Julian wasn't looking.

* * *

Bogdan Sokolov sat at his desk looking through the windows of his office at his collection of blunt-instrument goons. He cracked his knuckles and thought of murder.

With what, he reasoned, was nothing short of an act of defiance, the clock's minute hand sat stubbornly a few minutes before eleven o'clock. He looked down at his desk blotter, drew a deep breath and let his shoulders relax. This was not the time for rash decisions. How he would kill Julian Blessing was something that required careful consideration.

He looked up, and sat back in his chair with a start. A chair that had been empty seconds before now contained one Julian Blessing. Sokolov looked into Julian's steel gray eyes and didn't like what he saw.

Julian sat with his legs crossed and a modest smile on his face. His forearms were draped casually over the arms of the mobster's guest chair.

"You are going to die," Sokolov said with venom in his voice and an ugly sneer on his lips.

"We are all going to die, Mr. Sokolov," Julian said softly. "Now if you are done stating the embarrassingly obvious, can we move along to business? I am busy and so don't have time to waste," Julian said and the ease with which he said it shocked him far more than it did his host.

"That's it! You are dead fucker!" Sokolov exploded out of his chair, leaned over his desk and glowered at his guest.

Julian looked thoughtful and wondered why he hadn't soiled his trousers. He turned his gray eyes to Sokolov's face, looking at the man, into him. What he saw made him sick. The words were whispered and came out one at a time. "Sit. Down. Please." The mobster's eyes were hard and cold and Julian held the man's gaze relentlessly.

"You have two men standing outside your office door. Send them away. You won't need them and they can't help you anyway," Julian said.

Sokolov smirked and moved his head slightly indicating his men should move along. "Both men," Julian said with a slight smile, a smile he did not enjoy.

With nearly painful slowness, the Russian said, "You are more trouble than you are worth, Blessing. I kill you now." The man swiveled his chair to the right. Before he could reach for the top desk drawer, Julian said, "Are you thinking of taking notes?" Sokolov looked up, consternation etching his forehead, drawing his eyebrows together.

The Russian looked at Julian. Everything was wrong with this man. "What are you talking about?" the big man said.

"You're reaching for a pistol in your right hand drawer. In that drawer, there are pads of paper and a porn magazine. The thing you're looking for is in the upper left hand drawer. For now," Julian said and smiled a smile he did enjoy this time.

Sokolov tore the right hand drawer open. Pads of paper and a copy of Babes Over 40 magazine. The man, demented with rage, looked up at Julian. Turning to the left upper drawer, the Russian found more pornography and his coffee cup.

The mobster felt the words and looked up to see Julian looking at him, head canted to one side. *"I lied, sorry. Couldn't resist. Next drawer down,"* Julian thought. The Russian's shock was soon replaced with nostrils flaring and eyes narrowed into hard slits as he considered using his hands to murder Julian.

Sokolov reached slowly down one drawer, never taking his eyes off of Julian. Without looking, he reached into the drawer and felt the familiar frame of the small Sig P290, 9mm pistol. He left it where it was, but left the drawer open in case a change of heart came upon him.

It is a good policy to be wary of strangers who appear out of thin air, know things they shouldn't, and drop words inside people's heads. Culturally steeped in superstition, the Russian's wariness quadrupled.

Sokolov smiled a smile that never reached his cold, dead eyes. "I start to like you, Blessing. We do business, eh?"

"Oh gosh! Can we?" Julian said and the sarcasm ran in rivulets across the Russian's desk. "Let's just move along, shall we? Do you have Doctor Dwyer? I only require a yes or no answer." Julian raised his eyebrows and looked expectant.

A mocking smile appeared on Sokolov's face and Julian had to increase his concentration to stay focused. If he allowed it, his mind would turn to speculation-fueled sickening images of Ailís. He knew if left unchecked, he would obliterate the Russian without a single thought beyond rage if anything happened to her.

Sokolov swiveled and removed a large envelope from his credenza. He emptied the contents on his desk.

Julian recognized Ailís' purse. He bought it for her on a trip to Dublin. There was no need to open the Irish passport or to go through the wallet. They were Ailís' and he knew it, felt it. He knew something wasn't right too. Knowing what, would be something he would work on later. Now it was all about the man sitting across from him.

He watched Sokolov with infinite care. He followed the Russian's eyes every time he looked away. Julian refused to let the man escape his stare until he knew everything about Sokolov's signature.

"I'm still, waiting. Yes or no?"

"What do you think, Blessing?" Sokolov asked. "There are your woman's things. You tell me.

"Now, I think we make deal, eh? You could have value to me. You do a few things for me and I give you back your woman. Is simple, no?" Sokolov concluded with a shrug.

Julian looked thoughtful and then smiled. "I'll think about it. Well, this has been a pleasant chat, but it's time for me to go."

The Russian looked astonished. He had seen this kind of swagger before but never from someone like this. His hand moved slowly across the desk to the left.

Julian stood then turned his back on Sokolov. Without turning back he said, "Leave the weapon where it is. As I said, I will think about your offer. Right now, I don't think much of it, but that may change."

"You do more than think about it," Sokolov derided. "You do some things for me or I enjoy your woman until you do. Maybe I sell her to someone later. Is simple, no?"

Julian turned and, looking at the floor, walked back to the desk. He looked up and found a spot on Sokolov's forehead. The big Russian had seen a lot and done a lot and all of it was bad. He had looked at men who wanted to kill him and he had laughed.

He now looked at Julian Blessing and the hairs on the back of his neck stood on end. He began to lick his lips and blink rapidly. His breathing increased and perspiration broke out on his scalp and ran down his back. He managed to press a button under his desk.

Julian smiled slightly, left the spot on the man's head and sought out his eyes. With a terrifying intensity, Julian thought and Sokolov suffered. *"Feeling a bit warm are you? You should because I am boiling your brain right inside your head. And I am the only one who can make it stop. Keeping me alive and safe and happy had better become your second priority in life. I'll get to your first priority in a minute. Is simple, no?*

"You have made me unhappy with your whole 'fate worse than death' routine. Let me turn up the heat, and I'll show you what could be worse than death," Julian said.

Sokolov began to drool and sweat coursed down his face. Julian's breathing was slow and his heartbeat was steady. The Jesuit Book had taught him to eliminate everything that got in the way of achieving absolute focus. He wondered how long he could keep it up. He walked around the desk and sat on the edge next to the man who had threatened Ailís. Julian knew he would keep that focus forever if he had to.

The big man's throat began to constrict his airflow and he started to choke. His eyes began to bulge as his body started to shut down non-essential systems.

"Here." Julian reached into the desk drawer and took out the pistol. He placed it in the Russian's hand. *"That is your idea of power. Your brain is on fire and you can't even wrap your fingers around that thing. How much good is your power doing you now?*

"You think there is hope, don't you? Your men are running this way right now. Each of them would kill on your orders and most have. I've closed the door, but didn't even lock it. A closed door. That's all that is keeping them out.

"You know why all of them will stay on the other side of the door? Because they hope I kill you." He leaned next to Sokolov's ear. *"For them, it's called career advancement.*

"Listen to me, you pig. It is possible you have the doctor. It is possible you only have her purse. I could tell you to release her if you have her at all, but you may have some failsafe in place that would cause her harm. Maybe you don't.

"It is all about probabilities, possibilities and outcomes. I could ask if you had her and you would answer. You would probably tell me the truth, but there is always that tiny possibility you would not and a smaller possibility I would not detect your lie. Her life is not something I will gamble with.

"Because of that slight uncertainty, I'm not going to kill you. Right now. You had better hope I do not get the feeling something has happened to the doctor. The moment that thought comes to me, you will be dead a nanosecond later.

"Here is a little something to remind you never to threaten me. It might give your troops out there a little something to think about too." Blood began to run from Sokolov's ears as the veins in his neck distended while his body tried to replace the blood it was losing.

Julian took the Russian's pistol and threw it into a drawer. The drawer closed without Julian touching it. He left the desk and walked slowly to the office door. "Probabilities, possibilities and outcomes, Sokolov.

"If you have her, keep the doctor safe and comfortable. That is your first priority. Is simple, no?"

Before reaching the office door, Julian closed his eyes and concentrated. Two blocks away, he stepped back into normal time and began looking for the inspector and her sergeant.

* * *

Fr. Dominic stood respectfully at Cardinal Luciano's office door. There was no reason to knock.

"Come in, Dominic," the cardinal thought and the priest, still unsettled by the fact, felt it. He entered and stood before the massive carved desk, a desk that had been in this room for over three hundred years. The cardinal looked up, his eyes cold, gray and remorseless.

"Eminence, I trust you are having a productive day." Fr. Dominic didn't use the words 'good day'. In the cardinal's residence, no one had a good day. Ever.

The cardinal brushed aside the question. "I trust you would not be here without having something for me."

"Indeed, Eminence. The American, Blessing, has been to see Sokolov. Our contact within the Russian's organization could not, or would not, provide details beyond two.

"He said Sokolov met with Blessing and at the conclusion of that meeting, blood was running from the Russian's ears. The second detail was that Mr. Blessing disappeared."

"Disappeared? The blood from the Russian's ears was a nice touch," the cardinal said and smiled.

"Yes, Eminence. Apparently, Mr. Blessing was in Sokolov's office one moment and not there the next. No other information was forthcoming beyond the fact a doctor was called to the office."

The cardinal looked at his tooled leather desk blotter and suppressed a grin. "Interesting news. Anything else?" the cardinal said.

"Yes, Eminence. Our test appears to have been successful. A new, far larger amount has been withdrawn from the IOR." The priest used the initials of Istituto per le Opere di Religione – the Vatican Bank.

"This was planned, so it is not news," the cardinal said.

"True, Eminence. The withdrawal comes as no news to you, however, the amount might." The priest smiled, proud of his handiwork. He continued before he irritated his boss. "Two million, three-hundred thousand euros or," Fr. Dominic consulted the file folder he carried. "that would be nearly three million dollars as of fifteen minutes ago."

The cardinal sat back in his chair, looked at his assistant and said, "Nicely done, Dominic. If there isn't anything else…?" Cardinal Luciano left the sentence unfinished. This interview was over. Fr. Dominic bowed slightly and left the office.

The priest walked to his office, deposited his folder in a safe and went for a walk. "Nearly three million dollars stolen undetected and he calls it nicely done," Fr. Dominic smirked and shook his head.

CHAPTER ELEVEN

"I should be angry with you. I should be so angry with you that I ask Enrico to give you a good beating. I will dismiss my anger if you have something useful to report," the inspector said. "By the simple fact that you are alive, we can assume you did not see Sokolov or you pulled some more of your wizard-y shit."

Julian considered his options. Nothing useful = beating. Something useful = no beating. Seeing very few options to consider, he moved along.

"I believe Sokolov is a bad man and that he is laundering money and he may or may not have the doctor." Julian stood as though he expected a reward.

At the words, 'bad man' the inspector closed her eyes and began to rub the middle of her forehead. "Enrico," she said softly. "Beat this man, but only until your arms get tired."

"Oh, yeah, I nearly forgot. I got this for you," Julian said and tried to suppress a grin. The inspector looked up to meet Julian's cool gray eyes, alive with mischief. He reached into the pocket of his sport coat and withdrew a sheaf of documents for her.

With eyes like slits, the inspector took the papers. She didn't expect much. She unfolded them, took a bored breath and began to examine the first document – a spreadsheet. She took a second breath and this one she held for a very long time as she scanned the column headings, headings written in Italian. She began to look at the numbers and made quick work of looking through the other papers, handing them off to her assistant as she went.

The sergeant scanned the first paper, looked up with a hard expression and stared at Julian.

The inspector looked kind when she smiled and said, "Signore Blessing, do you mind if I call you Julian? Julian, where did you get these documents?" she asked sweetly.

"I got them from Sokolov's desk. I figured while I was there I should probably bring something back for you two," Julian said as sweetly.

The sergeant said, "Can I beat him now?"

"Sushhh, Enrico. Can't you see? We are talking with a foreign national, a tourist and a guest of our country. You can beat him later. I will help."

The inspector smiled more sweetly still and said, "Julian, you went to see the Russian and he gave you these papers, yes? Is that what you would like us to believe? Or you found yourself in Sokolov's office."

She continued. "You saw a stack of the most damning spreadsheets and memos imaginable and that Russian pig said, 'I'll bet your friends Bella and Enrico would find these interesting.' Is that what happened?"

Julian looked thoughtful. "Bella, Enrico," Julian began. The inspector's nostrils flared at the use of her Christian name. Her assistant put the papers under his arm and began bunching and unbunching his fists. Informality begged to be punished.

"I know something about finance. I used to be in that business. While I was doing my wizard-y shit, as you say, I saw the papers in Sokolov's drawer. I figured you could use them in your investigation, although how you got them would probably fall into the not-admissible-in-court category." Julian trumped the inspector's smile.

***

"Eminence, the bank has sustained another loss. This time the amount is substantial," a quintessentially average man in a black suit said.

Cardinal Manning drew a breath before he looked up. "You are saying the first loss of three quarters of a million was not substantial? Or the one before that? Tell me, what constitutes a catastrophic loss?"

"$2.9 million was the size of this loss, Eminence."

The cardinal inspected the man standing in front of his desk and did so for a full minute, a minute during which the man looked through his file folder.

"Signore, our losses so far are well over four million dollars. This is starting to look like carelessness and…" Manning stopped. Something about this unremarkable man's face had changed and not for the better.

"There is more," the cardinal said and his tone was flat and unfriendly.

"Eminence, I cannot say. The director general is coming to see you in a few moments. He will have all the information you request. The director sent me ahead to tell you what I know. That, Eminence, is all I know." Perspiration had erupted from the man's scalp and coursed down his cheeks and back.

A knock on the door preceded the entrance of the Vatican Bank's director general. The man jerked his head and the unremarkable man left the office.

"Cardinal Manning," the director said. "I have just come from a meeting of the bank's auditors. I must tell you the news could not be worse." Manning's polar stare over his half glasses had the president swallowing hard.

"Continue," the cardinal said.

"While trying to strengthen our electronic and physical security, at my instructions, the auditors began an examination of prior transactions. Their audit continues, but they feel they have found all past and present losses."

"Signore, you are doing yourself no favors by trying to free yourself from blame. The amount of the losses, if you please."

"Eminence, our losses to date amount to almost half a billion dollars."

The clock in the office pounded in the bank director's ears. Each tick was another nail in his professional coffin.

"Do you feel our security procedures have been increased sufficiently to assure there will be no further losses?" the cardinal asked in a whisper the president strained to hear.

The man licked his lips, took in a breath that might as well be his last and said, "I can only tell you, everything that can be done to safeguard the IOR has been done."

Another whisper passed Cardinal Manning's lips. "Get. Out."

The cardinal looked at the telephone on his desk. It was an instrument he would have to use very soon. The call he would make would wound his papal aspirations, but not kill them entirely.

He picked it up, touched one number on the phone and waited. "This is Manning. It is necessary for me to see His Holiness. Yes, thirty minutes will suffice." He hung up the telephone and considered a lifetime's scrambling, maneuvering, plotting, betraying and planning. Very careful planning.

* * *

"Julian, my friend, was your interview with Mr. Sokolov a pleasant one?" Fr. Soski thought and his grin made his mood palpable.

"Marek, it is always pleasant when old friends get together, no?"

"Oh, my. Can I assume you did not use him gently?" the priest scolded.

"I would have to say, Mr. Sokolov and I would be unable to come to an agreement on the meaning of 'gently used,' but he would be the first to admit he was definitely used." Julian's slight smile was rueful, but quickly turned solemn. I am unable to determine whether he has Ailís or not. The man is a ball of hatred and so is impossible to read except on the most visceral level.

"I can tell you, he is unhappy with me. The implications are clear. I feel the Jesuit Book would be safer in your care. I believe things are going to get dicey and I doubt, seriously, my ability to safeguard it. It is too important a work to put at risk."

The men sat on a stone bench in the shade of a large tree. The tree and bench were in the private garden Julian rented from his hostess at the House of Joy. The men shared a lunch of crusty Italian bread, olives, a hunk of cheese and some prosciutto cotto. Fr. Soski thought as he ate.

"Julian," the priest said. "Often the resources we need are right at hand. If you will get the door, I believe we can have our need for security and peace of mind met."

Julian smiled just before a discreet knock was heard on the door leading to the garden. Julian walked to the door. Joselina Conaletti stood on the other side looking pinched and distinctly unhappy.

"For the love of the Madonna, wizard, don't you know who that is, who you've brought into my house? Have you gone suddenly more stupid or something?" The woman's panic was inspiring.

"That is my friend, Fr. Soski. Come out, I'll introduce you," Julian said.

The madam looked horror-struck. "I am supposed to go out there and meet the Ghost! Rosa, the girl on the same floor as you, she told me a customer of hers knew a man who said he knew someone who once looked the Ghost in the face and was driven instantly insane. And this you bring into my house? Do you care nothing for me and my daughters? How can you do this to us!

"I told that useless Giuseppe Sarro to throw the both of you out and do you know what that knot head said? I'll tell you! He said he would rather dig out his eyes with a rusty spoon! That man is afraid of no one, but even he won't screw around with the Ghost." She made the sign of the horns so the priest wouldn't see.

"Signorina, please come and enjoy your lovely garden with us. My friend, and I are in need of your wise counsel," Fr. Soski thought and Joselina staggered as if head butted by a long horned sheep.

Julian smiled his most charming smile. The hallway behind Joselina was filled with her employees. He opened the door wide and the young women suddenly had a great need to be anywhere other than where they were.

"See what you've done." The woman looked at Julian and was venomous. "It is one thing to have you doing your wizard shit right on my front steps and now I have the Ghost inside my head! And, and, and now my daughters have abandoned me. Nasty whores, I will skin them all if I live through this. If I do not, I will haunt you forever wizard!" the woman hissed.

She entered the garden and, without touching it, Julian closed the door behind her. She jumped. Julian smiled.

Fr. Soski stood and turned to face her. She looked at the white hair, the opaque gray eyes and the pale skin of the tall, banister thin priest as he held out a hand to welcome her. He smiled and terror animated the soul of Joselina Conaletti when she touched the cold hand of the Ghost.

* * *

"You obviously have friends in very high places, Mr. Blessing. "Taking your leisure in the Vatican Gardens is not something every tourist has the opportunity to enjoy. I am impressed," Cardinal Luciano said and was impressed not at all.

"You asked to see me," Julian said. "I thought this would be a convenient place."

"Oh, yes, very convenient and very public. Do you and I really need to be this cautious with each other? I am getting the impression you do not trust me." The cardinal's voice was musical and light with its slight Italian tinged English.

"Eminence, do I have to be this cautious with you? The answer to that is yes. Do I trust you? Of course not. Not only is this a public place, but we are being watched," Julian said, strengthening the defenses around his thoughts.

The cardinal smiled and shook his head. "Mr. Blessing, I appreciate your candor. It is so American, so refreshingly naive. However, I cannot say your fabrications are especially original. In fact, we are not being watched. I would know, as you would know, if we were.

"Further, watched or not, you could easily fall over dead and it would appear, for all the world, that I did nothing but administer the last rights. And the world would, of course, be right. I am a man of God after all," the cardinal chuckled.

Julian set a slow pace as they walked down a long pea gravel path leading to a small fountain. Perfectly trimmed boxwoods lined the path and the air was honeyed with the smell of jasmine.

Julian stopped and cocked his head at his opponent, "You wished to see me?"

"Indeed," Cardinal Luciano said. "I wanted to report I have been diligent in my inquiries regarding Dr. Dwyer. Some obstacles are to be overcome, but her safety comes first, so I am sure you will be happy to assist in any way you can." The cardinal's smile was a smirk.

"And in what way can I assist, Eminence?" Julian asked and dreaded the answer.

"We talked of powerful people when we met at my residence, no? Well, these powerful people are in a position to find and free your doctor, if anyone can, but they need to know which side you are on," the cardinal said.

"I am on the right side, Eminence. And you?" Julian smiled a smile he did not feel.

The cardinal let the innuendo pass. "Mr. Blessing, there is a man. He is a man of great power and international standing. He is one of a handful of such people who are doing great harm to society. He is holding mankind back from claiming its true destiny. He is clever, this man. It appears to all the world he is the very model of piety and moral rectitude.

"This man must be," the cardinal paused, "dissuaded." The emphasis was heavy and driven home when the cardinal arched an eyebrow.

"Much discussion has been held on this subject. It is felt you are the individual in a position to accomplish such a thing." The cardinal went no further, but looked at Julian awaiting a response.

"I need to kill someone in order to secure the release of the doctor, is that what I'm hearing? Please, tell me I misheard."

"Mr. Blessing, it is you who used the word kill. I merely said dissuaded. I understand how your interpretation could be seen to be correct. Early in our relationship you indicated you were not inclined to join us. We accept and respect your decision, although we are disappointed of course. That said, you need not join as an active member in order to have your doctor returned to you.

"Successfully accomplish this task for us and you and the doctor are free to resume your lives far away from Rome. You may rest easy that you have completed an important mission for the greater good by protecting the world from an immense evil. In the process, you may just save this man's soul. Of course, we will bother you no further." With eyebrows raised and a broad smile, the cardinal looked pleased.

While Luciano waltzed around the subject, Julian's natural style was slam dancing. "And the target of this assassination is who, your Eminence?"

The cardinal looked at Julian in mock disapproval. Luciano held Julian's gaze, then looked away into the distance. Julian followed the man's eyes. Both men squinted slightly under the harsh Roman sun.

From a small door in the wall surrounding the garden, a compact group of clerics entered and stood aside. It was a small pond of black cassocks, some piped in the scarlet of cardinals, others in the purple of bishops.

A tall, kind and jovial looking man with wispy white hair, a kind face and, what Julian sensed as a shrewd, but generous spirit entered. He inspected the garden, closed his eyes for a moment and enjoyed the respite from a worrying world. This man wore a white cassock and a white zucchetto, a skullcap, and a simple gold pectoral cross on a simple gold chain around his neck.

This man was the Pope.

He glanced in Julian's direction. The cardinal placed his hand on his own pectoral cross and bowed from the waste. Julian inclined his head slightly, but never took his eyes off the leader of over one billion Catholics.

Julian picked the place, but Luciano had picked the time. The cardinal had known the Pope would appear and when. His Eminence was half a step ahead of Julian in this race.

The cardinal took Julian's arm. "A few more moments of your time, Mr. Blessing. I understand you have been to see a Russian gentleman of, shall we say, questionable character. A man named Sokolov, I believe. I must caution you. He is a dangerous man to know."

"Eminence, there appear to be many men in Rome who are dangerous to know. In the case of Mr. Sokolov, he also has been kind enough to offer his assistance in finding the doctor."

Cardinal Luciano ignored the jab. "Hmmm, I will have to trust you know what you are doing and what risks you are taking.

"Remember, men like him do not give of themselves freely. He will exact a price should he find that for which you are looking," the cardinal said, his face strained to look serious and thoughtful.

Julian nodded his understanding. "And that would make him different from you, sorry, your group, how exactly?"

Again the cardinal sidestepped the insult. "Doubtless, Mr. Sokolov has heard of your talents and will demand their use if he finds the doctor. It well could be he took her to begin with," the cardinal said.

"I offer this only as a word to the wise. We are alike in our calling and so I owe it to you to give the best counsel I can," the cardinal smiled and continued.

"The Sokolovs of this world would use you for selfish and malicious ends. My friends and I will, in time, find your doctor, but the request we would make of your services is nothing but altruistic. We seek only the betterment of mankind, while Sokolov wants only to enrich himself at mankind's expense. You see the difference, of course."

Julian saw the difference, but it was a difference without much of a distinction.

"I have thought over your initial offer and will think over what you have said today. I do not feel now is the time to make such a decision, at least until the doctor is found and returned safely," Julian said.

The cardinal laughed. "Mr. Blessing, I wish I could play your words back so you could hear them from my point of view. I must tell you, yours is prevarication on a Vatican level. Had you become a priest in your youth, you would surely be a prince of the Church by now. What they say is true, you learn quickly.

"If I could make a suggestion – do try to look a little earnest when you say such things. People might question your sincerity otherwise." Again, the cardinal smiled without meaning.

"If there is nothing else, Eminence," Julian said.

"For now, nothing," the cardinal said with a sneer. "Think well and quickly. I wait to hear from you, then we will talk further. For now, go with God, Mr. Blessing."

Julian nodded, turned and traced his steps back along the pea gravel path. The cardinal sat on the edge of the small fountain and watched him walk away. He watched and he wondered and he weighed the life of Julian Blessing. For now he was worth more alive than dead.

* * *

"Signore Marino, you saw and you heard?" Julian reached into his coat pocket and withdrew the listening device the sergeant had placed there. "He wants to take out the Pope! You have proof. Will you arrest him or will the..."

Marino, shook his head, no. The sergeant was situated on the roof of the Vatican Radio transmission center. He placed the listening device and binoculars in a small briefcase and looked at Julian.

He had secured the services of the sergeant. Marino brought with him ungodly swift and deadly physical responses to all occasions. The sergeant had no discernable signature. Marino's listening in would not have saved Julian from being obliterated, but he may have had proof of Luciano's complicity. At least that was what Julian thought.

The sergeant looked at Julian and shook his head again. "Arrest him for what? You are the one who suggested killing the Pope. The cardinal suggested you reason with His Holiness."

Julian ran over the conversation in his mind. He acknowledged what the sergeant said.

"Sergeant, may I ask you a question?" Again, Marino nodded once.

"Didn't Vatican Security object to you being on one of their roofs?" Julian asked.

"Bella told them I was here to protect the cardinal from you. The Vatican authorities trust no one. They have a sniper trained on me and another on you. Right now."

"Me? Hey, that's a good one." Julian chuckled. His was the only chuckle as he scanned the rooftops and windows, easily feeling the presence of, not two, but three counter snipers.

"Yeah, well, do you mind another question?" Julian said with a concerned look on his face as he scanned the rooftops of the Vatican. Marino nodded only slightly.

"I know this may sound pretty macabre, but you think those guys would, you know?"

The policeman looked at Julian several moments longer than Julian found comfortable before saying, "There are too many wizards in Rome, so yes."

A dazed Julian said, "That isn't exactly what I meant, but, okay, well, oh, look at the time. Nice chatting with you, Sergeant.

Thanks for, ah, being here. It made me feel a lot better. Arrivederci, no?" Julian's smile was weak tending toward pathetic.

Enrico Marino's face was as expressionless as usual. When a shaken Julian was off the roof, the policeman smiled. Slightly.

* * *

"Marek, bilocation? Really? What is it about Jesuits that you can't just say 'two places at once?" Julian asked.

"Because," Fr. Soski answered, "bilocation is far more accurate, more scientific. In this case, at least." The priest was clarifying things metaphysical for Julian and warning him of the dangers likely to assail him.

"Let us take Cardinal Luciano. It is both physically and metaphysically impossible for him to be in two places at once. He can, however, project a likeness of himself. You could, one day, be facing several cardinals each looking like Luciano. Thus, bilocation." Julian's friend smiled.

"Like a hall of mirrors." Julian looked pleased. The priest did not.

"Julian, what is it that causes you to reduce things to their simplest form?" the priest asked, not unkindly.

Julian looked sheepish and the priest laughed. "My friend, let us stay with bilocation, if you wouldn't mind. We'll leave the hall of mirrors simile for another time." Fr. Soski paused, looked expectant and continued.

"Regardless of our talents, all of us have one thing in common. The ability to focus binds us all together. That focus allows us to do what we do," the priest said.

"Bilocation is a serious threat. If you are focusing on a person, then suddenly you are confronted with two, three or four of that person, you have no choice but to shift your focus. If given enough time, you will sort out the real from the illusionary, but it may be too late by then."

The two friends sat in the priest's darkened office. Julian broke the silence.

"Marek, every time I speak of general principals, you bring us back to the hostile applications of those." Julian's statement was delivered as a simple observation. Fr. Marek steepled his fingers as if in prayer.

"Julian, as I have said before, I have watched you with some care. I continue to talk with others about you. You are the subject of much research and conjecture, a real celebrity, but I won't ask for an autograph quite yet." The priest smiled.

"The usual course is we learn to wield the talents we were born with. Through study and application over a lifetime, we gain a certain mastery of ourselves and our abilities. You, however, continue to learn and grow and you are doing it with shocking speed. I suspect this is because you don't know what you can't do." Fr. Marek's chuckle turned to a racking cough. Julian grimaced.

Fr. Marek caught his breath, apologized and continued. "You, Julian, have an unimaginable set of gifts. It is necessary that you know, yours is a brilliant light. You must also understand, there are those who would extinguish it. With the light comes the mist, the shadows and the darkness, my friend."

"Marek?" Julian asked. The priest wiped his mouth on a handkerchief and it came away speckled with blood. "Luciano, he wants me to murder the pope."

"Well then," the priest said, "we will have to make sure you don't do that."

CHAPTER TWELVE

"Eminence," Fr. Dominic said. Cardinal Luciano looked up from his book. His eyes narrowed, but did not respond. "Eminence, another test was run." The priest hesitated as the cardinal's look turned dark. "It was not successful."

The cardinal set his book aside, crossed his legs, but said nothing.

"It would seem the Vatican Bank has tightened its computer systems security and changed its protocols and procedures. What would make this worrying is these changes were made the moment our test entered the system," the priest concluded.

The cardinal considered a moment and then thought, *"Dominic, you said, 'would make this worrying,' as though I should or would be worried. There is nothing about which I need to worry. As the individual responsible for all things financial here, it is for you to worry."*

When the thought struck, Fr. Dominic shuddered and his eyesight blurred. When the cardinal addressed him telepathically, it left him feeling ill and with a migraine for days afterward.

"Eminence, I meant I would be worried only all traces of the transaction, on this side, disappeared the instant the changes were detected by the bank. There is no trail leading back."

"Well then, you should hope these changes disappeared quickly enough, no?" The cardinal picked up his book again and began to read.

Fr. Dominic bowed, turned and left. It wasn't until he was a fair distance from the cardinal's study that the young priest puffed out his cheeks and let out a breath.

Antonio, Cardinal Archbishop Luciano, looked up from his book and suppressed a contented smile. It was, he had always thought, easy to smile at the expense of others.

* * *

"Gentlemen, come in. Please take a seat." Cardinal Manning stood up from his desk as Julian and Fr. Soski entered.

The priest bowed his head in deference to rank. Without preamble, Julian said, "Eminence, your message sounded urgent."

"Urgent is it? Although, the Holy Father sees this as an urgent matter to be addressed quickly, I see it as nothing short of a catastrophe that will cause the bank to collapse if not repaired now. I am asking, begging for your assistance." The cardinal's features were distorted by nervous tension and nearly palpable anxiety.

Manning pressed the intercom and said, "Send him in."

A perfectly nondescript young priest entered the office and the cardinal motioned for him to approach.

Look out any window, at any time in Vatican City and you could find scores of priests who looked just like this one. Slender, tall, young, wearing a black cassock. A minute out of his presence and that would be the only description possible.

Julian examined the newcomer with care. There was something about this one. The way he stood, the way he walked – there was something ultimately ordinary, while being out of the ordinary, about this priest.

Soski glanced up at the young priest, then looked away without another thought.

146

"Edward, my boy, tell these gentlemen everything that is known about our difficulty," the cardinal said as he sat.

Soski looked at Cardinal Manning, while Julian looked at the floor, closing his eyes.

Fr. Edward Millburn drew a deep breath, adopted a pleasant expression, and began.

For just short of an hour, the priest recited a litany of loss and the methods employed to cause it. At the conclusion of his narration, he nodded to the cardinal and stood in a respectful silence.

"Thank you Edward," the cardinal said. The young priest bowed his head slightly and left three men sitting in silence, alone with their own thoughts.

"You see the problem, gentlemen. We have a mole, a leak, a quisling and I need that man found and quickly," the cardinal said, his voice low and his intensity palpable.

"I've heard enough. Shall, we?" Fr. Soski thought.

Julian nodded his head in agreement, then addressed the cardinal. "Eminence, we will need access to every inch of the bank at all times of the day and night and we will need to interview every person working here."

"You have whatever you need. Present yourselves to the guard at the door. From there the bank is yours. God speed your efforts. I need not tell you I need this handled quickly and quietly.

"Julian," the cardinal continued, "I've not forgotten about the doctor. I've leaned on everyone in the police and have engaged the Vatican's gendarmerie to make discreet inquiries. Neither you, or the doctor, is ever far from my thoughts or prayers."

The cardinal's guests stood, said their goodbyes and left the cardinal and the Vatican bank.

"Fr. Edward is the leak, of course," Julian thought, *"and the cardinal knows it, at least suspects it."*

"Yes, but the priest isn't alone. That presentation was memorized from first to last so the youngster wouldn't give anything away. He was on autopilot with almost no thoughts of his own. Someone knew we would be present today," Fr. Soski thought.

"Sadly, that's what I think too," Julian replied. *"I suppose we should start interviewing people."*

"There won't be much of an interview needed. A handshake and a brief word will eliminate nearly everyone and highlight anyone we need to have a serious talk with," Fr. Soski thought.

"Marek, a question if you don't mind."

Soski raised his eyebrows.

"Why are we both here? You could do what he needs or I could. Both of us will only speed the process marginally."

His face set in concentration, Soski thought, "That, my friend, is the real question. We are both here to witness something together or to keep one of us from being elsewhere."

* * *

"Come in, Dominic," Cardinal Luciano said and continued to look into the fire crackling in his office fireplace.

The priest rushed in. "Eminence, our source has just advised that the Russian, Sokolov, is soliciting at the bank. He is looking for an accomplice within the bank. When I say soliciting, I mean he is trying to blackmail or otherwise force," Fr. Dominic started.

"The man is unreasonably transparent. I suppose if he presented himself at the door of the Vatican Bank with a brass band, it would be somewhat less subtle than what he is doing now. He is starting to wear on me. Anything else, Dominic?"

"No, Eminence."

"Then you may go. I will not have need of you until tomorrow morning." Cardinal Luciano concluded the interview.

Fr. Dominic bowed and left the office never having dreaded a night off more. "What happens tomorrow morning?" He would ruminate on that for the remainder of the evening. By the morning thoughts would have turned to anxiety would have developed into full-blown dread. Terror wouldn't be far behind.

* * *

"Good morning, Marek ," Julian said as he entered the priest's office. In profile, Fr. Soski looked drawn and even more pale and his eyes looked distressingly weary. "What is it? What's wrong?" Deep lines on his forehead telegraphed Julian's concern.

Fr. Soski swiveled his desk chair around slowly. He said nothing at first. Julian could feel it, nearly see it.

"Do I need to say the words, Julian?"

"Yes, Marek . I want to hear what happened. I don't want to feel your words, I want to hear them."

"Fr. Edward Millburn, our presenter at the Vatican Bank, is dead. It is believed he died of a cerebral hemorrhage while at the opera last night." With his mind, the priest pushed a copy of *la Repubblica* across his desk to Julian. The newspaper was turned to page twenty, below the fold and following a restaurant review. Scant tribute for a member of the clergy.

Julian slowly, painfully teased the meaning out of the Italian language paper.

He took a deep breath, and then another, as Fr. Soski watched the emotions move across his friend's face.

"Luciano was present." Julian's statement was flat.

"I'm sure he was. Opening night of La Bohème? He wouldn't miss it. Odd though that a simple priest would have tickets to a sold out opening night performance, no?" Marek asked.

Julian nodded his head.

"The cardinal wants to get your attention," the priest said without emotion. "And possibly to send a message to others." Fr. Soski said and paused before continuing.

"Don't do it, my friend. It will only bring you pain. Don't look back." The priest could see it was too late.

Julian's eyes were heavy and his face twisted in sympathetic agony as he watched Fr. Edward place his hands to his head, stand up in a crowed opera house and die. He watched it twice in his mind, before the images faded.

"The cardinal has my attention," Julian said.

* * *

"Eminence, Fr. Edward Millburn? He's dead? I saw him just last night," Fr. Dominic said.

"So I understand, Dominic," Cardinal Luciano replied with a pleasant look on his face.

"But Eminence, I don't understand." Fr. Dominic's face reflected his inability to process his shock and his sinking despair. "Eminence, Edward and I were at seminary together. I recruited him for you. He was ecstatic about going to see La Bohème last night. He couldn't believe his luck in getting tickets. He can't be dead."

Luciano looked quizzical. "Recruited him for me, Dominic? Whatever for? As for La Bohème, it was inspired. I saw Fr. Millburn and thought of inviting him to my box. He seemed in some distress, so I thought better of it. As for your understanding, he was alive and now he is not."

"But," the priest was panicked, stunned, his thoughts tossed on a dark and violent sea. "Eminence, did you…"

"Did I what, Dominic?" The cardinal's voice held an edge that begged to cut. "I've done you the courtesy of telling you myself."

With his chin on his chest, Fr. Dominic attempted to collect himself. As tears brimmed his eyes, he stood erect, squared his shoulders, inclined his head to his employer and said, "It is very kind of you to tell me, Eminence. Will that be all?" He tried to smile, but the sadness in his eyes killed that in its infancy.

"It is all for now, Dominic," the cardinal said eying his assistant, looking inside the man, judging his capacity for betrayal.

The priest again bowed slightly and turned to leave. The door opened as he approached and he stopped when he felt the cardinal's words.

"Dominic, do not tempt me again," the cardinal thought.

The priest drew a deep breath and left the office. Sometimes, self-preservation is its own reward.

The cardinal waved his hand slowly and the large office door closed silently. Luciano shrugged with a smirk and calculated the number of days Fr. Dominic Giglio had left to live.

* * *

The guard at the front door of the Vatican Bank said, "Cardinal Manning asked that I send you both to him when you arrived."

"Well, we have certainly arrived," Julian said.

A priest hurried to the security station. "This way, gentlemen," and the trek to the cardinal's office began. As they passed the teller's windows, each employee looked at the two visitors, then looked away quickly.

"I suppose everyone knows who we are and why we are here," Julian thought.

"Who we are, no. They don't want to think about such things lest they call down the evil eye. Why we are here, most assuredly," Fr. Soski answered.

Their escort knocked lightly, the cardinal called out, and the doors were opened. Again, Cardinal Manning was ensconced behind his desk. There was no welcoming smile. He indicated chairs for his guests.

"The news about Fr. Edward is tragic. Tragic. I've been up much of the night, but I have come to no conclusions. Have you?" the cardinal asked.

Julian looked to his companion. Fr. Soski inclined his head and Julian began, "Eminence, a tragedy, yes. We should have anticipated it or something like it. That the priest was murdered, there is little doubt. In less doubt is Cardinal Luciano's involvement. Having served his purpose, Fr. Edward was discarded."

"It is the cardinal's usual practice and method, Eminence," Soski added.

"You have proof?" the cardinal asked.

Soski began, "There is no proof to be had, Eminence. This is a crime for which no fingerprints will be found. There will be no smoking gun, as they say. He had the motive and opportunity, but only we will ever know he had the means and that he exercised it."

"You believe Fr. Edward was complicit then? He is, or rather was, our traitor?" the cardinal asked. "Then we are done and I can report it as such."

"In a qualified way, we agree," Julian said. "We believe he was involved up to his neck. We believe he was working from the inside, obscuring the embezzlement. However, he was not alone and we are far from done," Julian said.

The cardinal let out a noisy breath and let his chin fall to his chest. He drummed his fingers on the desk in his anxiety and frustration."

"Eminence," Fr. Soski began. "I can only imagine the pressure you are under. With respect, Eminence, although concluding this matter quickly by settling blame on Fr. Edward, we would not be concluding it well. Should the bank name the culprit and continue to incur losses…" He left the sentence in midair.

Without looking up, the cardinal nodded and said, "I understand perfectly. Gentlemen, please continue with your task and I will continue with mine and may God have mercy on us all."

Julian and his friend walked down the marble corridor toward the bank lobby.

"Can you answer a question for me, Julian?" Fr. Soski thought. Julian shot his companion a sidelong glance and shook his head.

"What is wrong with all of this? I realize the cardinal is under pressure, but there is something amiss here. His reactions, his thoughts, his emotions are not wrong, they are just not right."

"I have had the same feeling. He is easy to read and doesn't appear to be protecting his thoughts in the least. I am getting a signature and it is the same each time I meet with him. Still, I agree with you. I don't know how to put it into words," Julian concluded. Deep lines creased his forehead and his eyes were fixed in concentration.

"We are none of us what we appear to be, Julian. In any case, how should we continue our investigation?" Soski asked.

"Marek, of plans, I have none," Julian answered.

They continued down the hallway in silence.

CHAPTER THIRTEEN

"There they are. You pick them up and bring them in. I've got a few things to do. I'll meet you at the station after you have questioned them," Inspector Belladonna Saviano said to her assistant.

"Oh, Bella, there are so many things wrong with that. First, you say that as if it is a perfectly normal thing to say. Second, what do you want to talk to them about? Third, none of that is going to happen. Ever!" her assistant answered. "You want me – me – to load the Ghost and that idiot wizard in this car? The wizard, I can handle, but the Ghost? No one tries that and is ever the same. Being an inspector has shaken your brain loose, Il mio amore."

"I don't know what I want to question them about. I know they have been up to something. I want to know what they are being called to the Vatican Bank for. There has to be a reason and it can't be good." The inspector tapped her lips with her index finger and came to a conclusion.

"Alright Enrico, do not be a big baby about this. Two men. Toss in back of car. Drive to station. Question. Probably release. And I'll meet up with you after. Simple, no?"

"No," her assistant said.

"I could order you," his inspector suggested.

"You could order me to fly, but that isn't going to happen either."

"You are a very difficult man, Enrico. Justice will not be served today and it will all be your fault." His partner was miffed.

"Well, speaking of serving, today Barnardi's has done justice to that Tuscan roasted vegetable ravioli you like," Enrico tempted.

"With the mushroom sage chicken?" said the inspector warming to the subject.

"My cousin can arrange that."

"Well, alright. I deserve it if only for enduring your meanness. Today justice will be served after all," the inspector said.

* * *

Julian sat in his room at the House of Joy. He sat with his eyes closed at the mirrored dressing-table-turned desk. He opened his eyes and tried to look into his reflection in the mirror. It would be nice to see the future, he thought, but he was making the future as each present moment passed.

What he saw instead was disturbing. Deep circles rimmed his eyes. The scar on his cheek, once red and angry after a beating he endured in Ireland, was turning into a fine line. It highlighted the planes of his face. It was a reminder to him that some things are important enough to fight for.

It was his own eyes he noticed most. Gone was the mischief that hid behind them not so long ago. Now they were all business. He shook his head and his face creased in concentration as he considered his situation and options.

He found himself defused. With all the balls in the air, finding Ailís was getting lost.

His mouth turned hard while his eyes took on a grim cast. 'But what of the rest?' he asked himself.

'Cardinal Luciano, the Vatican Bank, Cardinal Manning, the Russian, they all take up space, but do they matter?' he asked himself. He closed his eyes again, his shouldered slumped with fatigue.

'Find Ailís and get the hell out of here. That's an answer,' he thought, but knew as the thought passed it was not a solution, only an outcome. 'This will come down to the Russian or the cardinal. I will trade my life for hers, regardless. I will never hesitate and they know it.

'Luciano wants me to kill the Pope, but why does he need me? He could do it with ease.'

"Doesn't matter. If he has Ailís, he can have what he wants from me, unless that isn't what he wants," he said aloud and then continued to himself. "But what if Sokolov has her? What then? I couldn't read anything from him but hatred and bile. The only thing I can trust with him is that his word means nothing except when it comes to wanting me dead.

"What about the bank? The lives of depositors and the Church itself are at stake. If the bank continues to hemorrhage money, it could easily collapse, wiping out the savings of hundreds of thousands of people – parishioners, the clergy, churches, hospitals, schools, orphanages, retreat houses and retirement homes. All gone overnight.

"Then there are the institutions, pension plans and hedge funds," he reflected and the worry ran throughout his body, weighing him down, dulling his wits. If unchecked, it could leave him without the wherewithal to act when action was called for. He knew it would be called for and he had a dim, but ominous feeling it would be soon.

"Come in signorina." The proprietress' knock was halted with her knuckles inches from the door. She drew back, made the sign of the horns, crossed herself and entered.

"Here is your book, wizard." She handed Julian the Jesuit Book and turned to leave.

Earlier, Julian and Fr. Soski asked her to hide the book for safe-keeping. For safety sake, Julian told the old woman the Ghost had done something special to the book to make sure no one opened it. And lived.

A small, forgivable, but fun lie.

Joselina turned back. "Qual è il problema, stregone?"

Julian tossed an ugly look. "Okay," his guest said. "You say you aren't a wizard. Still, what's the problem?"

"What do you mean," Julian answered and tried to smile. "There's nothing wrong."

The madam looked at Julian, made a face and shook her head slowly. She returned and sat on his bed. "Wizard or whatever, I deal with whores and men who need such services. I deal in lost souls for a living and you sit there and tell me, nothing is wrong? What, you think I do not know better?"

Julian looked at the Jesuit Book. He ran his hand lightly over the cover and felt the coolness of the leather. He could nearly feel the words inside. Julian looked at and into Joselina. What he saw left him with a smile. Not everything he needed to know came from books.

"You are right, signorina. I am neck deep in trouble. In some cases, I know what to do. In others, I am lost. In some areas, it is not yet time to act. In other cases, well…" Julian left the sentence unfinished, his face reflecting his frustration and confusion.

"You must be fun at parties. Jesus, if I let you go around depressed like this, you will ruin my business. This is the House of Joy, remember?" She smiled and winked and Julian chuckled.

"I'm busy and don't have time to solve all your little problems. Give me one and I'll see what I can do," the woman said.

Julian looked at his guest. "Well if you think you are capable, I suppose I could give you a tiny problem to work on."

"If I weren't tired, I would come over there and show you capable, idiota," she sneered.

"Alright, calm down. Remember, you told me you are in frail health." Julian smiled at the thought and continued. "I have this friend, a doctor we met in Ireland," Julian began.

"She came to Rome and is missing. Several days have passed. I need to find her and do it quickly," Julian finished and sat back in his chair.

Joselina looked thoughtful as deep lines scored her forehead. "So, your Irish lover," she began.

"Friend," Julian corrected.

"Yeah, whatever you say. Why don't you try niece? That never works either. Anyway, she came to Rome to get happy with you. This is a thing I do not understand. Maybe Irish girls are that desperate, eh?

"No matter, I have heard something of all this. My Bella told me some when she dropped you off, but I have heard other noises on the street. Not so much noises as whispers, so you know powerful people are involved. I will look into this for you. For a price. Business is business. For wizard business I only charge double." Her smile was slight and it triggered a smile from Julian.

* * *

A scream cut the air. Concern notched lines into Joselina's face. She moved for the door as it flew open. "Momma, come quick!" A young woman stood in Julian's doorway and, her hands folded in prayer, addressed her boss.

"It's Rosa. I think the devil's got her!" The woman ran off without another word.

Joselina was through the door and down the hall at a demanding pace. Julian grabbed the Jesuit Book and followed.

The madam pushed her way through a knot of her employees blocking the door to Rosa's room.

A young woman in her mid 20's lay on the floor. Her muscles alternately contracted violently and relaxed only to spasm again. Her head lolled with each contraction. Julian pushed his way into the room, knelt beside the woman and in a quiet voice told Joselina to clear the room. She did it with a look which sent everyone elsewhere. Quickly.

He felt the words from the Jesuit Book as clearly as if they were spoken, *"You know what is needed. It is time."*

Julian looked at Rosa's face as her head jerked from side to side. Compassion took possession of his body as he began to rub his hands together. Julian could feel it. Rosa's mind was alive with activity as electrical impulses threatened to swamp her. The root of the loose energy running through her body was centered in her brain.

"Won't she swallow her tongue or something?" Joselina ventured as she knelt opposite Julian, but Julian didn't answer. "Right, shut up Joselina," she said a moment later.

Julian didn't hear her, couldn't hear her.

Rosa's convulsions were now more rhythmic and more violent. He could feel her, not her distress, but her. He took her face in his hands and closed his eyes. Julian began to exhale. He could feel the energy build, then travel down his arms, gaining momentum as it went. Once he had tapped into it, the energy seemed to gather its force from everywhere and everything.

He looked down at Rosa and his lips drew into a hard straight line as the power surged to his hands, then into the woman. Her body went rigid as Joselina gasped. Rosa's back arched, then she began to go limp. She took a stuttering breath as her mouth fell open. She stopped breathing and her face went slack.

Julian's right hand moved from Rosa's face and hovered over her chest. He drew a slow, practiced breath. The world went white. He stiffened as energy coursed from him into the young woman. He stiffened and the muscles in his arms contracted violently. He gritted his teeth as he tried to hold his hands in place.

Rose arched off the floor again. She drew a ragged breath and then another.

Julian took his hands away with infinite slowness and care.

The young woman's head rolled to the side and she looked at her employer through heavy lidded eyes. The words were a whisper, a prayer, "I'm sorry, Momma." Joselina bit hard into her lower lip, but her eyes betrayed her as first one tear, then another, coursed down her cheeks. She wiped them away with irritation.

Julian sat back on his heels, each breath he took, an effort. 'So this is what Moira and Bridget felt when they touched me, healed me in Ireland,' he thought.

His body felt heavy and slow as he took Rosa into his arms. It felt to him as though she weighed almost nothing. His own weight was incalculable. Gently, slowly he laid the woman on her bed. He reached out with his mind and drew Joselina to his side.

The older woman was a patchwork of thoughts and emotions. Julian felt bits and pieces of each and then thought, *"Please, sit with her for awhile. She will be confused and tired. Have a doctor come and look at her. Without treatment this will happen again. Epilepsy, maybe? I don't know. The doctor will know and will know what to do."*

Joselina drew back as her mind was invaded, even as she gathered Rosa into her arms.

Julian whispered with aching slowness, each word an effort, "I think I'll rest for a bit. I feel so tired." He smiled slightly and moved toward the door, the Jesuit Book in hand.

He touched the door knob and then thought, *"Joselina, you will, I know, but be gentle with her. She won't be up to working for a while."* He smiled and added, *"By the way, you're right, you do need an assistant. Rosa would be good at that. Don't worry, I can't read your mind. One of the ladies told me."* He turned the knob, left and shut the door quietly behind him.

Joselina's face softened as she looked at the young girl in her arms. She looked to the closed door and the older woman's face softened further. A tear for Julian joined the others.

CHAPTER FOURTEEN

Cardinal Manning sat at his desk, chair rocked back, hands clasped behind his head. "Come," he said in answer to a light knock, but otherwise he didn't change his posture.

The Director General of the bank entered and stood before the cardinal. "Another loss?" the cardinal asked.

"Yes, Eminence," the man answered in a voice as subdued as his dark suit.

"A large loss?"

"One hundred thousand more than the last theft," he said.

"Thank you. Keep me advised," the cardinal said. The Director General left.

Cardinal Manning sat forward in his chair, placed his hands on the desk and looked at the telephone.

He thought of the man at the other end of the phone - the Bishop of Rome, Vicar of Christ, Successor of the Prince of the Apostles, Supreme Pontiff of the Universal Church, of Italy, Archbishop and Metropolitan of the Roman Province, Sovereign of the Vatican City State, Servant of the servants of God.

The Pope.

He drew a breath, smiled, then reached for the telephone.

* * *

Julian used the telephone in Fr. Soski's office. "Sokolov, you left a message for me."

"Blessing," Bogdan Sokolov said into the telephone. "I want see you."

"I want a pony, but that really doesn't mean I'm going to get one," Julian answered and smiled. He could feel, nearly see, Sokolov become rabid. "By the way, it's 'I want to see you,' not, 'I want see you.' It makes you sound like an simpleton otherwise," Julian added.

"I will send car for you," the Russian said.

"'I will send a car for you,' but never mind that. Here is a better suggestion. You can meet me at the fountain in front of the Spanish Steps in an hour. Do I have to tell you to come alone or would you rather suffer if you don't? By the way, this is a better suggestion because it is the only way it is going to happen." Julian smiled and hung up.

* * *

Julian sat on the steps of Trinità dei Monti, the church atop the Spanish steps. At first, it was difficult for him to filter out all the signatures he felt when in a crowded place. With time, patience, and practice, he could separate the background noise. He practiced now.

Feeling Bogdan Sokolov was a piece of cake. The man's hatred of everyone, and distain for everything, made his signature impossible to miss. Even tourists without Julian's talent for reading people, found themselves repelled by the Russian. They felt it at a fundamental, visceral level. It was a reminder to Julian of how everyone had access to a larger reality and greater truths.

Pickpockets approached what they believed was an easy mark, only to reverse direction when they came within fifteen feet of Sokolov. Carriage horses' nostrils flared. Street venders selling trinkets always liked to see a nice fat tourist. Even these men of street-level commerce looked the other way and kicked themselves for not going into the restaurant business like the family wanted.

The Steps weren't crowded and Julian could detect only one other significant presence in the area. He stepped into a shaded area, relaxed and closed his eyes. He stepped out of time and walked down the steps at a leisurely pace, taking up a position ten feet in front of the mobster. Julian closed his eyes again and reentered linear time, much to the anger of Sokolov.

The man's eyes narrowed and his lips twisted into an ugly slash across a face deformed by a lifetime of hatred. Julian looked pleasant and could feel the Russian's rage deepen.

"Bogdan, my friend. Why don't we sit here on the fountain? No worries. I've got your back. I'll know long before anyone sneaks up on you. Maybe. Maybe not," Julian said and smiled.

"I will kill you someday, Blessing, and I will enjoy it," Sokolov snarled.

"You can certainly try, Bogdan. Now, what do you want? I don't have a lot of time for you today, so make it quick." Julian was enjoying enraging the man entirely too much, but not so much that he didn't feel the other signature on the square. Inspector Belladonna Saviano was seated in a horse drawn carriage further down the piazza. Watching and waiting.

Tourists sat down next to Julian and Sokolov, then decided they had made an obvious and potentially dangerous mistake in their seating choice. Julian smiled and the tourists moved along with a pace that set cameras clanking against their owner's chests.

Julian looked expectant.

Killing Julian, for Sokolov, was pleasure but he was here on business. "You are doing business with Vatican Bank."

"Okay, if you say so," Julian responded lightly.

"I have business to do with Vatican Bank," Sokolov said. His accent was thick and guttural and was not, Julian decided, going to be helped by the use of good grammar.

"Oh my, I'm really not the person to talk to about opening up an account," Julian began.

"Blessing! Do not fuck with me!" Sokolov growled. Spittle formed at the corners of his mouth and everyone sitting around the Fountain of the Old Boat, at the foot of the steps in , decided to go sightseeing. Elsewhere.

"Well, Bogdan, you certainly have a way with people," Julian said, watching the tourists run away. "Tell me what you want and I'll tell you what I will do."

"I want to get someone inside the bank. I want you to make it happen. Remember, I have what you want."

"I understand you say you have what I want. As yet, I've seen no evidence of that. Return what I have lost and I will think about helping you. If not, not." There was a smile on Julian's face, but it never reached above the corners of his mouth. His gray eyes communicated raw malice. Sokolov noticed and imperceptibly leaned away.

"So, I get you your woman and you get Bogdan what he wants? That is deal?" the Russian asked as his eyes went small and cunning.

Julian studied the big Russian. A minute passed as he looked into the man, looked into the cesspit of a soul that was the foundation of Bogdan Sokolov. What Julian saw sickened him more than it had before, but he continued to look. He wanted to hate this man with good reason. After a full minute, Julian had all the reason he needed to obliterate the Russian without remorse if the time came.

Julian nodded his head. "That is the deal," he said.

Julian's thought struck the Russian as an ominous whisper. *"Pay attention Sokolov. You have twenty-four hours. I would make returning what I have lost a high priority of yours or I will make you a high priority of mine."*

Julian stood and walked away.

* * *

As he drew level with the inspector's carriage and horse, Julian patted the horse's neck and crest and, without looking away from the horse, said, "Why don't you join me at Babington's Tea Rooms. They say Babington's has chocolate cookies people dream about for years after tasting."

The inspector narrowed her eyes and made the sign of the horns at Julian's back.

"Tisk, tisk, inspector. A modern woman like you? Such superstitions will do you no good at all." Julian laughed and turned toward the faded terracotta colored and completely nondescript tearoom with the finest cookies in the world.

The inspector's nostrils flared, she crossed herself, stuck out her tongue for good measure, and made the sign of the horns again. With both hands.

* * *

"So, wizard, you are out consorting with a man who is a known mobster and money launderer and murderer and degenerate, who wants to kill you and may have kidnapped the doctor, and who also is under constant police surveillance.

"I'm so glad you are taking advantage of everything Rome has to offer." Venom dripped from her voice.

"Want a chocolate cookie?"

"Are you trying to annoy me? And yes I do. And tea. The expensive stuff, not what the tourists drink."

Julian ordered for them both.

"So," he said, "were the documents I gave you of any interest to your bosses?"

"Don't ask questions you know the answers to. As much pain as it causes me, they probably saved me from the secretarial pool."

"I'm glad. You wouldn't make a very good secretary. Much too cranky. So what do we do next?"

"What is it about you and this 'we' you keep talking about? We are not going to do anything next or ever. You have done too much for everyone's good. What did Sokolov and you talk about?" she demanded.

"Oh, nothing much. I told him he had twenty-four hours to return the doctor. In exchange, I would get him a mole in the Vatican Bank. You know, just chit chat," Julian smiled and continued.

"Oh I wanted to ask, what do you think about that whole assassinate-the-Pope thing? I'm sure the good sergeant told you."

"He told me. He also told me, the cardinal said no such thing. Luciano spoke in generalities that could have applied to anyone or no one. It could have been a test to see what you would do," the inspector explained. "Cardinals are funny that way. They are forever saying a great deal without saying anything. In that way, they are a lot like you." Her smile was one of her nastiest so far.

"It doesn't really matter. I'm not going to do it, of course. As for Sokolov, the mole will probably be the head of bank security or something," Julian answered. He looked unconcerned, but felt anything but.

"Blessing, I keep telling you, the list of coincidences just gets longer every day. I have lived here all my life. No one close to me has ever been kidnapped. I've never been abducted and taken to clandestine meetings. I've never been called to conferences with one of the most powerful moneymen in Italy. No one in organized crime has ever asked me for a favor. I've never stolen important documents from mobsters and, this will strike you as very odd, never has anyone ever asked me to kill the Pope."

"Not bad for a tourist, eh? No wonder you need my help." Julian figured payback for destroying his hotel room was in order.

"You've been here not quite a week. Just think what you can accomplish if you stayed a month. You lived in New York. It is a wonder to me the place doesn't look like our Forum!" The inspector's hands shook with pent up frustration.

"You seem unhappy, Inspector," Julian said looking as concerned as watery solicitude would allow.

She hung her head and her hair hid her face. "Enrico said to me just this morning, 'Bella,' he said. 'Why don't we just arrest the wizard and have done with him?' I asked on what basis we could do such a thing. He said we could charge you with being an unlicensed prostitute.

"That would get my friend Joselina in trouble, so I told him no," the inspector said. "I am rethinking that."

The waitress arrived with their order, "Cookie?" Julian asked.

The inspector looked up, scowled and took her cookie.

* * *

"Well, this should be interesting," Fr. Soski chuckled as he and Julian walked down a narrow street.

"To you, Marek, everything is interesting. Why is this especially so? What does your friend know or what will he tell us?" Julian asked.

"I'm glad you made that distinction. This is Rome and what people know and what they are willing to share are very different things. No, this is interesting because my friend asked for a meeting in Piazza di Campo dei Fiori."

They entered the piazza and Fr. Soski pointed. "That is why it is interesting."

Julian and his companion were standing in front of the statue of Giordano Bruno.

"Nice. This fella is a bit dark for me, but nice statue. So?"

The priest considered before saying, "He may be feeling a bit dark because this fine gentleman here, Giordano Bruno, is being burned at the stake. The Church took a dim view of heretics at one time.

"The Inquisition was especially put out with those who, after weeks of torture, refused to come to their senses. 'Their senses' being the inquisitor's senses. People can be so obstinate sometimes." The priest chuckled again. "The inscription says, 'To Bruno, from the generation he foresaw, here, where the pyre burned.' You can be sure that is appropriate to the occasion.

"It is Rome my friend," the priest continued. "Everything has significance. Nothing is ever what it seems. Our meeting is with a man who is able to uniquely blend subtlety and theater and do it well.

"We are currently standing on what was, in the distant past, Rome's execution grounds. He did not pick this place because it was convenient. It is out of our way and his, but more importantly, it is out of the way." The priest stressed 'the' and then began to cough.

"He is examining us from the window of that bar over there. Don't look. You won't see him.

"He'll be along when he feels it is safe. Although this piazza is a Mecca for pub crawlers, it is practically deserted this time of day," the priest said and then continued in a voice drenched in seriousness.

"Julian, we must take this man seriously. Do not try to read him. He is not one of us, but he has a level of self-awareness and a knowledge of people that would make you think he is.

"He will tell us what he will tell us and he will leave. Do not ask questions, just listen to every word and watch every movement, every gesture. Everything about this man is important." The hacking cough began again and the priest wiped his mouth. Blood came away on the handkerchief.

A very tall, lean man in his mid fifties entered the square from the bar nearest the statue. He locked eyes with the priest then turned and walked toward a restaurant. There was no hurry in his stride. He wore an impeccable black suit and gray silk tie. His beard was going a dignified white.

The man knocked once and entered La Restorante Carbonara. He left the door ajar.

"Ah, we are not alone," Fr. Soski said. "We have an audience."

"I can feel something, but can't locate him. A policeman I think," Julian responded.

"Right," the priest said, "there." A flowerpot from a second floor window crashed to the cobblestones and the plainclothes policeman jumped. He was at the far end of the square near a bar that was just starting to fill up. All the patrons turned to look at the man.

Marek and Julian entered La Restorante Carbonara a short time later and sat at a table. The man they followed was nowhere in sight.

"Just wait," Fr. Soski said. "He will be along shortly or he won't. If we hear the back door slam, we will be leaving immediately and should be ready to counter any threat we encounter." The priest's eyes were unblinking. Julian nodded once, took a breath and held it.

The moments ticked by in the restaurant's dark stillness. The kitchen doors opened and the man entered, smiled broadly, crossed to their table and embraced Fr. Soski as Julian stood.

"Marek, why is it you never visit anymore? Mamma asks for you often," the man chuckled. "What am I to do with you? Look at you. Thin as a strand of linguini. You don't eat enough."

"Ricardo, the smell of your mamma's food makes me fat. You know I can't resist," the priest laughed and began to cough again. The bearded man's eyes tightened and he lost his smile as he concentrated on Fr. Soski. The coughing spell passed and the man turned to Julian.

"Please call me Ricardo, Mr. Blessing. I must warn you, too much association with the good father here will be the ruin of you." The man smiled his introduction, but the undercurrent of what was just said wasn't missed by Julian.

"It is a pleasure to meet you, Ricardo. No Mr. Blessing here. Please, call me Julian," he said.

"Pleasure? It is nothing of the kind. I will prove to you it is never a pleasure to meet me, Julian."

"Wine, Ricardo?" Fr. Soski asked. They all agreed and the priest nodded to an old waiter standing respectfully against the far wall of the restaurant. He was a man who saw nothing, heard nothing, knew nothing and had done so all his life.

The wine arrived, was uncorked and poured. "Salute," Fr. Soski said and they all sipped their wine in silence.

Julian gathered impressions of the man, but went no further. Relaxed was the only word Julian could find that would fit. This was a man who would be comfortable in any boardroom in the world or behind the counter at any deli or in any Swiss bank. He was a man infinitely comfortable with who and what he was. "Now, who and what are you," Julian thought and Fr. Soski tried to hide his smile.

"Ricardo, what brings a busy man like you to us today?" the priest said in a whisper as his voice began to tire.

"Oh, Marek, no time for small talk? It is not the Roman way, you know. Still, as you say, I am busy and being seen in your company is not good for my spotless reputation," the man said and smiled easily.

The smile faded and his brown eyes grew tight as he turned his gaze to Julian and made a careful study of his face. Ricardo began slowly. "Julian, I have been asked to extend to you an invitation. There are," he paused, "people who would like to meet and talk with you.

"The subject of the discussion is unknown to me of course. Doubtless you know or can guess the essence if not the substance of it all. Perhaps they have news of home for you. I am simply a humble messenger. It would not be unreasonable, however, to surmise these people are," he paused again, "influential and a request to meet is a grave honor. You must be terribly important to receive such an invitation.

"I feel sure you will give their request very serious and very careful consideration. They did ask me to pass along something I find most curious. They want me to assure you that they will ensure your safety. That said, this is Rome and assurances are easy to come by. We are each responsible for ourselves, no?" Ricardo continued.

"It doesn't just apply to you. We all live in a dangerous world, wouldn't you agree? Sadly, often times we are unable to protect ourselves and we must place our trust," again he paused, "elsewhere." Ricardo turned and looked at Fr. Soski.

The man sat back and smiled. Slightly. He laid an envelope on the table.

Julian nodded slightly. He pocketed the envelope and all three men sipped their wine and said nothing.

* * *

Julian and Marek stepped back into the sunlight of the piazza a short time after the messenger had departed. The priest had put on his sunglasses and hat inside and Julian was forced to squint into the brightness. Office workers were just filtering into the square and Julian could detect nothing untoward among the score of signatures. The policeman was gone.

"*Well, I thought that went rather well,*" Fr. Soski thought and Julian turned to face his friend.

"*What went well? What happened? Far more than I know, of course. So tell me, Mr. Rome, what is all this about, I mean aside from the super villains and their invitation?*"

"*First of all, the messenger was, how shall I say this, the night time mayor of Rome. Although the title may sound comical, the man is not. Let me assure you, he is one of the most influential and trusted men in the country. His eyes and ears are everywhere. By the way, I have asked him, and can assure you, he is working on finding the doctor for you.*"

"He was asked to act as messenger because he is well known for his discretion and absolute trustworthiness. Also, your invitation calls for safe conduct. Involving Ricardo is a guarantee. No one would dare go back on that. Your hosts know that and they know you now know it, too.

"Still, he only accepted to act as messenger because I am involved and the sender wants you to understand exactly how important the message is. Hiring such a messenger does not come without its political price. A very, very high price. It is a price they are willing to pay.

"You have been summoned to sit before an inquisition and you had better pray to your god because he is the only one who can keep you from being burned at the stake. Not now, of course, but later when your safe conduct has expired. You really must pay more attention, Julian. How are you ever to become a Roman? I despair for you sometimes," Soski said.

CHAPTER FIFTEEN

Parked in front of the House of Joy sat a purposefully nondescript car that could be only identified as an undercover police car. Julian felt the inspector's presence well before he saw the car.

"Hi guys." Julian put on his best effervescent self. He felt far from bubbly.

Enrico Marino reached for the door handle intent on punishing Julian Blessing. The big man snorted, "'Guys.' Did you hear him? That's it. I need to hurt him so he doesn't do that anymore." The inspector touched her partner's sleeve and shook her head.

"Blessing, Blessing, Blessing – what exactly am I going to do with you? Aside from this morning's meeting with Sokolov and the secret meeting you are coming from, what else is on the agenda for today? While I am dying to know, Enrico is dying to beat you, so there is that," the inspector said and arched an eyebrow that rivaled her curled lip.

"Secret meeting? My friend and I went for a walk. You know, kinda sightseeing. Anyway we stopped in a place and had a glass of wine, then we continued our stroll. Nothing secret about that, right?"

The sergeant reached for the door handle again. "In a minute, Enrico. I promise," the inspector said.

"Wizard, Popes ask politely for meetings with Ricardo Covi, but he meets with someone like you," she threw the word 'you' at Julian, "for drinks at some out of the way restaurant that doesn't even serve cannoli, I might add.

"Tell me, wizard, how is this possible? That he would meet with the Ghost, doesn't surprise me. That he would waste his time with you is beyond me. So tell me Blessing, and do not tell me you don't know what I'm talking about. Believe me, you will beg to tell me if I let Enrico out of the car." Her lip curled further than Julian thought lips could curl.

"Was that who that was? Marek and I ran into a guy. He said his name was Ricardo and I figured he was just some guy. I thought he might own a clothing store. He had on a great suit. Never figured him for, you know, somebody. Go figure."

Julian took his hands out of his pockets and let them hang loosely at his sides. He relaxed his shoulders and looked at the ground so the inspector wouldn't see his eyes as they hooded over.

"Sorry," the inspector said as she removed her hand from her partner's sleeve. "I tried to help you." Enrico opened the car door and one foot hit the street.

Julian's look was penetrating, but not unkind. He said, "Me too. Sorry, that is." He stepped out of time and vanished. He reappeared inside the House of Joy, looked out his window and watched as the inspector covered her face with her palm then started beating the dashboard.

The inspector's partner scanned the surrounding area. "Me too," Julian whispered again. "I wish you could help."

***

The envelope contained an address and time. Julian checked the paper again as he faced a building that could not look less like the lair of a group of super villains. Few structures in the Centro Storico qualified. Old Rome was not a place that allowed such things. Walled and gated, a two story brick home accented with bright yellow shutters smiled sedately behind a boxwood hedge. Lavender trees flanked the house, ivy clung to the wall in places, and irises with purple and yellow blooms filled the flowerbeds.

Julian rang the bell beside the gate and waited for the speaker to come alive. There was a muffled click and the gate opened slightly. Julian closed the gate behind him and proceeded up a brick walkway that led to the front door.

A heavy set, older man with gray hair and a dark suit opened the door and bowed slightly as he gestured for Julian to step into a room off the foyer.

The room was light with a large window looking onto a garden. The walls were cream colored with built in bookshelves, filled to overflowing, on every wall. Framed, delicate woodcuts and etchings elbowed for space.

The furniture was a diverse collection whose only connective theme was comfort.

Watching him from a large red sectional sat Antonio Cardinal Luciano.

"Well, aren't I surprised," Julian said.

"Be assured, no more than I," the cardinal said and Julian believed him.

The cardinal's thoughts were protected as usual, but his emotions were not. The man was a jumble of conflicting feelings trying to sort themselves out. Julian sat, closed his eyes, and cleared his mind. He smiled. The cardinal didn't know why he was here and didn't know what part Julian had to play in all of this. Julian smirked. He felt the cardinal's emotions at a fundamental level and he enjoyed the man's discomfort.

Still, something sat heavy and out of place in the house, a presence, a sense, a force he could not identify.

A young man appeared in the doorway. His English was clear, but carried a heavy Italian accent. "Mr. Blessing, your Eminence, if you would follow me? Coffee is being served on the terrace."

The cardinal's eyes narrowed and he boiled with rage at the breech of etiquette. To address a layman before a cardinal was unheard of in his world. In unmistakable terms, he was being told he was not in his world now.

Again, Julian smiled and thought to himself, "So, pride's your weakness. I'll bet it's not the only one. Not as invincible as you thought, eh?"

Julian was quick to head for the door, leaving the cardinal to bring up the rear.

French doors opened onto a shaded terrace. A herringbone pattern of aged bricks laid a carpet under a collection of wicker and wrought iron furniture covered with forest green cushions. Across an expanse of lawn, a private forest of varying shades of green and gold unfolded at the end of the terrace. A coffee and tea service waited next to magnificent porcelain coffee and teacups on a nearby buffet table. Cream and sugar anticipated use in silver containers.

"Gentlemen, please, help yourselves and join us." The voice was as relaxed as its owner.

Julian was feeling better by the minute. That 'gentlemen' was another slap at the cardinal. It was followed promptly by no intention of serving him as protocol dictated.

Four men sat easily in the comfortable wrought iron chairs. To Julian they looked like a foursome of CEO's fresh from the golf course.

The undercurrent of power, strength, authority and cunning wasn't lost on him. His senses went to a higher state of alert and his defenses were strengthened. Still, reading these men individually was impossible. They sat behind an impenetrable barrier, but seemed relaxed, nearly carefree in attitude and posture.

"So glad you could join us this afternoon." It was an American accent and belonged to a man in his late sixties with silver hair, heavy build and an overly large smile. He didn't offer a hand for Julian to shake so he sat and waited for the inquisition to begin.

"I'm sure you were busy and am so sorry more notice couldn't be given to you," the man said.

He continued, "Cardinal, you know everyone, but let me make introductions for you, Mr. Blessing."

'Cardinal' – another slap. Julian considered and thought whatever Luciano did had landed him in the deep end of the shit pool.

"May I present Mr. Clarke, Monsieur Colbert and Señor Rodriguez. Me? I'm Tan. Bob Tan. Gentlemen, this is, of course, Mr. Blessing." The man spread his arms and his smile was contagious. Julian decided that although the man was CEO material now, he started on a used car lot somewhere early on.

"Mind if I call you Julian?" the man asked politely. The other three men looked on smiling and expectant.

Definitely a car lot, "Of course, Bob. Julian is just fine."

"No sense beating around the bush here, Julian. You're a busy man and we realize that. Hell, we're all busy. See what the world has become? Nobody has time anymore."

So far nothing was being said, but a lot of words were being used to say it.

"Julian, we've got a problem. Couple of problems really. You've got yourself one too. Not enough time and too many problems, eh? Anyway, we were thinking we could help each other." The man stopped and waited. Julian had seen this before, had practiced it himself – the next one who talks loses.

"Right," Tan continued. "We are not men of insubstantial means or clout. Your doctor friend has gone missing and we are prepared to put everything we have behind finding her for ya."

"I would appreciate that, Bob," Julian said and waited for the other shoe to drop. He expected it would land hard and hoped it wouldn't be on him.

"No problem. If she is to be found, we'll find her," Bob said and beamed.

"You're a business guy like the four of us." Another slap at the cardinal who seethed.

"You understand give and take. Sure, we'll help you all we can, but we've got some problems only you can help with." The man was a volcano of ersatz enthusiasm and a lake of simulated sincerity.

"It's like this with us. We are businessmen so it is all about profit and loss. You understand. I'm not tellin' you anything you don't already know.

"Keeping that in mind though, all of mankind is our business. As people progress, our business progresses. Society starts going backwards and, well, you know the rest. Unhappy shareholders.

"We've found that you guys, you and the cardinal here and the others like you, are on the same side as us. Still, you're disorganized. Each of you operates independently. You try to do good and succeed most times. Still, your efforts are uncoordinated.

"We want to join forces. We'll provide the organizational structure along with nearly inexhaustible capital and human assets. Are you following me here?" Bob took a breath and asked.

"Yes, Bob, I understand." Julian looked to the cardinal. The man's eyes were quick and keen and his level of anxiety was rising rapidly. "Why don't you continue? I'm following so far."

"Manny, why don't you take it from where I left off?" Bob addressed Señor Rodriguez.

"Julian," the man's relaxed and expressive Spanish accented English was hypnotic. He was everything Bob was not. No bluster or backslapping. No glad handling or offers of a drink. This was business. Polite business, but business all the same.

Señor Rodriguez continued, "I'm not telling you anything new, as Bob said. The world is in chaos and we believe we can make it right again. We have learned a great deal, both about the business of mankind and about the business of business. Further, we have learned you, and those like you, hold a key to the future of people, both individually and collectively." Rodriguez paused and smiled, inviting Julian to ask questions. None were forthcoming.

"You have demonstrated a level of talent that has garnered you a lot of attention within your community. It doesn't take talent however to see into your future. In time – and that time will not be long coming – you will take up a strong leadership role within your group." Again, another pause and another smile, and another blow to the cardinal's pride.

Julian was staring into his coffee cup. He looked up at each man individually before he spoke. "Gentlemen, as you said, we are all busy, all have problems and time is of the essence. Please, tell me what you want. I understand you perfectly so far. Without preamble, just tell me what you want of me." Julian's voice was far more relaxed and pleasant than he felt.

Monsieur Colbert leaned forward in his chair. He smiled and slowly set his coffee cup on a nearby iron table.

"Mr. Blessing, we want your assistance in two very important areas." The two previous speakers rose, walked to the coffee service, refilled their cups and returned. Monsieur Colbert waited.

"The first is we need your help recruiting people of your kind. Perhaps that is putting it badly. Please forgive me. Let us say, people like you. We feel that with very little effort, you could easily form a cadre of talented people who could advance our aims exponentially.

"If I'm not mistaken, those aims are also your aims as they are those of his Eminence. Do you not agree, Julian?" Colbert threw Luciano a bone. The cardinal did not receive it with good grace.

"I'm not yet sure your aims are my aims. Right now, my aim is to find my friend and return home. To the degree you can advance that cause, our aims are the same. Beyond that, you've not given me anything specific, so I cannot say," Julian offered and the cardinal's mouth twitched toward a suppressed smirk.

"To be sure, as Bob said, we will put everything we have into this effort for you whether you choose to join us or not," Colbert said. "But we will be drawing down time and resources to do so, time we could use in pursuit of our objectives. The question is, what are you willing to contribute to the efforts?" Monsieur Colbert sat back and waited.

"I'm sure you all understand," Julian began, "what you present is only a picture in broad brush form. The details are missing. Without those details, I am unable to form a cogent response. For now, I will say I understand your desires and to the extent of my ability support them in principle," Julian weasel-worded and then continued.

"I will tell you, the group to which I belong is effective because it has no centralized leadership. We are a group of free agents. Trying to recruit from that pool would be disappointing. Besides, I am new to the community and so cannot, and would not, claim a following of any sort.

"Can you give me something more specific that you want accomplished that does not depend on my ability to recruit for you?" Julian rose, poured himself another cup of coffee, and indicated the coffee samovar to the cardinal. Luciano glowered his displeasure and declined. Julian shrugged and returned to his seat.

With a velvet voice, Señor Rodriguez took up the case, "Luc, if I may?" Monsieur Colbert nodded.

"Julian, this is not something I mention lightly. It goes against every principle to which we have dedicated ourselves," Rodriguez said.

"Go on, Manny," Bob encouraged. Mr. Clarke made a slight gesture and silenced Tan.

"To date, we have found ourselves thwarted at many important turns in moving society forward," Rodriguez said. "This was more than troubling to us, so we dispatched agents to find the reason," Rodriguez said.

"The information we received back was staggering. While we all signed on to assist the world in reviving it's potential, a powerful group that has been operating for centuries has set its sights on enslaving mankind.

"The people involved in this reprehensible conspiracy are those we all trust most. Politicians, civic leaders, members of the clergy of every denomination, the wealthiest and most powerful businesspeople, the social elite – members from all of those walks of life have a vested interest in seeing that mankind is kept sedated, powerless and subservient.

"It took time and cost many lives in the process of finding out who leads this group." Rodriguez's voice dripped with frustration. "We have succeeded and the leader of this group is someone of immense standing and power, I am talking of..." Julian interrupted Mr. Rodriguez.

"Let me save us all a lot of time," Julian said. "You would like me to assassinate the Pope for you." Julian sat back, crossed his legs and looked like he hadn't said, 'assassinate the Pope' out loud.

"Moreover, it was made pretty clear that the safe return of the doctor was dependent on my success. At least that is my understanding."

The four members looked at Julian with hard eyes. Eyebrows knitted, Mr. Clarke asked softly with a cut crystal British accent, "And you know that, how?"

"His Eminence told me," Julian said.

All eyes, except those of Mr. Clarke and Julian's, turned to the cardinal. For his part, Luciano was outwardly calm, but Julian could easily sense the rage rolling off the man.

"Mr. Blessing," Mr. Clarke said, "we, of course, do not require an answer today. I will tell you, there has been a misunderstanding. We will assist you in any case. For our part, we must mobilize our forces in order to pursue your current difficulties. We will begin the search for the doctor immediately. On that, you have my word. The four of us have given you a great deal to think about. May we call on you later to continue our discussion?"

"Of course, sir. I will do all I can to be available for you. In the meantime, I will consider carefully what you've said," Julian said inclining his head.

"Thank you for coming. Can we arrange transportation for you?" Mr. Clarke asked.

"That is very kind, but the day is perfect and I need time to think. I've not really explored Old Rome and the walk will do me good," Julian said with an ease he did not feel. He stood as did they all, except the cardinal. "Will you join me, Eminence?"

"I'm sorry, Julian, but the cardinal will be helping with some agenda items we need to go over," Bob said.

"Good meeting you, son." Bob shook Julian's hand vigorously. The hand was firm, but somehow cold, lifeless.

After saying his goodbyes and thanking the group for its hospitality, Julian followed his previous escort to the front door and out to a freedom he thought he only had a 50/50 chance of ever enjoying again in spite of any guarantees of safe conduct.

* * *

He joined Fr. Marek Soski on a bench several blocks away. Julian sat, blew out a long noisy breath, and asked, "You heard?"

"Not one word," Soski answered mildly.

"What? You were supposed to be backing me up. What if something went wrong?" Julian demanded staring at the priest. "You were supposed to ride in and save the day. Remember?"

Fr. Soski said, "You entered that place and it disappeared. I heard nothing and felt nothing. It wasn't as if a wall went up. It was as though that piece of property didn't exist. I have not the slightest idea what or how it happened. I could see it, but it wasn't there. As far as backup goes, you, my very good friend, were in the hands of God. Or all on your own, which ever way you want to look at it." Fr. Soski shrugged and tried to look contrite.

* * *

The priest took out his iPhone and called for a cab, and when it arrived, the driver nearly drove off. No one, he felt, drove the Ghost around and lived. He put his foot on the accelerator and the car died. The man looked up to find a deathly pale priest in an overcoat, hat, gloves, and sunglasses staring at him over the hood of the car. The driver swallowed hard, jumped out and opened the back doors for his guests. Once installed, the driver made the sign of the cross and the taxi sped into the heart of Rome.

"*And so?*" Fr. Soski thought while the cab driver knew only that he had a particularly silent fare.

Julian considered before he returned with his own thoughts. *"A few things became clear, but not many. Some things became muddier. Typical of Rome I'm discovering.*

"First, because we should start with dessert," Julian said, *"Luciano was there and will be lucky to escape with his skin. Next, the main course. There were a group of four men, Tan, Rodriguez, Colbert and Clarke. Ethnically diverse if nothing else. Clarke was in overall charge. He is the one who spoke the least. The others were busy trying to convince me, a) I should become a recruiter for them and b) the little matter of me assassinating the Pope. The Pope is the bad guy in all of this and he is thwarting the group's efforts to make the world a better place.*

"They were all about 'doing well by doing good' of course. Always a good place for those who are interested in doing well at the expense of others. Extrapolating from their line of reasoning, there are multiple thousands of ways they can harvest the world at large and make money – with our help." Julian stopped, reflected, then continued.

"There is already one of us on their payroll and he, or she, isn't so much formidable as terrifyingly powerful," Julian said. Soski turned in his seat to look at his friend.

Julian continued, *"As soon as I crossed the threshold, all my attempts to do anything were stopped. I could get something off the cardinal, but only the rawest most violent passions. Of which he had plenty."* Julian chuckled.

"The group entered into all of this today with a sort of paranormal bodyguard. Try as I might, I could read none of them. While Luciano was clear in his intent to open up a six-pack of industrial strength whoop ass, it was clear he couldn't, wouldn't or was afraid to try.

"The others took up physical space, but nothing more. No signatures, no nothing. Even the house and the staff were blocked off to me. That would account for you not being able to sense anything from the out-side. What do you think?" Julian asked.

"Industrial strength what?" Soski responded. *"Never mind, I would rather not hear you explain that. One of us acting as a shield. Now that is something a little more than disturbing.*

"I have an idea that is far beyond reasonable," Fr. Soski said. *"Think about what you said. Think about what I said. What if only you and the cardinal existed? What if you and he were sitting alone in that house? No group, no coffee. What if it was all an illusion? You stepped through the gate, took one step into a pocket dimension, and the rest was a false impression.*

"Had you or the cardinal done anything untoward…" Fr. Marek left the thought unfinished.

"A chimera, a mental hologram. That's sickening," Julian thought and felt his mind roil in confusion.

"Could I so easily be deceived?" he thought to himself. *"Could a world be created for me in my own mind? One shared with the cardinal?"* Julian's teacher had said it was possible.

"It would turn our world upside-down," Soski said. *"A world, I will remind you, we have already turned inside-out."*

Julian said, *"While we're upside down and inside-out, let's consider something else. If they have one of us powerful enough to do what you've suggested, why do they need me?"*

Fr. Soski thought and Julian received the thought with crystal clarity, *"That is the only thing we do know. They need you because you are expendable. It would also launch the church on another inquisition, with us being the modern day heretics and witches. A nice distraction, don't you think?"* the priest said. *"Distracted from what though?"*

"Marek, I have tried to avoid it, but it is something that must be considered. This Group, is it the same institution Professor Agostini uncovered?"

"I pray I am wrong, but fear I am right," Fr. Marek said. *"I believe it is the same and that terrifies me. I need to talk with some people. There is an explanation to all of this and we need to find it quickly."*

CHAPTER SIXTEEN

"Your thoughts?" Mr. Clarke asked.

A man in a plain black suit and clerical collar, considered, then said, "There is almost no chance Blessing will do as we ask unless we give him no choice. He will do anything to protect the woman. He would give up his own life freely. He would murder a thousand popes. She is his weakness and she must to be found."

"You have no way of tracking her?" Mr. Clarke asked.

His companion arched an eyebrow, smiled, and his words were acidic. "If I could, she would be in our possession now and this would all be behind us."

"I mention it," Mr. Clarke said, "not to offend, but because I have never known you, as our Consul, to be stymied."

Clarke had used the Group's title, Consul. It was a vestige, the highest position in the ancient Roman Republic. It was a designation used in great deference then and now.

"Are there larger issues, other agents or powers involved? Cardinal Luciano for example?"

"No offense taken, my friend. The thought has occurred to me as well. Something, or someone, is obscuring the woman's presence, her essence actually. It is as though she does not exist. That sort of protection would draw much power. To be sure though, I will work my way through this.

"As for the cardinal," the man snorted his derision, "his Eminence is an easier situation to handle. He will be expunged once he has served his purpose. People never fail to fascinate me, Mr. Clarke. They embrace the light and shun the darkness. What they can't afford to admit is the light is a fantasy and the dark is the only thing that is real."

"The good cardinal," Mr. Clarke followed the thought. "Even for all he knows, all he is, he spurns the light, but he is incapable of grasping the reality of how dark the darkness truly is. He and Blessing stand in the mist between the two."

"The difference is," the Consul said, "Blessing knows roughly who he is and definitely where he is and why he is there. He grows more adept and powerful every day.

"The cardinal believes he is out of the light so he must be in the darkness and he stopped growing long ago. The very definition of a stupid man, don't you think?"

* * *

The Vatican Bank was a blizzard of activity. On the surface, all looked calm and businesslike but Julian could feel the hum of energy just below the surface. The employees, from tellers to directors, were terrified.

"You asked for me, Eminence. If you want to know what progress I've made, the answer is, none. Fr. Soski and I have interviewed and profiled every employee of the bank and we have not discovered the mole, let alone the method. We are at a standstill." Julian stood at Cardinal Manning's desk in a respectful silence.

The old cardinal sat back in his chair, closed his green eyes and drew in a deep breath. "Julian, I am running out of options.

We are currently drawing from our reserves to keep things afloat. Our buoyancy is failing fast, my son.

"The Pope would like my head and will have it, but he knows replacing me will do nothing but delay stopping these attacks and bring the spotlight onto the Vatican itself. Again. For this reason he will keep this quiet. Although not important in itself, I will be free to continue working on this without fear of being replaced.

"There are a group of cardinals who sit on the bank's advisory board. This same group advises the Pope on all matters financial and economic. Julian, I want you to interview each of them.

"You and Fr. Soski have been through the bank like a dose of salts. I know because the managers have complained. Not loudly. This is, after all, the Vatican bank." The cardinal eked out a slight smile.

"The members of the council are all that remain. If not them, then the attacks are originating without assistance from the inside. My auditors say that is nearly impossible. A man on the inside is needed for any external assault to work." The cardinal's Irish accented English was present, but subdued.

"Eminence, Cardinal Luciano is a member of that body, no?" Julian asked.

"He is and I know he presents a special case for you and Fr. Soski. We will leave him for last, but sooner or later, he must be confronted. About that, son, he will not be entirely pleased," Cardinal Manning said.

* * *

"Thank you for calling, Bridget," Julian said to his Irish mentor. "I wish I could say I've made progress. Hell, I really wish I could say we were on our way back home. Things here seem to get murkier by the minute and I am no nearer finding Ailís than I was." Julian avoided telling his mentor about being ensnared by the Group, Sokolov and Cardinal Luciano.

Her diction, as always, was perfect. The cadence of her Irish accented English was unhurried and hypnotizing. "You are in error, Julian. The murkiness has always been there, no more, no less. You are just now plumbing its depth. Do not let the darkness distract you. Whatever you do, do not despair. Going through that doorway leads in only one direction.

"You have allies who will assist you beyond your ability to understand now. Hold to two things - you will bring this to a conclusion and you are not alone.

"I cannot see it and that in itself is strange," Bridget continued. "There is something in the way, blocking my vision, but I feel you are nearing your goal of finding Ailís. I can tell you no more."

Between them, the air did not need to be filled with words. Julian considered, then spoke slowly. "Bridget, there is an unimaginable power larger, and far more deadly, at work here. I feel one of us has been turned. My problem is, I can't believe someone so powerful would have gone unnoticed."

Bridget could feel his anger, his frustration and his fear. It wasn't from his voice or what he said. She could feel the raw emotions and the swirling thoughts. It was palpable to her, real, and her face twisted with the pain of it.

"Julian," she began, "you have changed during your time in Rome. You have grown. The rate and direction of your growth has surprised even me. I am not so easily surprised.

"The result is, now, more than ever, you must become the master of your thoughts, your reactions and your emotions. What you are facing requires you to have no doubts, no fears. Know the unreality of the reality that has been presented to you.

"You have heard it before. You and I, and those like us, are tasked with dispelling the mist. In this case, you must make sure you project the strongest light possible. Your life, and that of others, may depend on it. You are strong and you are capable. You are talented and bright. Use all of that to intensify the light and know, you are never alone," she concluded.

"I will try, Bridget. I will do my best," Julian said.

"I know you will and that is all that can be asked of you," Bridget whispered.

She hung up and her heart ached. She knew some of what he faced. When new and raw, she had faced it too. She had nearly died and would have if her teacher and mentor had not given up their lives to save hers. The grief and the guilt had been so great she had prayed to die. Now she prayed Julian would survive better than she had.

She said to herself in an undertone, "It is all that can be asked. But sometimes our best is not enough."

* * *

Rain beat a steady tattoo on the windows of Fr. Soski's office. The office was, as always, swathed in its perpetual twilight. Julian looked into the gray middle distance from a gap between the curtains. He turned to his friend seated at his desk.

"Well, Marek?" Julian asked in a whisper nearly drowned out by the rain.

"I do not see any other possibility, Julian. A conspiracy spanning two thousand years or more and they did it all in secret," the priest said and ruminated on the possibilities. "The group we are dealing with is the 'they' in all of this. Your professors, Agostini and Bragonier, their research leads to only that conclusion. Proof we do not have, but their investigation is the next best thing."

"The coins were the nexus of a criminal enterprise that puts all others in the shade," Julian said. "The question is how was it held together for so long and in secret. The answer is we, those like us, have been involved from the start. There is no way of knowing who is involved now, so trusting anyone will be impossible," Julian said.

"Impressive. I don't know five people who can keep a secret for twenty minutes. So what's next? Julian, at best we can only try to avoid being killed," the priest said.

"Well, let's call them the Group for lack of anything else. If the Group wants the Pope dead, we have to assume..." Julian was interrupted.

"We must assume one thing first," Fr. Marek said and Julian nodded. "Our assumption was the doctor was being held by either Luciano or Sokolov. There is a new piece on the chessboard. The Group may have her. Their motivation has a higher priority and a greater likelihood.

"This Group, the good cardinal, and a Russian mobster all want you dead," Soski said, "as soon as you've rendered some small service. In this case, assassinating the Pope. By the way, it would be a worthwhile conjecture this is not their first pope."

The rain intensified as the storm passed overhead and thunder boomed in the distance.

"Yes," the priest continued, "we can assume something else. Life insurance for you must be hideously expensive. You seem to attract all the wrong kind of attention. Julian, please work on that, will you?

"I wonder if we should cue the ominous music soundtrack now?" Fr. Soski said. Rather than lighten the mood, the sharp contrasts between life and death were only accentuated.

* * *

Sapienza University had been scrubbed clean by the overnight rain. The jaunty buildings and staid structures seemed to take on new confidence.

The professor had called. There was news, a clue and it was sufficient enough to perturb an imperturbable man. Agostini was unwilling to share it over the telephone. Julian climbed the stairs to Professor Agostini's office. The long days and sleepless nights were wearing deep lines into Julian's face and dark circles lay heavy under his gray eyes.

"No!" The word was a scream, a hope, a prayer and came from the second floor. Julian moved, taking the stairs two at a time. He reached the second floor and began to run. The word came again, "No!" as Julian reached the only open door on the second floor.

Gio knelt beside the body of Professor Agostini. The older man's body was twisted, contorted into a painful shape. He lay face up. His chest was collapsed as though all the ribs had been crushed. Rivulets of blood had run from his ears and eyes, but had dried quickly as the man's life faded, then was no more.

Julian looked up and saw heavy scorch marks on the filing cabinet where the professor kept his notes. Everything inside, including the professor's research, was ash now.

Gio, his knees drenched in blood, vomited, but continued to kneel beside the professor. Rocking back and forth the young man whispered over and over, "No, no, no."

"Gio," Julian said as he lifted the young man away from the lifeless body of his professor. "Leave him, now. Let's wait outside." Julian's voice was whisper soft and gentle. He guided Gio to the hallway as campus security arrived on the run.

Crime scene investigators arrived, measurements were made, photographs were taken and fingerprints lifted. The coroner arrived and took possession of the professor's body.

The university security personnel stood by while members of the Carabinieri questioned Julian briefly. They were far more interested in Gio who they had handcuffed and sitting in the hallway. The officers took copious notes and asked questions in rapid fire Italian. Unsatisfied, they stood the young student up and started toward the waiting squad cars.

"This isn't happening," Gio said to Julian. "It can't be happening. I didn't do this thing."

"I'm sorry, Gio. It has happened and you didn't do it. I know that and the authorities will too. There is nothing more to be said." There was much to be said, but Julian wasn't prepared to say it. "Say nothing until you talk with your lawyer. I'll find the best there is. No matter what, say nothing and know you're not alone."

His past viewing ability gave Julian no clue what had happened. He could see the office clearly. He watched as Gio had arrived for his appointment. It flickered into being and then was gone, obscured by some dark presence. In the present, it manifested itself as Julian had found it. A dead professor and a grieving, terrified student. And a world of information gone.

Julian watched as the police car pulled away from the curb with Gio in the backseat. He began to walk. He could have hailed a taxi, but he needed time to think, time to see through this darkness.

* * *

"Wizard." Julian came slowly to himself. He blinked rapidly and shook his head trying to clear the thoughts and images. He had traveled several blocks along the busy street.

He was subdued when he answered, "Inspector, what can I do for you." A statement not a question.

She sensed the difference and cocked her head. "Behind you is a small park. Go there, pick a bench you like and sit. We'll be with you in a moment."

"No." Julian spoke the word simply.

The inspector's brow creased and she said softly, "Please."

The unmarked police car pulled away from the curb and was lost in the traffic as Julian drew a noisy breath and turned into the park.

He found a shaded bench and was joined a short time later by the inspector and her sergeant.

"What are you doing here?" Julian asked, not interested in the answer and his mind a thousand miles away.

"We monitored a emergency call at the university. A body had been discovered. A murder they say with a suspect in custody. No concern of ours, but it was noted. The Carabinieri get all the interesting things to do while we deal with finance. And you. It is unfair.

"Driving down the street, who do we see but you, a few blocks from the same university where a body has been found. Enrico and I looked at each other and instantly knew you were involved. What have you done?" She was reading Julian in a fundamental way. He was distant, he was serious, hurting.

She dealt with him gently, while the sergeant looked on and watched for the slightest flare of any reaction or emotion. He found nothing in Julian except an empty sadness.

"Tell me what has happened and if or how it involves you," she said softly.

Julian looked at the ground and saw nothing at all. His mouth a hard, tight line. The space between his eyes deeply etched in thought. He answered quietly, "Inspector, there are things you do not want to know, apparently things that will get you assassinated. Leave it alone. Your world is dangerous enough, but much easier to live in than mine."

"That may be. You said assassinate while I said murder," the inspector said. "There is a difference between the two, no?"

"Yes there is a very great difference. Very great and no difference at all. A good man is dead," Julian said without intonation or emotion. "Still, you are the police. If you say murder, it must be murder."

"Don't be like that." The inspector's words were hard-edged.

Julian turned to the young woman, thought hard for a moment and said, "Inspector, can you do me a favor? I have no right to ask, but you are the right person to ask."

The inspector thought, looked to her partner who shrugged. "Ask your favor," she said. "We will see."

"The young man who was arrested for this crime, he is a friend and needs a lawyer quickly. You know the good ones from the bad ones. I need only the one who will get my friend out of jail. I don't speak Italian, as you have reminded me. I need you to call whatever lawyer you think best for the job," Julian said.

"The thing you ask is easily done. But in return…" She left the sentence suspended in air and looked guarded.

"I will give you some information and I will save your life." Julian looked into the inspector's eyes and she leaned away. Simultaneously, her partner leaned in.

"I can tell you," Julian began. "The young man in custody didn't do it. You don't like the word assassinate and I don't like murdered. Let's settle. The professor was silenced to keep him from telling me something. His death was meant as a warning, an example to me, and it eliminated some vital information."

Julian continued, "I can tell you, people are behind this who will never be caught. You have no idea how powerful they are." Julian smirked. "I would like to tell you who they are, but I can't. I don't know. They are shadows. They are nightmares.

"Now I will save your life." Julian looked from the inspector to her sergeant. "Both of your lives, actually. Please, make the call and then distance yourself as quickly as possible. Do not look into this case even informally. Do not speculate. Do not think of it again. Put it from your memories forever."

The inspector's brows drew together in concentration. She looked to her partner. His shrug was a little less lackluster than the last one.

"I will do this for you and promise to stay well away from the case. I must warn you though, the Italian justice system is not an easy one to navigate. It is based on Napoleonic law which, itself, is based on Roman law. It is not for the state to prove a suspect guilty, but for him to prove his innocence.

"I will tell you another thing," the inspector said. "In Italy, money buys influence. Influence buys power. Power buys happiness. There are many happy people who want to stay that way."

"Cost is not an issue. My friend needs to walk on this. There will be no justice for the professor. I want there to be no injustice befalling my friend. He did not do it. You may depend on that."

"Again, wizard, you have told us absolutely nothing of value. We will make the call, but one day we will call on you for a favor," the inspector said, "and, regardless of what we ask, you will deliver."

Julian closed his eyes and nodded.

Chapter Seventeen

He accepted the inspector's offer of a ride to the House of Joy. He made a call he dreaded. He telephoned Professor Bragonier. The man's moan came from a tormented soul. He passed the phone to his wife, Bridget. Julian explained again the circumstances of Professor Agostini's death. Julian added horrific details he hadn't shared with Bridget's husband, would never share with him.

"I am sorry, Julian. There is little else that can be said," the woman whispered.

"Bridget?"

"Yes, Julian." She could feel the pain in his tortured silence.

"You have the Sight. I know you can't see what is going on now, but going forward..."

Bridget waited for him to continue, waited for the questions she knew would come.

"Going forward, beyond right now – will Ailís survive this?" Julian whispered his question.

"She will," Bridget said and felt sure in her answer.

"Will I?" Julian asked.

"There is a cloak around you, Julian. It covers all of this business and, I'm afraid, I cannot explain it and cannot really see beyond that. Your survival will depend on the choices you make. Beyond that, I cannot say."

"Thank you, Bridget. It's good to know what I'm facing," Julian said.

But she could see, not everything, but enough. She did know, not everything, but enough. She could say, but nothing that would change Julian's choices.

Bridget Bragonier hung up the telephone and, for the first time in a very long time, wept.

* * *

"If it isn't Mr. John Clarke. You indicated there was some urgency, my young friend." The heavyset older man with the simple suit and the clerical collar seemed pleased to see his protégé.

He was seated in an underground passage in the lower reaches of Castel Sant'Angelo. The passageway was safe, secure and a secret known to few who had not been murdered to keep the secret.

"You are looking particularly smug today, Consul," Clarke said using the Group's ancient title for its leader.

"The Passetto di Borgo is the secret passageway connecting St. Peter's to Castel Sant'Angelo. Not a secret any more, of course," the Consul said.

"Today, tourists walk in the same pathway as many popes. Oddly, no one ever noticed this parallel passageway we built. The things our little group has accomplished have been remarkable, no?"

John Clarke thought a moment. "I take it you selected the place we eliminated our first pope for a reason."

"I did, actually. Generations of us followed generations of them right to you and me, right here in the present day. We murdered

John X here in fact. Yes, the castle has the residence and refuge of popes, a prison, barracks and an execution chamber.

"Still, we mustn't neglect our butchering the next two popes, Leo VI and Stephen VIII. The woman who killed them all did so in order to install her son on the Throne of Peter." The Consul continued with his history lesson. An historical place, don't you think?

"She was a very busy lady and advanced our cause substantially. We owe much to her. When it was time, she was killed by her apprentice as I will be killed by you." The Consul smiled with a kindness that never reached his eyes. "You know all of this, so what brings us together today?"

"I have a concern, two actually," Clarke said. His British accent was elegant, his language precise. "We have employed every available asset to locate the doctor. Our search has been fruitless. As you have said, without her, Blessing will not comply with our wishes. Can you assist?"

"I agree, he will not," the Consul said. "As for finding the woman, in all likelihood I could do it. Doing so, however, would require lowering the shadows that protect our business. There are many who, right now, are probing the shield I maintain. Any weakening would leave us exposed," the Consul said.

"I understand. Could we not threaten Blessing in another way? His mentor in Dublin comes to mind," Clarke said. His bright gray eyes sought out the steel gray eyes of his superior, his mentor.

"Let me tell you something," the Consul said. "Send an army of kidnappers or assassins against that woman and your army would be no more. She tangled with us decades ago. She escaped, but two of her companions did not.

"Those three obliterated a score of our people in the process. She did not get away unscathed, but the experience left her vicious. Over the years she has become unreasonably powerful. She can detect anything you send against her or hers at a great distance and would not hesitate to eliminate the slightest threat.

"To make it more difficult, she has the sight. She would know well in advance, my friend. She is a very large reason I cannot lower our guard." The older man sat and ruminated before saying, "You mentioned a second concern, John."

"Luciano," Clarke began. "He has become troublesome in one way, dangerous in another. I feel this is getting worse by the moment. He lacks discipline and so is prone to wild outbursts and unpredictable behavior.

"We left him to recruit Blessing. The cardinal's arrogance put paid to that. He then went on to forewarn Blessing about our intentions, viz this current pope. As a result, the young man was prepared for us."

Clarke went on. "As you know, the cardinal is talented. His ability to protect his thoughts is formidable to be sure. Still, there is something he is doing beyond that and beyond his thefts from the bank. I don't know what it is, but I know it will not benefit us. My belief is he is setting himself up to supplant you. That, to my mind, makes him dangerous." Clarke sat back, took a deep breath and closed his eyes.

The passage way was closed in, the atmosphere thick and laid like a blanket on thoughts, feelings and conversation.

After five minutes, the Consul said, "His Eminence is clever to be sure, John. He knows I could easily pierce any defense he can put up. He also knows I cannot and will not do that without exposing us all. His largest obstacle now is that he does not know who I am.

"For all his cleverness though, he has left himself badly exposed. He allowed Soski to live. We made use of that by making sure he gave Blessing the book.

"Blessing," the Consul said. His eyebrows knitted together in thought. "He lacks the cardinal's experience and viciousness. However, having absorbed the book's teachings, Blessing is far more powerful than either he or Luciano knows." Again the passage filled with ominous thoughts.

"*What of the cardinal?*" Clarke thought.

"*We will continue with the plan only slightly modified; we will accelerate the timeline,*" the older man said.

A moment passed, then another. "*And the pope?*" Clarke thought.

The Consul responded, "*This would be an ideal time and with Blessing's help, he could be the catalyst for a new inquisition. A perfect distraction actually that would serve our cause. Still, if not this pope, perhaps the next one.*

"*One pope is much like another?*" Clarke thought and smiled.

"Exactly."

* * *

The Gregorian University was quiet. Early evening had deposited an inky darkness and the air was heavy and still. A dim light shined from the second floor corner office of Fr. Marek Soski. The room was still, but the atmosphere was filled with thoughts.

"*Do you think Manning knows more than he is saying?*" Julian thought. "*What are you getting from him?*"

"*My experience with Vatican politics tell me he does know more, but my readings of him show him as confused as we are. We have not had a great deal of contact over the years, but my feeling is there is much more wrong about the cardinal today than when I met him. Perhaps the embezzlements have changed him. It would be understandable. The fact is, I don't know,*" the priest speculated.

Julian laced his fingers on top of his head, leaned back and looked at the coved ceiling. Fr. Soski steepled his fingers, set them against his lips, and thought to Julian, "*What do you think we should do next, my friend?*"

"*Marek, I would like to answer, but I have a problem,*" Julian acknowledged. "*I don't care. I don't care what happens to Manning. I don't care what happens to the Vatican or its bank. I don't care about Luciano or Sokolov. I don't care about the Group or their agenda. I want Ailís back and I want to get her back home to Ireland.*" Julian's mental tone was somber, but carried conviction bordering on anger.

"*And you, Julian? You have left yourself out of all of this.*"

"*Again, I don't care. Her safety is all that is important. She is innocent in all of this. Whatever price must be paid will be paid,*" Julian responded with his thoughts as he sought out the pale eyes of his friend.

"*If I said I didn't understand, or that you should not be so hasty or selfish, I would be lying and you would know it instantly. I am not a good liar for one thing and it isn't the truth for another,*" Soski said.

"*Marek.*" Julian stopped and considered for a moment. "*There are others of us in Italy, perhaps some even in Rome. Isn't there some way we could...?*"

"*A paranormal army? Is that what you are suggesting, Julian? Really?*"

"*I'm up for whatever it takes. I've got to find her and I feel I'm running out of time. If anything happens to her, the sacking of Rome will look like a picnic.*"

"*I understand your frustration, but the answer to your question is, no. There are others of course, but they are not here and we are. Right now, our priorities are not their priorities. It is you and me, my friend. We are all there is and we are enough.*" The priest's smile was small and sad, and offered a glimpse of a darkening future.

* * *

"Eminence," Fr. Soski said. "What we can say is there is no one currently in the bank who is providing assistance to anyone outside. We have found quite a number of people who are stealing office supplies, but no more."

Julian added, "Administration is assembling a list of names of those on vacation and leave, or who have recently resigned, been dismissed or reassigned. We will work our way through it." Julian's heart wasn't in it and the cardinal and Soski could feel it.

The cardinal looked older, more beaten than stressed, more anxious than frustrated. "I thank you for your efforts, gentlemen."

Soski tilted his head as though he was listening to something or for something. Julian sat back in his chair, closed his eyes and let his chin rest on his chest. When he raised his head, his eyes were heavy lidded. Deep furrows formed at the corners of his eyes and across his forehead.

Something was wrong, off somehow. It shimmered into existence then was gone, but it had been there. Something powerful and dark and Julian knew it.

Manning sighed deeply and said, "I am off to a briefing. Please keep me advised of your progress." The interview was over.

In the hallway, Soski looked at Julian and shook his head. Julian acknowledged and they both proceeded down the marble stairs and into the polluted Roman air.

"*You felt it, of course,*" Fr. Soski thought and Julian replied with his own thought.

"*Oh yes. Now if I only knew what it was. A dark power of some sort. It came into existence quickly, then was gone. It didn't last long enough to track it to a source. However, residual energy was thick in the air.*"

"*This is moving beyond me, Julian,*" the priest thought. "*I need to talk with some people. In fact I have much to discuss with them.*"

* * *

Julian awoke to a melancholy day in Rome with a tantalizing hint at bright sunshine later. He showered, shaved and sat at his desk before dressing. He ran his thumb down the scar on his cheek. He looked drab and tired. The mirror mocked him, scolded him. He had accomplished very little beyond discovering far more questions than answers. He had not done enough even though he was doing all he could.

Julian's mouth turned into a hard, tight line. "It changes today," he said to himself.

He reached out for the Jesuit Book. His hand hovered over it and he could feel the power contained inside. Julian let his hand rest on the book and again he said, "It changes today. Good or bad, it changes today."

CHAPTER EIGHTEEN

Bogdan Sokolov let his chin drop to his chest as he pinched the bridge of his nose. His head jerked up as he heard Julian say, "Time's up."

Julian was sitting on the other side of Sokolov's desk. A place where five seconds before, there had been a distinct lack of Julians.

"Sokolov. Your twenty-four hours have passed and at your request, I granted you another day."

Sokolov's mouth twisted into a nasty snarl. "Blessing, I will kill you now."

"Okay," Julian said and his face was placid and pleasant. "Do you have a fire extinguisher nearby?'

"What?" Sokolov spat. He opened a desk drawer and fire erupted out, licking at the edge of his desk. The Russian managed to get the drawer closed and, open-mouthed and enraged, looked at Julian.

To Sokolov, nothing about what this American did or said aligned with anything in human experience. There was nothing the Russian could do which Julian wouldn't counter simultaneously. Intimidation and bribery were jokes. There were no surprises possible. Speed meant nothing. Animal cunning was worthless. Raw force and brutality wouldn't work and that combination had been his go-to solution for most of his life.

"Produce the doctor," Julian said. His gray eyes captured and held Sokolov's attention. The eyes were unflinching and remorseless and deadly.

The Russian took a breath and held it. He exhaled noisily and said, "Blessing, I will do as you say, but I want something from you. It isn't much, but if you do it, you get your woman back today, yes?" Sokolov said and tried to look sincere.

"What is it you want?" Julian's response was measured, the words emotionless, and his look never left the Russian's face.

"I want you to introduce me to this Luciano. You know him, no? I think I can do business with him. He is with the bank and I need someone inside. Start at top, no?" Sokolov tried to resist the unseen force that was pushing him back in his chair.

"Sokolov, you are without doubt the stupidest man I know. You have taken being dim-witted to new lows. The Russian mafia is hard up for leadership if you are still alive and walking around." Julian squinted at the big man who was struggling to get out of his chair.

"I just want to make sure you understand. If I take you to see Cardinal Luciano, he will kill you. If you think dealing with me is bad, you'll think I was your guardian angel compared to Luciano. Take my word for it, you don't want to meet with the cardinal," Julian concluded.

Breathless from trying to free himself, Sokolov reiterated, "Introduce me to this priest and as soon as my business is done with him, I will make one call and your woman goes free."

Julian tried again to read the big Russian. The man was a bag of hatred, anger and bile. Beyond that, Julian couldn't tell if Sokolov was lying or not. Still, Julian had a suspicion, a feeling too strong to ignore, but upon which he could not act without corroboration. He knew how to get that corroboration.

"You know, Sokolov, let me make you a deal. I will introduce you to his Eminence. At the conclusion of the interview, we will walk out, you will make the call and you will have her put on the phone so I can talk with the doctor. If you do not do these things – I want you to pay special attention to this part – you will burst into flames. I will not hesitate and there will be no further negotiations. Am I making myself clear?" Julian asked.

"Fuck you!" Sokolov shouted as he continued to struggle to free himself. Julian shook his head and looked resigned and sighed. A high bright flame erupted from the center of the Russian's desk blotter. Julian tossed a bored look at the man. Sokolov recoiled from the heat. Julian moved his hand and the fire moved closer to the Russian.

"Done. That is deal. Cardinal first, then your woman." The fire disappeared as quickly as it appeared leaving only a large scorch mark and a furious Sokolov whose eyebrows had been singed off.

"Shall we go?" Julian said to Sokolov. "You can drive." Julian released the mobster.

* * *

Fr. Soski sat in his office. His head was resting on the back of his chair and his eyes were closed. The priest was feeling the thoughts of his teacher, another Jesuit living in retirement.

"Ronaldo. As always, I appreciate your help. Our time is short. I must find Mr. Blessing and…"

"Marek," the teacher interrupted. Soski paused and had a feeling of foreboding. It was difficult to hide anything from his teacher, his friend, his confessor. This was such a time.

"I can not help you with Mr. Blessing." The man's voice turned hard. *"Marek, it is your time that is short and you have made it so. It is the path you are intent on traveling. I am asking you not to do this thing you are planning. Mr. Blessing's path is his own. That is true of all of us. You, however, have embarked on the wrong course. It is one of your own design and it will end badly. Revenge is never true or right or wise.*

"I will confess, I cannot see into this business and I cannot see the future, but I can feel the steps which will lead to a bad end for you, your friend, and others," Ronaldo concluded.

"Thank you for all you have done for me old friend. I have always appreciated your wisdom. Those times I have not followed your advice, I have regretted it. Unfortunately, in this instance, I have no choice. It must end here, it must end now," Fr. Soski thought and then continued. *"About that other matter?"*

Knowing his advice would be ignored, Ronaldo sighed and answered his student's question. The response was detailed and missed nothing. It spoke of how much can be found when you find nothing. The older man finished and the air was thick with thoughts.

"You are sure of that?" Fr. Soski thought.

"Marek, I have been at this a long time, since before you were born. I tell you only what I felt. That was not a simple matter. Everything was obscured. At first, I was clearly seeing the man you told me about, then nothing. He simply winked out of existence.

"It was just a flicker," the teacher continued. *"It was the briefest of moments. The man was there then he was not and then he was there again. I would like to tell you more, but there is no more to tell."*

He was a man of late old age and he sat on a sofa in his office. His eyes were closed and he could feel all of his student's confusion, frustration and ever-present physical pain. The man saw through

Soski's milky gray eyes, eyes once alive with mischief and promise and what he saw left him sick at heart.

"*My friend,*" the teacher thought, "*you have spoken to me of Mr. Blessing and spoken often and with much affection. I know of him of course. I know his mentor, Mrs. Bragonier and his teacher, Mrs. Hagan,*" the teacher said. *If this ends badly, I need to know the Jesuit Book is safe. Another thing, in the event...*"

"*Ronaldo,*" Father Soski interrupted. "*The book is safe. It will be delivered to you if,*" the priest paused, "*if Julian has no need of its use. To answer your other question, yes, please notify Mrs. Bragonier whatever the outcome. She will know what to do.*"

"*Thank you, Ronaldo, addio. You have been a good friend to me,*" the priest said and tried to keep the tears away from his thoughts.

"*Marek, the phrase is,* 'ci rivedremo,' *because assuredly, we will meet again,*" the teacher thought and, for the moment, was able to keep the heartache from his mind.

The connection was gone. Fr. Soski squeezed his eyes shut and a tear coursed his scared cheek. He said only one word.

"Manning."

The telephone on his desk jarred Fr. Soski. "Yes," he answered and paused. "Do not send him up. Bring him up and do it as quickly as possible, please." He hung up and concentrated on his closed office door and awaited Fr. Dominic Giglio.

* * *

Did you hear me Fr. Soski?" the terrified priest asked.

Fr. Dominic had opened with the words, 'It wasn't my fault. I stumbled on it all by accident.' The young priest had been nearly hysterical. At that moment, Fr. Soski had begun matching the young priest's thoughts to his words. They matched. This was not subterfuge.

"I did, Fr. Dominic, and I thank you. Now go. Find a place where there are a lot of people. Get in amongst them and do not think about the cardinal. Do not think about me. Do not think about you. If possible, do not think about anything," Fr. Soski whispered and his guest had to lean forward to hear him.

"Your thoughts will lead his Eminence to you." Soski's indulgent smile froze Fr. Dominic to the core. The priest with the milky gray eyes said emphatically, "And he will kill you."

* * *

"I have anticipated this, but are any of us ever ready?" Fr. Soski said to himself and dread chilled his soul. He hung his head. The priest closed his eyes and thought, "*The moment of the ending was dictated long ago. Now we close the chapter, but the book is not done, only my part in it.*"

He stood, took a calming breath, gathered his hat and overcoat and left the office.

* * *

"Notify the Cardinal Secretary of State that I wish to have Cardinal Luciano taken into custody to await the pleasure of His Holiness."

The young priest who received this message had been in Rome for a month. He stood paralyzed at Cardinal Manning's words.

"Is it deaf you are, father?" the cardinal asked in his best jovial Irish English. Cardinal Manning smiled.

"Uh, no Eminence. I will call the Secretariat immediately."

"Son, no, no, that isn't the Vatican way. Take yourself off to the Secretariat and see the Secretary of State. Simple. Speak with no one else. His is the oldest office in the Curia. One does not flip out one's iPhone and discuss such a thing. Do not worry; he will contact the Inspector General of the Corpo della Gendarmeria. From there we need worry no more."

That said, worry cut deeply into the priest's forehead. "Eminence, what if the Cardinal Secretary won't see me?"

"Won't see you is it? He is waiting for you now. Telephones do have their uses." The cardinal's smile, pleasant enough, never reached his green eyes.

The priest bowed slightly and left with a message that would change the complexion of the Vatican, the lives of thousands and the Catholic Church irrevocably. The young priest-messenger had no way of knowing his coming actions would change the world. He hadn't been in Rome long enough.

✳ ✳ ✳

The Basilica of St. Peter cast long late afternoon shadows across Cardinal Luciano's residence. The air was thick with humidity, incense and foreboding. Hushed footsteps on thickly carpeted stairs and whispered conversations preceded Julian, Sokolov and their guide as they approached the cardinal's office door.

"Come," the cardinal said, a moment before a young priest knocked.

"Eminence..."

"Yes, I know. Show them in," Cardinal Luciano said casually. "Do you know where Fr. Dominic is? No matter, tell him I will have need of him tomorrow."

"Yes, Eminence." The priest hadn't seen Fr. Dominic all day. And he never would again.

Julian and Sokolov entered the cardinal's darkening office. The cardinal motioned his guests to chairs in front of the cold fireplace and he smiled an ingratiating but wintry smile.

Sokolov, a career criminal, scanned the room as he entered making note of doors, windows and anything he might use as a weapon should this cardinal prove to be a problem.

From the moment he crossed the threshold, his eyes never left the cardinal's face. Julian had employed his time in Rome, and the Jesuit Book, to build a thick wall around his thoughts. He wondered now if his defenses would be enough to keep the cardinal out.

'Everything you need to know, you will find on his face. Everything you need to see, everything you need to fear, you will find in his eyes. There you will find the answer too, the key.' Julian recalled the words from the Jesuit Book to himself.

"Gentlemen, I usually do not receive guests on such short notice." The cardinal's voice was relaxed and his Italian accented English was soft, expressive and ironical. "Since, it is Mr. Blessing, I have made this exception. Sadly, the press of business will be calling me away rather soon, so there is some haste." The cardinal smiled his humorless smile.

"Church business, Eminence?" The derision in Julian's voice sounded mild.

"Oh, Mr. Blessing, I exist to serve the Church only, as you know. Therefore, all my business is Church business."

"There is something I want, priest," Sokolov stated. His face mirrored his disgust.

The cardinal looked balefully at the Russian. "Mr. Sokolov, I can see you are a man built in mind and body for quick and often violent action. I must tell you, these are traits I do not admire. I see, also, you are missing your eyebrows and smell of smoke." The cardinal looked to Julian, but he only shrugged. "Still, I will listen to your request," the cardinal said and Julian's mouth twitched.

"I want a man in Vatican Bank to help my business. You are that man," the Russian said and Julian shook his head and waited.

"You seem to be a man of many wants. Life, unfortunately is filled with many disappointments," the cardinal said mildly. "I am a man with few real wants, but what I want, I always receive.

"For example, I want you to remove yourself and your organization from Rome. No, let us make it from Italy altogether." The tone was mild and smooth and the cadence was relaxed. Julian could feel the edge even if the Russian could not.

The following silence was punctuated by the ticking of a clock near the cardinal's desk and time seemed to move slowly before Sokolov said, "Eat shit, priest."

The Russian's accent was thick, but now doubly thick with distain. "I have business here and my business is no business of yours. There are things you do not understand. They are things that will get you killed. You can be dead any day I choose it, no matter who you are. So I'm not going anywhere.

"Anyone can be dead any day I say." The big man looked pointedly at Julian then back to the cardinal. "You understand? Bogdan Sokolov won't be leaving Rome anytime soon, your holiness." The Russian bowed slightly. "I have no time for this. I thought we could do business. We cannot. Blessing, we are going."

Julian remained seated with the Russian towering over him.

Cardinal Luciano sighed. "I will find the answer tedious and uninspired, but I must ask for the sake of good form. Tell me, Mr. Sokolov, how would you propose to have me killed?"

"Simple," the Russian said. "I would not. I have Blessing do it." The man's smile dripped condescension. "I have Blessing by balls. I have his woman, the doctor. To get her back, he will be my bitch and do what I say. If I say you are dead, you are dead."

"Mr. Blessing," the cardinal said, "do you see the trials you and I, and those like us, must endure?"

Julian said nothing. His eyes never strayed from the cardinal's face. Across that face passed the flicker of a shadow. Julian saw it and he knew.

The cardinal's face darkened, but only slightly. He felt sure Julian had seen something, but what and how much was still in doubt. Much depended on knowing now. "If you would be so kind, Mr. Blessing, please explain the realities to Mr. Sokolov. Remember, use small words and speak slowly. He isn't terribly bright," the cardinal said.

The angry blood rushed to the Russian's face, the veins distended in his neck, his breathing ran quick and sharp.

Julian looked up briefly into the eyes of the big man then returned his gaze to the cardinal. For the first time that day, Julian smiled. He had found his corroboration. "You don't have the doctor. You never did."

"You know I do. I show you proof. I show you her things."

"Sokolov, you really are an idiot," Julian said. "The evidence you showed me happened to fall into your lap at the very moment you needed something to convince me. An odd coincidence, don't you think?

"Listen," Julian continued, "There are no coincidences. You were handed the evidence you needed so that you would take the fall. The thought was, I would kill you when you failed to produce the doctor.

"But, as I said, you never had the doctor." Julian paused a moment. "His Eminence does." Julian knew what he needed to know. Ailís' location was being protected mentally. Luciano dropped his guard for a nanosecond and Julian could feed off the cardinal's feelings.

Color drained from the Russian's face and his eyes became small and ferret like.

"Bravo to you, Mr. Blessing, and I do believe the situation is becoming clearer to your companion with each passing moment. Do sit down Mr. Sokolov. You look tired.

"First, he discovers he has no leverage whatsoever," the cardinal observed, "and soon he will learn he has no option but to obey. Life is sometimes full of sad surprises."

The cardinal turned his attention to the Russian who remained standing. "In the strictest sense I suppose, you and I are in the same business. There is a difference though.

"While you lightly launder a few millions of dollars, I cleanse entirely hundreds of millions. You have become an annoyance, a distraction, and you are attracting the wrong kind of attention. Be gone from Italy by, shall we say, two days from now?" The cardinal looked expectantly at the Russian who only glared. "Good, with that settled, you may go."

The big man was rabid with rage. "Priest, I am going to…" Sokolov clutched at his chest. His eyes bulged and pain etched his face deeply. He gasped for a breath that would not come. The Russian fell to his knees and his jaw went slack. Moments passed, annunciated by the ticking clock and the Russian's approaching death rattle.

Julian said coldly, "Enough. You've made your point. I'm sure he understands."

"But do you understand?" the cardinal asked and sat back further in his chair. The Russian fell to his knees gasping for breath, filling his lungs with air he thought he would never breathe again.

"As I said, Mr. Sokolov, you may go. Mr. Blessing shan't be going with you. He and I, you see, have other business matters to discuss."

* * *

"Bella," Marino asked his inspector, "where has the wizard taken himself off to?"

"Which wizard? This town seems to be full of them lately. It's like there is a wizard convention. It doesn't matter. I have a very bad feeling about all of this. I've no evidence to support it, but today is the day," the inspector said.

"The day for what, amore mio?" the sergeant asked.

The inspector turned and looked into her partner's profile while he drove. Marino looked concerned. "Bella, what is it? Today is the day for what?" Enrico Marino, a man who feared little in life, watched his partner's eyes turn to a sea of equal parts reminiscence and regret and he was afraid.

Bella took in a breath, held it then exhaled slowly. "Let us go see Cardinal Luciano. We have questions. He has answers. Today is the day we act." She sighed heavily. "Today, tesoro mio, someone will die." She smiled over at her partner, reached over and set the back of her fingers on his cheek.

* * *

"Mr. Blessing," Cardinal Luciano said, "crassness is for the likes of Sokolov. The man is a simpleton and so crudeness works best when dealing with such scum.

"He is someone with whom we need not concern ourselves. Normally, he would run back to his cave, brood for a bit and fester for a bit more. He would then do something stupid. Stupid things attract the wrong kind of attention."

The cardinal continued, "This cannot be allowed. To save us all a great deal of inconvenience, Mr. Sokolov will reach the street and die from heart failure. Sadly, we all succumb to heart failure in the end." The cardinal sat back in his leather chair and smiled.

"And?" Julian asked.

"Well, you and I need not be crass with each other. We are from a different stratum, a different species, no? I need not threaten and berate you. I will ask you to assist me, you will comply and your doctor will go free.

"Isn't that better than being tactless with each other?" The cardinal's cold smile oozed insincerity.

CHAPTER NINETEEN

Fr. Soski entered the cardinal's residence through a little-used door accessed from the underground parking garage. He closed his eyes, cleared his thoughts and took a deep breath before continuing with his task. This door would close and lock behind him. The door and the hallway beyond were alive with energy, obscuring Ailís and keeping her shielded from outside intervention. She was effectively invisible. He moved ahead. There was no going back.

***

An enraged Bogdan Sokolov descended the stone staircase from Cardinal Luciano's residence to the street. He reached the bottom step, turned and spit.

His right-side-up world lost focus as he suddenly found himself clutching his left arm before his universe exploded in a cascade of pain and fear. A hammer blow of more intense pain brought him to his knees.

Lightning flashed down both arms to the tips of his fingers and back up into his chest. He began to lose consciousness. He was suffocating. His vision narrowed until everything seemed far away.

His hearing became distant before his sight finally narrowed, then blinked out. Sounds mingled, blended into one fading noise, then silence. He was nowhere, but fully aware. Except there was nothing to be aware of.

Alone in a void, his attention turned to the only thing it could find. Bogdan Sokolov. He remembered the events that had shaped his life. He saw it all - the man he killed when he was ten; at thirteen, the first woman he raped, the first kidnapping of a government official, the torture of many and the deaths of scores of others. Bogdan Sokolov remembered it all, saw it all and with a sneer, died.

* * *

"What is it you want, Eminence?" Julian asked.

"There, you see? That is better, no? I will give you the Pope's itinerary and you will kill him tomorrow.

"You and I will then leave Rome. There will be some consternation here we should avoid. Dead popes occasion such things but they provide delightful diversions. Unhappily, I am not all seeing or all knowing. Trying to defend oneself on multiple fronts is tiring. Our talents will complement each other, I feel.

"After you have accomplished your task, and while I move ahead with my plans, you will protect me from those who would thwart those plans. In the meanwhile, your doctor will be free. You, of course, understand?" the cardinal concluded.

It was taking all of his energy to protect his thoughts, but Julian did take time to smile. It was a small smile. A knowing smile.

The cardinal had given himself away. The prelate was right; he was not all seeing and all knowing. Their talents were complementary. Not the same. He had stated his one flaw in plain language.

The smile slid easily from Julian's face. "I want to see the doctor. Now would be a good time."

"Of course. I admire you Americans. You have such a sense of immediacy. You are right, sooner is always better than later. If you will follow me." The cardinal rose, stayed behind his desk, and indicated a discreet door hidden in a fresco. The door that led from his study to a hallway beyond.

* * *

Fr. Soski thought, and Ailís could feel the thought, "*Doctor, please put the chair down. I am a friend of Julian's. You know that; you can feel what I am saying is true. Since you seem to have a plan, I'm not really rescuing you, but I am speeding the process. I will open the door now and I will get you away.*"

He looked at the door. The lock mechanism clicked and the door swung open.

* * *

"Che bellezza!" Enrico Marino spat out in disgust as he and his partner approached Cardinal Luciano's residence.

"Isn't what just great? Oh, my," the inspector said as she looked past her partner. "Enrico, shouldn't you do mouth to mouth or something?"

Marino looked at his inspector as if she had gone mad. "A gangster? Mouth to mouth? Really? Is that your idea of a joke?"

"Well, he might be alive, no?"

"That," Marino pointed at what had been Bogdan Sokolov, "that is dead. Even if he wasn't, we would wait until he was."

"So, dead one way or the other? Well that throws a kink into the investigation. The paperwork alone will take us days." The inspector shook her finger at Sokolov. "You are a very inconvenient man. Most are, except for my Enrico of course, but you are more inconvenient than others."

* * *

Ailís stumbled, feeling her way along the corridor, following the tall, thin priest. A week in captivity had left her muscles slow to respond and her mind sluggish.

Julian stepped into the hallway and felt her confused and distorted signature immediately. He spun on the cardinal. With hands outstretched, he raised a wall of pure energy that stunned and blocked any immediate counter attack. "Ailís! This way. Hurry!" Julian caught sight of Fr. Soski followed closely by the doctor.

Soski moved through the door and into the cardinal's study. He forced a blast of energy ahead of him that pushed back the cardinal's defenses.

Ailís was within a few feet of the door and Julian shouted, "Run! Get out now!" He took her by the hand and moved her through the office and into the hallway while Soski held the cardinal at bay. "Keep going until you get to the street." Fear hid just behind her eyes as she nodded and ran.

With unfocused eyes she moved along the hall and made it to the huge double doors. She clung to the door jam, then staggered through and outside into a world she thought she would never see again. She reached the first steps before she heard the crash of furniture from inside.

Clutching the graceful curve of the stone stair railing, and with halting steps, Ailís Dwyer lurched down the stairs toward the inspector and her sergeant. She tried to see through pinpoint pupils. Her arms and legs wouldn't work in unison and her voice followed none of her commands to shout a warning.

Bella reached Ailís first and sat her on the steps. There was no doubt in the inspector's mind who this was. "Dottoressa Dwyer, can you hear me?"

Ailís' head lolled to the side as she tried to focus, tried to speak. She felt tired, sick, heavy and afraid for Julian.

"Enrico," Bella shouted her command. "Entirely too many people are falling out of this building! Call dispatch. I want everyone out here. We need two ambulances now and another couple just in case. I want the Carabinieri tactical unit, the fire department, the coroner, some traffic control cops. Have them get onto the Vatican. Get anyone else you can think of, anybody who will answer the phone. Get them here now, Enrico, then follow me."

Her partner was already on his cell phone, "Bella, no!" he shouted. "Shit!" She disappeared into the cardinal's residence as his call connected to dispatch. He shouted his orders and received confirmation of their understanding.

Enrico took the doctor's face in his hands as she pointed to the body of Sokolov. "É morto. There is nothing to be done, Dottoressa. You rest." He settled her gently against the stone railing.

He looked up at the towering residence and licked his dry lips. He then drew his sidearm and he ran. "Bella, wait!"

* * *

The cardinal's counter attack was rapid and skillful. He pushed back Soski's wall and the priest was thrown violently into a set of tables, careened off a leather couch, and onto the floor.

Julian could feel it. The cardinal was reaching out with his mind. His target was Ailís. Julian sent out a pulse that changed Luciano's focus and made the cardinal swear. Julian was the cardinal's immediate threat now, a far more formidable threat.

Julian's actions were automatic in the exchange that followed. The Jesuit Book had seeped into his flesh, his bones, his soul. Every cut and thrust was parried with near surgical precision.

Luciano was shocked by the skill Julian demonstrated. New-found skills do not easily overcome experience and the cardinal demonstrated that with a blistering array of attack and counter attack strategies. He couldn't overcome Julian, but he might outlast him.

* * *

"Not this time, Eminence." Fr. Soski spat the ecclesiastical title. The priest gathered himself, exhaled completely, then filled his lungs as he gathered energy around him. He stood and a ball of white-hot energy found its target.

Luciano was too busy being furious to be stunned. His cassock was smoking from the aftershock of energy. He had inhaled some of the superheated force and his lungs and chest burned.

The electrical charge the cardinal directed at Soski should have killed the priest, but an offsetting energy flow from Julian caused the cardinal's attack to go wildly off target. It exploded a bookshelf, turning the mahogany to kindling and the books to pulp.

The cardinal was holding his own, the way any cornered animal would, with far more attacks than defensive moves. For their part, Soski and Julian could feel Luciano weakening. Still, he was a very dangerous enemy.

All three men were panting with the effort of assaulting and defending. Julian caught sight of a slight movement. The cardinal's image had wavered for just a moment. Julian thought and Soski felt it, *"Hall of mirrors."*

As an identical image of the cardinal began to form, Julian and his friend unleashed a barrage of superheated energy. The false image dissipated and the cardinal went to one knee.

In response, he unleashed a torrent of force that pushed his opponents back enough, allowing him time to stand and build his next attack.

* * *

The inspector threw her jacket back clear of her holstered weapon. She could feel the hum of energy coming from the door at the end of the hall. She would have Enrico at her back soon. Still, it is never a good idea to leave one's flanks exposed. She threw open each door she passed. What she found were terrified priests huddled beneath desks.

Her sergeant appeared at her elbow. "Enrico, get them out on the street. I'll keep looking." Both of them eyed the large doors at the end of the corridor.

"Don't go in there without me. Capire, Bella?

"Capito, Enrico, capito," the inspector said.

* * *

Soski's thought was powerful to the point of being painful. *"Eminence, I can't tell you how good it is to be home."* Sarcasm dripped from Soski's pores. *"You remember, this is the room where you tried to murder me."* The white haired priest walked slowly, inexorably toward the cardinal. The cardinal's mind raced considering and reconsidering, weighing and balancing options for escape or attack.

"Julian, the cardinal wanted the Jesuit Book. I politely declined. You have noticed, the cardinal is a man who becomes cross when he doesn't get what he wants. Sadly, he is also a man with insatiable appetites. He wants what he wants when he wants it. Those who stand in the way of that are enemies to be destroyed. You see, my friend," the priest's eyes locked on Julian's, *"the cardinal has no discipline. Well, very little anyway. Unlike you and me, he has no ability to sustain an attack. He gets bored easily, I suppose. Did I mention his vanity? It is legendary."*

Luciano, with feral reflexes, struck when he believed Soski's mind was directed toward Julian. The attack was sharp and sustained, but was easily deflected by a confident, empowered, and ready Fr. Soski.

The priest's counter attack was well thought out. It was as relentless as his steps. As he advanced, his assaults changed, morphed and insinuated themselves into the very heart of Cardinal Luciano and the room hummed with the energy signature of each man. Retribution. Punishment. Death. Those were Soski's thoughts and his motivation.

Julian had understood every clue Soski laid out. He diagramed Luciano as you would a sentence. Julian stood, wiped blood from the corner of his mouth with the back of his hand. And smiled.

Advance, attack, faint, counter attack – Julian and his friend's advance on the cardinal was relentless, focused, driving, merciless. Each attacked a different weak point, then shifted and picked another.

The cardinal was no less formidable. His attacks and counter attacks were ferocious and forceful with each move calculated to inflict the most amount of damage to mind and body as possible.

The attacks diminished as each man paused to gather strength to begin again.

"Enough!" Inspector Belladonna Saviano shouted as she entered the room. "You and you," she indicated Julian and Soski, "you two back away now. Cardinal Luciano, sit. We are all going to get comfortable and then we are going to sort out who is going to prison and who is not.

"Cardinal, I said sit. Now." She continued to advance on the cardinal as her partner entered the room, weapon drawn.

"My dear, I think you are wrong," Luciano said panting from effort. Julian and Soski detected the shift in the cardinal's energy signature. They tried to raise a barrier, but it was too late. The cardinal unleashed a staggering, sustained burst of energy.

The inspector was hurled back against an alabaster plinth. Enrico was flung out the door of the study back into the hallway. Fr. Soski was knocked to one knee. Julian was catapulted into a bookcase. He rose slowly, coughing blood. He held his ribs against the pain. As he gained his footing, he felt Soski unleash a firestorm of raw, unrestrained, soul blistering energy. Julian surveyed the damage as his senses returned.

Enrico rushed to his partner. She lay crumpled on her side, blood running from her ears and mouth. He rolled her gently into his arms and felt her bones crack and grind against each other. He looked to Julian in panic and incomprehension.

Julian looked to Fr. Soski. The priest nodded once and resumed an attack that was merciless and would grant no quarter.

Julian moved from one piece of furniture to another, supporting himself as he staggered to join the sergeant and his inspector while Soski and the cardinal dueled.

Julian moved Enrico aside gently. He knelt over the inspector, closed his eyes, and rubbed the palms of his hands together rapidly feeling the energy build. He placed his hands on her chest. Bella's body jumped once, but moved no more.

Julian repeated the procedure. "Come on, concentrate. You can do this," he whispered. Nothing. Again. Nothing. Enrico captured Julian's hands in his. He looked into Julian's face, closed his eyes and shook his head. The sergeant had seen death before, had seen its many faces. His inspector was gone.

The veins in Julian's neck were distended and his breath came in short gasps. He turned his eyes on Cardinal Luciano. He only had one thought. Murder.

Julian watched as his friend, Fr. Soski, crumpled under the force of Luciano's latest attack.

"No." Julian hissed as his world went white. His attack was stunning in its complexity and Julian watched the cardinal's face as it went from incomprehension to a black rage. Electricity crackled and stung. The room constantly moved between an oppressive darkness and blinding light. Crashing, exploding, parried, dissipated, absorbed balls of energy moved around the room like lightning.

He continued to close on the cardinal. Julian was a daylight nightmare. His was a hatred-fueled vehemence, his face was a map of malice. Julian wanted to be as close as possible when the cardinal was destroyed.

The cardinal was thrown against a wall of porcelain vases, picked up and thrown again. His senses were addled, his eyes were taking longer to focus after each attack and he knew his mind was bending under Julian's assault.

Julian glanced at Soski. The priest was on his knees, doubled over in pain. Luciano used that moment to strike with everything at his disposal.

The room went suddenly alive with rippling, high voltage heat. The priest fell to the ground while Julian was thrown over a leather couch. Both men were dazed and both knew they would not be able to withstand another onslaught. They lay panting, unable to focus for several moments.

Enrico had been pushed back against a wall, still within reach of his inspector. He gathered his senses and looked at the cardinal. The prelate was badly battered and bleeding, his left arm hung limply at his side, and his right leg wouldn't support his weight. But he was not beaten. Not yet.

Julian struggled to gain his footing and stood. He was greatly diminished, but iron willed. Fr. Soski was unable to rise at all.

Julian felt the cardinal's scorching hot fingers close around his mind. The pain was excruciating, blinding, and slowly squeezing the life out of him.

Enrico reached for his sidearm. The holster was empty, the weapon lost in the attack when he entered the room. He saw Julian rise. The sergeant looked at the face of his inspector, closed his eyes, said his goodbye and reached for her Beretta 9mm. He stood, squared his shoulders and, with effort propelled by revenge and revulsion, stood over his partner's body.

Julian closed his eyes and as he opened them, he could see only one thing – the cardinal, a rabid animal that needed to be put down. The cardinal and Julian felt each other build one last burst of energy, one last attack. Julian thought, and Luciano felt the words, *"I may lose, I may die, but it is you who will beg for death. For all those you've maimed, all you've killed."* The discharge of energy scythed the air in a narrow band of glowing heat.

The exchange threw each man in the air and against opposite walls. Both tried to rise. Both tried to gather the last of the energy that animated each of them.

Julian's ears rang, he tasted blood and every joint ached. His legs were numb and would not answer his commands. He slumped back and rose again. His energy signature was nearly gone, he could feel his mind straining while trying to maintain some of itself and hold the cardinal off.

Luciano lay crumpled in front of his desk. He felt the edges of his mind collapsing after Julian's assault, an assault that was weakened but had not abated. He knew the full force of Julian's attack would come soon. His own had to come sooner.

He struggled to his feet and saw Julian unprotected and exposed. Dragging his leg and leaning heavily to one side, the cardinal approached Julian. It was time to end this uncooperative and dangerous American's life.

The cardinal's legs were knocked out from under him and he hissed one word. "Soski." He turned his attention to his former assistant and struck. The weakened priest was flung aside and crashed into a bookshelf and did not move again.

The cardinal made it to his feet first, but Julian was fast behind him. Regardless of condition, everyone in the room was thunder struck when they heard the words.

"I will see you in hell," Enrico said in an even voice. "Godetevi il viaggio." Enjoy the ride.

The first shot was deafening and struck the cardinal in the lower torso. It was followed quickly by two additional shots. Any of the three shots could have killed the man, but Enrico had pulled them. He wanted the cardinal to know, to understand, to suffer.

Luciano was at a loss. He couldn't sense the man who was standing only a few feet away and about to kill him. He looked down and saw the contrasting dark blood ooze from his chest onto his crimson cassock. His pectoral cross was blood spattered. He reached out his hand to fend off his executioner. The energy he produced was like static electricity. Nothing more potent would come.

Enrico, standing over his partner's body, looked down at her placid and pale face. "For you," he said with tenderness. He snorted in derision at the cardinal. Enrico looked into the man's gray eyes, saw the look of incomprehension on his face, and waited for it to turn to terror. When it did, the sergeant squeezed off two more rounds.

Antonio Cardinal Archbishop Luciano died as the last bullet exploded his heart. Enrico knelt and placed Bella's weapon in her hand, lovingly curling her fingers around the grip, slipping her finger inside the trigger guard. The sergeant walked the few feet to the cardinal's body and spat onto the face of evil.

Julian's ears rang. He'd watched the sergeant squeeze off two rounds. He saw the recoil, but could hear nothing. The heavy smell of burnt gunpowder was the last conscious memory Julian had before blackness overwhelmed his senses.

CHAPTER TWENTY

"Mrs. Bragonier, this is Fr. Soski. I am a friend of Julian's. He has spoken of you often and always with great affection. He gave me your number in case something should happen to him. Something has happened." The priest's voice was strained and laced with exhaustion.

Bridget's voice was even and calm as she dug her fingernails into the palm of her hand to control herself. "Father, it is good of you to call."

"Mrs. Bragonier, first, let me say Dr. Dwyer is with Julian at hospital. The doctor is unharmed. However, I cannot speak to Julian's condition. I will be going to see him as soon as possible. I will ask Dr. Dwyer to call you with a medical update right away," Fr. Soski said.

Bridget was making a conscious effort to control her breathing and her thoughts. Her voice trembled only slightly when she said, "Although I thank you, this is not the reason for your call. How can I be of assistance?"

"As you mentioned to Julian, there has been a very dark shadow over this entire affair. I feel that has lifted. Would I be correct in this?" the priest asked and choked back a cry as pain coursed through him.

"Indeed, the shadow is gone or nearly so. There are things I can see clearly, but much is still obscured. I feel that will clear soon, however," she said.

"It is difficult for me to speak and my time is brief. I need you to pull a story from my mind. Is such a thing possible?" the priest asked and continued. "I would not normally ask such a thing, but circumstances make it necessary."

Fr. Soski continued, "There are things I need Julian to know and I fear I won't be able to tell him myself.

"I am sorry to disturb you, but I believe you are the only one whom I can trust with this. You, dear lady, are the only one Julian will believe. Can it be done?"

Bridget thought for a moment. "Fr. Soski, what you suggest may be feasible, but I have never heard of it being done." Another moment passed as the seed of an idea took root. "Still, all things are possible if we are game to have a go. If we fail, it will not be from lack of trying. Are you in a place where you can enjoy some privacy?"

"I am. My office is secluded and no one will interrupt," the priest said with a wry and weary smile.

"Good, then hang up the telephone and let us begin," Bridget said.

* * *

For over an hour, Fr. Soski thought through recent history as though Bridget was sitting across from him in his office.

Bridget bit her lip as she felt the priest's story unfurled in her mind. The tale he told was appalling, but each sentence was drenched in the suffering Fr. Soski was enduring in order to tell it.

She rested her head on the back of her sitting room chair. The priest rolled out a story of nearly impenetrable complexity.

"Father," Bridget began when the priest had finished his rendition of events, *"you may depend I will tell Julian all that you have said. I, however, would like to clarify a few points. I look for this clarification not for myself, but because Julian is sure to ask. If I may?"* Bridget said.

The priest took a slow shuddering breath and thought, *"Of course."*

"If I understand, Cardinal Luciano, embezzled hundreds of millions of dollars from the Vatican Bank."

"The cardinal was also a member of a shadow organization, one of whose members, you believe, is also one like us. Julian had suggested such a thing a day ago." Bridget paused and then continued with a thought. *"Father, I must tell you, although I believe you, what you suggest is a thing that is inconceivable."*

"I agree," Fr. Soski said simply.

"I would like to make sure I have followed your story accurately. Cardinal Luciano was a dupe, a pawn. You suspect members of this dark organization used his thefts as a diversion, drawing attention away from a far larger embezzlement.

"The cardinal kidnapped Dr. Dwyer and was able to hide her from the organization, from Julian, from all of us. Without the doctor for leverage, the organization was unable to co-opt Julian, but the cardinal believed he could. Do I have the essence of this?" Bridget asked.

"Madam, you are letter perfect. Thank you for this. I know it has been taxing for you. However, Julian may never know the truth of it, but for you.

"Mrs. Bragonier," the priest picked his thoughts with care. *"Although truthful with you, I was not altogether candid."* He swallowed hard as the pain racked his frail body. Bridget reacted to his pain. *"As I said, I have not seen Julian yet, but I must warn you, you will find him greatly changed as a result of his encounter with Cardinal Luciano."*

"I understand," Bridget said. *"From what you have said, it would be impossible to be otherwise."* Bridget could sense the priest's pain as a sudden, prolonged cough tore at him.

There was a long pause as the priest tried to catch his breath in short gasps.

"Dear lady," Fr. Soski began. *"You are all Julian said you are. Please, take care of him. I feel he will need a great deal of assistance. There are specialists who…"*

Bridget interrupted, *"Father, I understand completely. I know such an individual and he will be available when Julian returns to us.*

"You may trust," she continued. *"He has many, many people here who care deeply for him. His recuperation is what is most important now. The love of those he knows will go a very long way to restoring him."*

"Thank you." The priest was deathly tired. There was nothing else to say. He paused and then said, *"Mrs. Bragonier, go with God. Goodbye."*

The connection was gone.

* * *

At the approach of Fr. Soski, Ailís disengaged herself from the Italian doctors at Hospital San Pietro where Julian had been brought. The priest looked gaunt and unnaturally pale. Each breath was labored and his milky gray eyes were pinched in pain. The priest rubbed the back of his neck in an effort to dissipate the pressure.

Ailís looked up into a face haunted by pain and suffering. She saw a man full of regret and sadness, a man sick at heart.

Fr. Soski took her hands in his. "Doctor, may I see Julian, please?" the priest whispered, simply, kindly.

Ailís hesitated only a moment then said, "This way, Father," but the priest did not move.

"I can feel it in you, Doctor. Tell me what is wrong. Beyond the obvious, what troubles you?" Soski asked and resumed walking with slow shuffling steps to Julian's room.

Ailís thought for a moment. "Father, I must warn you, Julian is nearly catatonic. He will not speak, not even to me. He will not react to any kind of stimuli. You're one of them, you're like Julian. You can reason with him."

Soski smiled gently and said nothing.

"Father," Ailís stopped in the hospital hallway in front of Julian's door, "if you can, you must convince him to..." She looked into the priest's face, pleading.

"Convince him to come back to you, Doctor?" Fr. Soski asked in sympathy with her. "I will do my best. My fear is that it may not be enough, but I will try." The priest pushed the door open, but turned back to Ailís and placed his hand on her cheek. "Please know this. Julian loves you above all else. He was willing to do horrifying things if it would guarantee your safety. There was never a moment when you were not in his thoughts. It will always be so."

The priest's face softened. "You want him back the way he was. Doctor, that is impossible. All of us have been changed by what we have lived through. It is the way of all life, no? We each have been wounded by this, you included. In time, both you and he will survive, I feel certain of it."

Fr. Soski paused, then continued with a thought. *"Unlike others, my talents do not include seeing the future. But I will tell you this, your love will endure. Know it, feel it with every atom inside you.*

"Julian will always be a part of you as you will be with him. It was your capacity for love that attracted you to each other. It is your love that will hold you fast." He turned and entered Julian's room.

She looked at the floor before taking a shuddering breath.

Julian stood with his back to the window. His eyes locked onto those of his friend when he entered.

"Julian, my time is short. There are things you must know," the priest thought and his friend felt it.

Julian closed his eyes and the priest felt the ache in Julian's mind, in his soul.

"Luciano had to be stopped, but we assigned an importance to him that blinded us to other dangers. I will take responsibility for that," Fr. Soski said and went on. *"The Group has refreshed its coffers with another stolen fortune."*

The priest's face twisted into a grimace as pain tore though his body. Panting from the spasm, he continued. *"I spoke with Mrs. Bragonier. She says what I suggest, what you and I know, is not possible. I believe she is incorrect. The Group is headed by one of us, protected and nurtured by one, perhaps more of us."* Fr. Soski swallowed hard and tried to breathe deeply. The racking cough served only to shorten each breath further.

The priest looked up at his friend. Julian's thought was weak, but the words were unmistakable.

"Cardinal Manning," Julian thought and Fr. Soski nodded. Julian continued, *"Bridget said she couldn't get through the darkness obscuring all of this."*

"Julian, Manning was the darkness, is the darkness, and that is how you will find him." Fr. Soski said. *"For now, Manning has gone to ground with a fortune. The total loss is estimated at nearly a billion including the millions he took from what Luciano embezzled.*

"The Vatican Bank is scrambling. With luck, and if it can call in enough favors, it will not collapse. If it does, millions of people and

institutions will be wiped out. That would ripple through the world-wide economy. Chaos is the only result possible. Chaos is their objective, Julian."

The priest allowed Julian to absorb what was said. *"Had they more time – a papal assassination would have allowed that – more funds would have been stolen. That would have ushered in a new dark age. By stopping them, you have frustrated their aims. This will neither be forgotten or forgiven."*

The men stood in silence, each with their own thoughts. Fr. Soski guided Julian to his hospital bed. A knock was heard at the door and Ailís looked into the room. "Father…"

"I am nearly done." His smile was sardonic and sad. "A few moments more please." The door closed silently.

"Julian, I must be going, but I have something else that needs to be said.

"You blame yourself for this. Don't do this my friend. Don't punish yourself by cutting yourself off. The people around you, the people who love you are a lifeline. They are the way back. By turning them away, you will surely lose your way, lose yourself." Soski moved closer to his friend.

"I have been where you are, further in some ways. I have had my mind nearly destroyed as you have. I have had my body broken. I feel I can say I know where you are. Stay where you are and you will be lost, my friend. Lost to us. Lost to yourself. Think carefully before you take your next step. It may be irrevocable.

"Remember too, if you can keep to nothing else, the love you have for Ailís and hers for you is vital. Even if it is whittled away to the merest splinter, you must hold on to it. It may be your only way back."

Fr. Soski could feel it. Julian would find his way back, but it would be the hardest, most painful way possible. Julian's friend smiled his sad understanding, turned and left.

* * *

"Father?" Ailís called after the priest as he left Julian's room. "Tell me."

"Doctor, there will be a long road back for him," the priest rasped with effort.

"I am afraid he is in a place you cannot go. You can lay hands on him, but you cannot touch him. None of us can. He is an ocean away from us all. He has endured so much, Doctor. More than that, he sees himself as being responsible for a great many deaths. Although painful for us, he believes by shutting himself off, he is sparing us his suffering. By removing himself, he believes he is protecting the ones he loves."

Ailís began to speak, but Fr. Soski overrode her with a glance.

"He is wrong in all of this, of course, but he will have to learn that in his own way, in his own time." The priest took out a handkerchief and began a racking cough. Ailís became alarmed when the man took his now bloodied handkerchief away from his mouth.

"Father, you must come with me now." She took the sleeve of his overcoat, but the priest just smiled.

"For now, dear Doctor, your place is with him. Stay awhile. He may not acknowledge you; in fact he won't, but you need to stay with him," Soski said. "It is my hope, you and Julian live long and happy lives. Go with God." He laid his hand on her head and she crossed herself as he prayed.

Fr. Marek Soski turned and left her at Julian's door.

She entered and sat at the bedside with what was left of the man she loved.

* * *

A portly man in his late sixties with sharp features, green eyes and slate gray hair looked into the mirror and adjusted his tie. He brushed at the shoulders of his blue pinstripe suit coat and smiled a crooked smile at his reflection.

He called over his shoulder to his protégé and continued to inspect himself. "Are we ready, Mr. Clarke?"

Clarke didn't answer at first. He continued to look out the window of the second floor bedroom in a sedate home in the heart of Old Rome. He looked into the side yard with its brickwork patio, wrought iron furniture and park like setting. "I think I shall miss this place," he said.

The older man took one last look into the mirror. He smiled as he watched his green eyes flicker slightly and gradually change to piercing gray.

"We really cannot call you 'your Eminence' anymore," Mr. Clarke said and smirked. "And Mr. Manning is just not on. Consul isn't an especially good idea either."

Terrance Cardinal Patrick Manning said, "I'll think of something." The Consul looked at his reflection once more, then said, "Shall we go?"

"Have you decided where?" Clarke asked.

"I think we'll hide in plain sight. Our group always has," the older man said and chuckled with a slight shrug.

Both men descended the stairs, and entered a waiting limousine.

CHAPTER TWENTY-ONE

A leery and ferret eyed Joselina Conaletti entered the room hesitantly and approached Julian.

"How can I help you, signora?" Ailís asked. Joselina shot the doctor a sharp look and Ailís immediately bristled, but let the woman approach Julian.

"My business is with the wizard," the madam said without ever taking her eyes off of Julian's face.

She addressed him softly. "I heard what happened. I hear everything of course. I came as soon as I could.

"You and the Ghost asked me to keep this safe and return it if anything, well, you know." She reached into her voluminous handbag and withdrew the Jesuit Book. She placed it gently in Julian's hands. He felt the cool, smooth leather under his fingers, but only closed his eyes in response.

The madam touched Julian's face and smiled. "Come and stay with us anytime," the older woman said before the thought came through to her quietly. *"Joselina, thank you. You are a good person and I thank you for keeping my book safe. You deserve better boarders them I have been,"* Julian thought.

The madam snorted. "As long as you pay in cash you're welcome at my house." She winked and turned to leave. Before she reached the door, she twisted back and looked at Ailís. "Dottoressa," Joselina said. "bring him back. It will be good for you both next time. I promise." The older woman smiled warmly. "Maybe we can teach you not to hang around with wizards." The older woman smiled. "We'll find you a nice Italian boy, no?" The door closed silently behind her.

* * *

Ailís tried to get Julian to lie down, but he wouldn't move. She sat in a chair in front of him and held his hand in hers. His eyes, once so clear and intense, were now a dull cloudy gray and as cold as his hands.

The door opened slowly. Enrico Marino entered quietly. He flipped his police identification card at Ailís, who stood as he approached.

"Officer, I am afraid Mr. Blessing is in no condition to talk," she said.

"Dottoressa, this is official police business. He doesn't need to speak. I will talk and he will listen. I require nothing else," the sergeant said. Ailís nodded and moved into the shadows near the door.

The big man sat in Ailís' chair. Julian's eyes only moved from the Jesuit Book to take in Enrico's face etched deeply with misery. Julian could feel only a part of the man's grief. The pain was excruciating and Julian welcomed it. He wanted to burn away his guilt, double his own suffering.

"She was why I couldn't sense you," Julian thought and Enrico looked puzzled and then smiled slightly.

"You gave yourself completely to her. You lived your life for her, for your Bella. But there is more. You never told her," Julian thought and

hung his head feeling the man's agony, touching an immeasurable well of misery.

Enrico slowly reached into his outside coat pocket. He withdrew a small satin bag and shook it's contents into his large palm. He held it out to Julian. Enrico had no more tears but Julian had a vast reserve of them. His shoulders shook as he wept in silence. Ailís lurched, hesitated and left the room instead.

Enrico said kindly, quietly, "I have carried it for many years. I was going to give it to her tomorrow. It took me all this time to build up the courage."

He smiled a painful smile. "Now, for me, there is no tomorrow. There is only this day for the rest of my life." He put the ring back in its bag, sighed heavily and said, "I was sent here to take a statement from you. Instead I will give you your statement." The big man knew it by heart and delivered it without emotion.

Enrico took on his official police voice. "'Braving a fierce and deadly attack by Antonio Cardinal Archbishop Luciano on her partner, Fr. Marek Soski and me, Ispettore Belladonna Saviano was forced to shoot and kill the cardinal.

"'Before dying of his wounds, the cardinal killed Ispettore Saviano. She selflessly sacrificed herself in the defense of others. She died a hero and an inspiration.' I will make up the other details later." Enrico looked closely into Julian eyes and said with kindness, "Hai capito?"

Julian blinked back his tears. "Sì, capisco. *Yes, I understand. Your Bella was a hero. As are you. I am more sorry for your loss than you will ever know. I am sorry I wasn't better, stronger. I am sorry for us all. Her death, all of the deaths,"* Julian paused. *"I am responsible."*

Enrico nodded his acknowledgement of Julian's thoughts and feelings. He stood and walked toward the door. With his hand on the door pull and without turning around, he said, "Wizard, you did not cause this. You are not to blame. Two men brought this to our door. Both the Russian and the cardinal are dead. They left us no choice so we did what needed doing. Learn to forgive yourself, sí, amico mio?" The sergeant was in the hallway approaching Ailís when he felt Julian's words.

"Amico mio," Julian thought. My friend.

Enrico smiled slightly and nodded to the doctor as he left.

✳ ✳ ✳

They were side by side on a bed in the second floor bedroom of a stately home in Old Rome.

Both men were naturally posed. One, a butler in the very recent past, looked regal in the crimson cassock of a Roman Catholic cardinal. A man of peace at peace.

The other, a young man in a plain black cassock was as neatly arranged, but the look of frozen terror on the face of Fr. Dominic Giglio was anything but serene.

Both men lay still.

Dead still.

✳ ✳ ✳

A mile away, a limousine proceeded at a leisurely speed through the outskirts of Old Rome.

John Clarke turned in his seat and looked out the back window as a fireball erupted, throwing bricks and mortar hundreds of feet up and out. Exquisite furnishings were turned to deadly shrapnel instantaneously. The explosion shattered glass in nearby homes and scythed mature maple trees in half. A sedate neighborhood was turned into a battlefield in a matter of seconds.

"I think I shall miss that place," Clarke said.

* * *

Ailís led Julian down the companionway and away from the arrival gate at Dublin's international airport. His pace was slow, and painful to watch. His eyes were fixed on a point in the distance, a point, a horizon only he could see. He held a leather bound book tightly in his hand.

A serious Sean Maher, in his Garda Síochána uniform, met them and expedited their passage through customs and immigration.

Sean looked at his friend and ached with the changes he saw. Gone were the easy stride and the ready smile. Vanished, the mischief in Julian's eyes and the kindness that had been his hallmark from the time they first met in Cappel Vale on the rugged Irish coast.

At the far end of the terminal stood Moira Hagan looking stern and Bridget Bragonier looking kind. Julian's teacher and his mentor.

Bridget reached into her purse, took out her cell phone before it chirped, and stepped off a few paces. Moira stood her ground, but softened as she felt the weight Julian carried. Her student had suffered and continued to do so. She bit her lip and bunched her fists to stop the trembling of her hands.

Julian stumbled, but Ailís and Sean caught him before he fell. He turned to Ailís and said in a slow nearly inaudible whisper, with tears in his eyes, "He's gone." Sean steadied his friend then stood next to the Hagan.

Ailís looked into Julian's face, a face she knew so well. She looked into the warm gray eyes grown cool with agony as tears brimmed them, then rolled down his cheeks. "Who is gone?" she asked.

Julian hung his head and he shook with the sobs. Ailís took him into her arms, but he did not embrace her. She felt him take a ragged breath, square his shoulders and stand upright.

She noticed his arm and hand trembled as he took a tighter hold on the book. Tears continued to course his cheeks, but his face, a face bathed in anguish moments before, was now expressionless, distant and cold.

Sean closed his eyes and swallowed hard as he felt the Hagan take his hand and hold on tight. She needed his quiet strength and in that, Sean was the strongest man she had ever known.

Bridget Bragonier, tall, slim and regal, placed her cell phone back in her purse. She approached Julian, looked into his face and her smile was sad with the empathy she felt for her friend.

She traced the scar on his cheek, the wound Ailís had stitched so carefully in Cappel Vale so many months ago. He was willing to suffer for what he believed then and he suffered more now. So much had changed, since then, for him and now, for them all.

"You know," she said simply, but Julian did not acknowledge her comment. "Of course you do. I am sorry, Julian. Words will change nothing. This is something that for you will heal, but will never be forgotten," she said.

She moved her hand to Julian's heart and her face instantly turned the color of ash. Moira tried to move forward and Sean held her hand tightly. She turned on him with venom. She softened and began to weep when she saw the big man close his eyes and shake his head imperceptibly.

"No. Julian, do not do this," Bridget said. "I forbid you to allow this to happen." There was iron in her voice, a voice of authority tinged with kindness and washed in wisdom.

Julian's face never changed. His eyes distant, his thoughts unknowable, his heart was closed and cold. He blinked slowly once and the tears stopped and began to dry on his cheeks.

Ailís looked on bewildered. Everyone seemed to know what was happening to the man she loved so much – everyone but her.

"Who's gone? What's happening? Someone tell me what is going on. I demand it," she said with force.

Bridget turned to the doctor. "Fr. Soski died not long ago." It was said plainly, gently. "He died of a cerebral hemorrhage combined with a great many internal injuries."

Ailís' stood in open-mouthed silence before she said, "But that's not possible." Her forehead was etched with incomprehension. "I was with him a few hours ago. He was injured, but..." She stopped and closed her eyes. She had looked at the priest and had not seen him as an injured man, but as a man who was Julian's friend, a man who could return Julian to her.

She turned away in bitter recrimination as an older man approached the group. Ailís had a dim recollection of the man, a vague recognition, but nothing more.

"Come with me." The man was gentle and said it softly. He had Bridget's kind authority in his voice. His words were neither a request nor a command, but more a statement of what needed to be done.

"I know you," Ailís said and she squinted in concentration, but the man never acknowledged her. He continued to look with soft, knowing gray eyes into Julian Blessing and what he saw is what they all felt. They felt Julian's slow decent into grief and the overwhelming reproach and sadness that was swamping his soul.

Sean stepped up and took his friend by the arm and supported him as they followed the older man toward the terminal doors and into the bright sunlight outside.

Ailís was standing between Bridget and Moira. She moved forward to follow Julian, but the two older women held her back.

"What are you doing?" she demanded. "I have to go with him." Her cry was plaintive, imploring, demanding.

Moira nodded and Bridget was the first to speak. Her voice was genteel and soft. "Ailís, you cannot go with him. That man is a specialist. He has experience dealing with this. He knows what to do and how to do it. Your place is not with Julian, not now."

"No, I have to," Ailís began, but Moira spun her around and said with force, "Listen to me, my girl. While Bridget is refined and will deal gently with you, I will not. Mind you, you probably could use a little gentleness now, but I've none to give, lass.

"Hear me well. The man you see there is not the man you knew. He is nothing like that man and may never be again. You have a practice in Cappel Vale to attend to and a son who needs you. You cannot help Julian, not now anyway. You haven't the tools and wouldn't know how to use them if you did." Moira said it and softened with the pain she saw on Ailís' face.

"Where your man is and where he is going, you cannot follow. None of us can." She stopped and kissed Ailís' cheek.

"Ailís," Bridget said. "Moira is right. You have a part to play in rebuilding him, a vital part, we all do. And we will each play our part when the specialist thinks the time is right."

Moira took up the line, "And not one moment sooner. This must run it's course and we are not to interfere. Do you understand, girl?"

Ailís' agonized wail drew the attention of passers by and Moira sent them on their way with a glance.

A member of the Garda approached. "Ah, ladies, is there a problem I can assist you with?" the constable asked cheerfully.

Moira spun on him and he backed up a step. "Problem, is it? If you consider yer bits shriveling up a problem, boyo, then indeed."

"Moira," Bridget warned with easy grace.

"Ach, than you deal with him or I'll sort him out straight away."

Bridget reached out and touched the constable's arm and the man's eyes went large as he stiffened. The electrical jolt that went through him made him swallow hard.

"Constable?" Bridget searched the man's uniform for his nametag. "Constable Monahan, thank you so much for stopping. It is an emotional time for our friend, as you can see. Although we appreciate your concern and thank you for it, you need not worry about us further."

She removed her hand from his sleeve and he backed up another two steps. His retreat was stopped when he bounced off the immovable Sean Maher.

Sean took the constable's arm in a grip that caused the man's hand to go numb. "Come along lad. No need to be a bother to the ladies now is there? Of course not." As they walked away, Sean looked back to indicate Julian had been driven away.

Ailís, weak from exhaustion, fell into the arms of her friends. She whispered a mantra of despair, "I've lost him."

Moira said, "For now, the boy is lost to himself."

Bridget picked up the thought, "In time and with our help, he will find himself again and you will find him. However, what you find may be far more than what you now think you've lost." Ailís looked confused. Bridget's smile was one of hope while Moira's face reflected her deep concern. Both woman harbored secrets they would not share with Dr. Ailís Dwyer.

Not yet.

The End

THANK YOU

»On behalf of the author and Penman House Publishing, thank you for purchasing and reading Echoes Through the Vatican.«

Please take a moment and leave a review of this book at Amazon.com. Don't forget to recommend this book to others.

Your support in this way is much appreciated and helps enormously.

Look for other titles from K. Francis Ryan

- Echoes Through the Mist – Available now

- Echoes Through Ireland - Due 2015

* * *

Additional Penman House titles

Aaron Aalborg

K. Francis Ryan

- <u>They Deserved It</u> – Available now

- <u>Terminated</u> – Available now

- <u>The Destroyers</u> – Due 2015

- <u>Black Smoke White Light</u> – Due 2016

* * *

Available titles can be found at Amazon.com.

For more information go to: www. http://penman-house
-publishing.blogspot.com.tr/

PenmanHousePublishing@gmail.com

About the Author

K. Francis Ryan is a freelance writer who coaches writing-challenged business professionals around the world. His experience as an internationally accredited stockbroker, a police officer and a feature writer for a small town newspaper is evident the writing of his novels ECHOES THROUGH THE MIST and ECHOES THROUGH THE VATICAN.

Mr. Ryan is currently working on the third novel in the Echoes Quartet, ECHOES THROUGH IRELAND.

He lives on the side of an active volcano in an even more active earthquake zone in the Republic of Costa Rica. Surely that's not nearly as horrifying as it sounds, right?

www.ingramcontent.com/pod-product-compliance
Lightning Source LLC
Chambersburg PA
CBHW050020180626
46810CB00002B/497